Lethe, he thought.

Yes, Billy?

Could you show me Thayla again?

Bill felt the spirit smile inside, and suddenly the darkness gave way to a brilliant light. The silence yielded to the glorious song of the goddess Thayla, who stood on a cracked plane of rock. Light shone from her like a beacon against the darkness, a wondrous sun in the blackest firmament. The song and the light were one and the same. Her voice rang out, rising and falling in beautiful melodious waves, washing over him like the warm surf. Until he cared not who he was and why he was there.

He merely wanted to stay forever.

Lethe's memory of Thayla was flawless, the sensation of the experience overwhelming Billy until he knew that he must join his guardian angel in his quest to help Thayla. The beauty must not be destroyed.

But we're in no position to help, he thought. *When we wake, we will be in Aztlan.*

If *we* wake.

ENTER THE SHADOWS SHADOWRUN®

SHADOWRUN

BEYOND THE PALE

Book 3 of the
Dragon Heart Saga

Jak Koke

A ROC BOOK

ROC
Published by the Penguin Group
Penguin Putnam Inc., 375 Hudson Street,
New York, New York 10014, U.S.A.
Penguin Books Ltd, 27 Wrights Lane,
London W8 5TZ, England
Penguin Books Australia Ltd,
Ringwood, Victoria, Australia
Penguin Books Canada Ltd, 10 Alcorn Avenue,
Toronto, Ontario, Canada M4V 3B2
Penguin Books (N.Z.) Ltd, 182–190 Wairau Road,
Auckland 10, New Zealand

Penguin Books Ltd, Registered Offices:
Harmondsworth, Middlesex, England

First published by Roc, an imprint of Dutton Signet,
a member of Penguin Putnam Inc.

First Printing, March, 1998
10 9 8 7 6 5 4 3 2 1

Series Editor: Donna Ippolito
Legend of Thayla: Tom Dowd

 REGISTERED TRADEMARK — MARCA REGISTRADA

SHADOWRUN, FASA, and the distinctive SHADOWRUN and FASA logos are
registered trademarks of the FASA Corporation, 1100 W. Cermak, Suite B305,
Chicago, IL 60608.

Printed in the United States of America

Books are available at quantity discounts when used to promote products or services. For information please write to premium marketing division, Penguin Putnam
Inc., 375 Hudson Street, New York, NY 10014.

For my college professors,
Don Taylor and Richard Lyons,
who taught me the basics of writing fiction.

And for my real world teachers,
Dean Wesley Smith and Kristine Kathryn Rusch,
who showed me how to make it my work.

ACKNOWLEDGMENTS

I'd like to thank Steve Kenson for allowing me to use Talon, and Caroline Spector for loaning Aina to me. They add depth and focus to the novel. Credit should also go to Mike Mulvihill for his great help with the plots and characters in this trilogy, especially with regard to this final book.

My usual appreciation goes out to my readers, Jonathan Bond, Nicole Brown, Marsh Cassady, Seana Davidson, Jim Kitchen and Tom Lindell for insightful critiques of the manuscript. I'd like to extend a special thanks to my agent, Don Gerrard, and to Dorothy Jean Saint Germain for their welcome help in financial matters which arose during the writing of the manuscript. And finally, much gratitude goes to Donna Ippolito at FASA for excellent editing and for making this trilogy possible.

NORTH

CIRCA 2057

North America

- ⊛ National Capital
- Seattle • City
- - - - International Boundary
- .... State Boundary (U.S.A. circa 1990)

TSIMSHIAN

ATHABASKAN COUNCIL
Edmonton
Lake Louise

ALGONKIAN-MANITOU COUNCIL
Saskatoon

Vancouver

SALISH-SHIDHE COUNCIL
Seattle
Spokane

Regina

Winnipeg

Pacific Ocean

Portland
Salem
Eugene

Helena
Butte

SIOUX NATION
Billings

Fargo   Duluth
Bismarck

Hell's Canyon
Boise

Sheridan
Idaho Falls

Rapid City

Sioux Falls   St. Paul
Minneapolis

TIR TAIRNGIRE

Eureka

Reno

Salt Lake City
Provo

Cheyenne

Des Moines

Omaha

San Francisco

CALIFORNIA FREE STATE
Bakersfield
Santa Barbara
Los Angeles

UTE NATION
Las Vegas

Boulder
Denver
Colorado Springs
Pueblo

Topeka

Kansas City

Wichita

PUEBLO CORPORATE COUNCIL
Santa Fe

Tulsa

Tijuana

San Diego

Phoenix

Tucson

Albuquerque   Amarillo   Oklahoma City

Roswell

Little Rock

El Paso

Ft. Worth   Dallas
Shreveport

San Angelo

Pacific Ocean

San Marcos dig

Austin
Houston

San Antonio

Corpus Christi

Chihuahua

AZTLAN

Monterrey

Culiacan

Durango

Ciudad Victoria

AMERICA

CIRCA 2057

Hudson Bay

Ft. Albany · · Waskaganish

QUÉBEC

Sept Iles

Gulf of St. Lawrence

Charlottetown

Québec

Fredericton

Halifax

Thunder Bay

Lake Superior

Sault Ste. Marie

Ottawa

Sudbury

Kingston

Montpelier

Montreal

Augusta

Lake Huron

Lake Michigan

Milwaukee

Lansing

Toronto

Detroit

L. Ontario

Buffalo

Albany

Concord

Boston

Hartford

L. Erie

Cleveland

Newark

Manhattan

Atlantic Ocean

Chicago Gary

Indianapolis

Cincinnati

Philadelphia

FDC

UNITED CANADIAN AND AMERICAN STATES (U.C.A.S.)

Springfield

East St. Louis

Charleston

Louisville

Roanoke

Richmond

Norfolk

Knoxville

Durham

Raleigh

Nashville

Memphis

Charlotte

Wilmington

Birmingham

Atlanta

Columbia

Jackson

Montgomery

Charleston

Baton Rouge

Mobile

Albany

Savannah

Jacksonville

CONFEDERATE AMERICAN STATES (U.C.A.S.)

Orlando

Tampa

West Palm Beach

Miami

Gulf of Mexico

Key West

CARIBBEAN LEAGUE

Delta Clinic

PANAMA

The year is 2057 . . .

And magic has returned to the earth after an absence of many thousands of years. What the Mayan calendar called the Fifth World has given way to the Sixth, a new cycle of magic, marked by the waking of the great dragon Ryumyo in the year 2011. The Sixth World is an age of magic and technology. An Awakened age.

The rising magic has caused the archaic races to re-emerge. Metahumanity. First came the elves, tall and slender with pointed ears and almond eyes. They were born to human parents, just as were dwarfs shortly thereafter. Then later came the orks and the trolls, some born changed, like elves and dwarfs, but others goblinized—transformed from human form into their true nature as the rising magic activated their DNA. Manifesting as larger bodies, heavily muscled with tusked mouths and warty skin.

Even the most ancient and intelligent of beings, the great dragons, have come out of their long hiding. Only a few of these creatures are known to exist, and most of them have chosen a life of isolation and secrecy. But some, able to assume human form, have integrated themselves into the affairs of metahumanity. They have used their ancient intellect, their powerful magic, and their innate cunning to ascend to positions of power. One is known to own and run Saeder-Krupp—the largest megacorporation in the world. Another—Dunkelzahn—is the most controversial creature ever to have been elected to the presidency of the United Canadian and American States. Dunkelzahn was

*assassinated in a mysterious explosion on 9 August 2057—
the night of his inauguration.*

*The Sixth World is a far cry from the mundane environ-
ment of the Fifth. It is exotic and strange, a paradoxical
blend of the scientific and the arcane. The advance of technology has reached a feverish pace. The distinction between man and machine is becoming blurred by the advent
of direct neural interfacing. Cyberware. Machine and computer implants are commonplace, making metal of flesh,
pulsing electrons into neurons at the speed of thought. People of the Sixth World are a new breed—stronger, smarter,
faster. Less human.*

*The Matrix has grown like a phoenix out of the ashes
of the old global computer network. A virtual world of
computer-generated reality has emerged, a universe of
electrons and CPU cycles controlled and manipulated by
those with the fastest cyberdecks, with the hottest new
code.*

*It is an era where information is power, where data
and money are one and the same. Multinational mega-
corporations have replaced superpower governments as
the true forces on the planet. In a world where cities have
grown into huge sprawls of concrete and steel, walled-off
corporate enclaves and massive arcologies have super-
seded two-car garages, vegetable gardens, and white
picket fences. The megacorps exploit masses of wage-
slaves for the profit of a lucky and ruthless few.*

*But in the shadows of the mammoth corporate arcolo-
gies live the SINless. Those without System Identification
Numbers are not recognized by the machinery of society,
by the bureaucracy that has grown so massive and complex that nobody understands it completely. Among the
SINless are the shadowrunners, traffickers in stolen data
and hot information, mercenaries of the street—discreet,
effective, and untraceable.*

*The Sixth World is full of surprises, not the least of
which is the recent discovery of a Locus by Aztechnology,*

a megacorporation with a dark and bloody core. The Lo-cus serves as a focus for metahuman sacrifices. It gives the puppeteers who control Aztechnology the power they need to construct their metaplanar bridge to the tzitzimine—demons who live off torture and suffering. When the bridge is completed, the demons will come into this world and ravage it. Aztechnology believes it will be rewarded as the tzitzimine scourge the land, bringing a millennium of pain.

Only Ryan Mercury can stop them. He is an undercover operative who worked for the recently assassinated great dragon, Dunkelzahn. Ryan must take the Dragon Heart—a magical item of immeasurable power—to the metaplanar bridge and give it to Thayla, whose song protects the world from the demons she calls the Enemy. The Dragon Heart will give Thayla the power to destroy the bridge.

Recently, Thayla's power over the bridge was breached by Señor Oscuro, an agent of Aztechnology. And at the same time Ryan Mercury struggled to overcome the selfish personality inside that inspired him to keep the Dragon Heart for himself. The evil part of him that allowed the cyberzombie, Burnout, to steal the artifact.

Ryan defeated Burnout, throwing him into the depths of Hells Canyon, but the cyberzombie reached out and snatched the Dragon Heart. Burnout plummeted into the chasm, taking the salvation of the world with him.

As the cyberzombie fell into the canyon, the powerful spirit, Lethe, possessed him in order to protect the Dragon Heart. Like Ryan, Lethe wanted to get the artifact to Thayla, but the spirit had seen Ryan claim the Heart for his own and had decided that Ryan could not be trusted.

Falling into Hells Canyon, Lethe found himself caught inside the cybermantic magic that kept Burnout's own spirit from leaving. Over time, the spirits of Lethe and Burnout grew connected; Burnout gave Lethe a physical presence and allowed him to be in contact with the Dragon Heart. And Lethe expanded Burnout's spirit, bringing him back from the edge of sanity, stabilizing his psyche.

Ryan tracked the possessed cyberzombie, but was unable to defeat him and retrieve the Dragon Heart. In the final confrontation between Ryan and Burnout, they fought to a stalemate until Ryan sacrificed himself in order to get the Dragon Heart back.

It was Lethe who intervened, using the power of the Dragon Heart to save Ryan at the last second. During the fight, the spirit saw the truth that Ryan no longer desired to keep the Heart for himself. That Ryan was willing to give his very life to complete the mission given him by Dunkelzahn—to carry the artifact to Thayla.

Now, however, Ryan knows that in order to finish the mission, he will have to contact ancient and powerful beings. He knows he must come head to head against the purest evil. This is the only way he can prevent the Enemy from coming across prematurely and ravaging the world.

Señor Oscuro and his pawns have already burned their wedge of darkness into Thayla's light. They are poised to attack her until her song is silenced. Until she is dead and they can finish building their bridge to oblivion.

Now that Ryan has the Dragon Heart, he must get it to Thayla before she is buried under Oscuro's onslaught. Ryan is unwavering in his commitment to his mission. He knows it will take more than he's ever given, perhaps more than he can give.

Perhaps more even than his life.

Prologue

His name was Billy Madson, and he was a boy in the body of a machine.

A boy with a guardian angel hovering around him. Protecting him. Calming him when the vicious memories came rushing back, the violence and the killing. Memories of his previous incarnation—a cyberzombie who was called Burnout.

The angel surrounded and buoyed Billy. The angel was the only reason Billy still lived. The angel's name was Lethe, and he had saved Billy's life. He had shown Billy the images of terrible beauty, blinding light and a song that brought tears to the boy's eyes. A voice of such power and purity that even Lethe's memory of it, filtered through Billy's mechanical body and into the recesses of Billy's mind, had moved him back from the edge of death.

Back among the living.

Now, Billy lay on his back, shackled unceremoniously to a metal operating table. Technicians and doctors had probed and studied him, apparently interested in the technology of his body. A few hours ago, they had left the room, leaving him attached to machines that monitored his brain patterns and the electrical activity of his cyberware.

The room was quite secure, he knew. His mind had automatically analyzed it for avenues of escape. He had done this without thinking, the possible scenarios running like a subroutine in the back of his mind, and he had marveled at himself for it.

I am built to kill and to destroy. A combat machine.

"Someone's coming," Lethe said, his soothing voice dropping into Billy's mind through a device in his cybernetics called the IMS—Invoked Memory Stimulator.

Billy opened his eyes to the darkened room. It was night, and moonlight shone through the barred and fenced-over windows, the crisscrossed shadows rippling over the floor and table next to him. Like hatch-marked silver.

"Not the same as before," Lethe said. "I sense stealth and barely contained aggression in those who approach."

Billy yanked at the heavy bands that anchored his legs, arms, chest, and head to the table, but he couldn't even turn his head, and much of his connection to his cybernetics had been disrupted by the doctors. "Can you tell if they're coming to kill us?"

Billy sensed laughter through the IMS. "No, my friend, I cannot read minds. I can only sense auras. Here they come."

The door to the room opened and someone entered, perhaps several people. Billy could hear them only when he cranked up the sensitivity on his cybernetic ears to their maximum. He could sense the slight pressure shift in the room as well.

"Señor, aqui!" The words were barely audible, subvocalized into a throat mic or headware, but Billy understood what they meant. "Over here, sir."

The Azzies have found me, finally.

Several people surrounded him. Billy couldn't see them and suspected that they had hidden themselves magically. He felt pressure against his chest and a compartment popped open. Then something was jacked into him, running diagnostics.

Billy knew that in his past life as the cyberzombie, Burnout, this had happened to him on a regular basis. Just a routine systems check. The portable deck was speaking to his brain, telling him exactly which parts were malfunctioning, which parts worked, and how much damage he had sustained in his quest to destroy Ryan Mercury.

A quest that now seemed so distant, so remote as to be

unimportant. In fact, it was Ryan Mercury who had brought Burnout so close to death that he had lost his identity. Or rediscovered it. His previous incarnation had died in the massive fire in Dunkelzahn's arboretum only hours ago, and Billy was not sad about it.

Perhaps Ryan Mercury did me a favor by almost killing me.

The irony did not escape Billy.

The diagnostic program indicated that his homing signal had been destroyed, probably when he had fallen into Hells Canyon. Another confrontation with Mercury that seemed like eons ago even though it had only been a week or so.

"Remarkable," whispered one of the invisible people standing over him. "He has sustained a huge amount of abuse, but he lives on. I think we should abort termination and take him back with us."

"Sí," came the response.

The paralysis started in his toes and moved up rapidly, system by system through his knees, legs, waist. Up through his torso and chest it traveled, the sheer absence of feeling. No tingling numbness, just a digital erasure of his sensory perception.

His taste turned off with a click, then his sight, hearing, until finally he was alone inside a vast ocean of darkness. A brain in a sensory deprivation tank.

Lethe, he thought.

Yes, Billy?

Could you show me Thayla again?

Billy felt the spirit smile inside and suddenly the darkness gave way to a brilliant light. The silence yielded to the glorious song of the goddess Thayla who stood on a cracked plane of rock. The light shone from her like a beacon against the darkness, a wondrous sun in the blackest firmament. The song and the light were one and the same. Her voice rang out, rising and falling in beautiful melodious waves, washing over him like warm surf. Until he cared not who he was and why he was there.

He merely wanted to stay forever.

Lethe's memory of Thayla was flawless, the sensation of the experience overwhelming Billy until he knew that he must join his guardian angel in his quest to help Thayla. The beauty must not be destroyed.

But we're in no position to help, he thought. *When we wake, we will be in Aztlan.*

If we wake.

23 August 2057

1

Ryan Mercury woke. The fragments of his dream crashing through his skull like broken shards of a ceramic sculpture. A shattered nightmare of sharp edges and cold, hard clay.

Ryan shivered. The pre-dawn air filtered crisp and cool over his body as he slipped out of bed and walked across the chilly marble of his recovery room. In the aftermath of his confrontation with Burnout, he had been given a small, quiet room in the west wing of Dunkelzahn's Georgetown mansion.

Ryan had recently used the Dragon Heart, which sat on the night stand next to his bed, to heal the bullet wound in his chest and the burns that covered his entire body. Now it was time to see what he looked like.

As he moved across the cold floor, he stared into the full-length mirror at his dark reflection—an apparition of shadows. A tattered mummy fluttering in the dim light cast by the reddening sky outside.

Ryan stood tall, trying to forget the dream, trying to discard the images of the horrible creatures attacking the goddess, ripping into her luminous flesh, like acid-soaked razors into unmarred skin.

With effort, he pushed the memory of their putrid stench from his mind and focused on the immediate. He looked at his reflection in the mirror as he slowly peeled off the bandages. He unwound the white gauze carefully, feeling no pain as the dried fabric pulled away from his healed skin. The Dragon Heart had worked its wonderful magic, bringing him to full strength in the passage of only one night.

Ryan's body emerged in front of him from beneath the bandages. A two-meter chunk of humanity, dense and strongly muscled. Ryan was pure flesh, no cybernetic or biological augmentation. He gained all his extraordinary strength and quickness from well-toned natural muscle and reflexes that were enhanced by magic. Magic that came from the Silent Way—the physical adept path he had learned from the great dragon Dunkelzahn.

His hair caught the dim light from outside, its auburn color reflecting red. And as he leaned in close to examine his face, he saw that his silver-flecked blue eyes were clear. All the bloodshot fatigue had been washed away by the Dragon Heart's magic.

Amazing, he thought.

Tiny hairline scars crisscrossed the flesh of his shoulders and head, left over from the cuts made by flying glass shrapnel. It was difficult to believe that it had all happened last night. His confrontation of Damien Knight, his battle with Burnout, his effort to save Nadja. The explosion that had nearly killed him.

Ryan finished unwinding the bandages, feeling like a freshly emerged butterfly, his new skin sensitive and cold in the slight breeze that blew in through the open window. He threw the bandages on the bed and dressed in a plycra nightsuit.

Since I can't sleep anyway, he thought, *I might as well get up and run through some katas.*

As he pulled a dark shirt over his head, his wristphone rang. He walked to the bedside table, picked it up, and looked at the tiny screen to see who was calling.

The code for Jane-in-the-box flashed across the top of the screen. Jane-in-the-box was the human woman who had been Dunkelzahn's decker for many years. Now that the dragon was dead, she worked for Nadja Daviar and the Draco Foundation. And sometimes, she ran the Matrix for Assets Incorporated, Ryan's team of shadowrunners.

Ryan strapped the phone to his wrist and punched the Connect button.

Jane's persona appeared—a cartoon image of a blonde human woman with pouting red lips, giant blue eyes, and huge breasts encased in red vinyl. Ryan knew that the real Jane, who decked from a physical location deep underground in Dunkelzahn's Lake Louise lair, looked nothing like the icon on his small screen. She was rail-thin and somewhat homely, had an acerbic wit and a razor-sharp intellect.

Jane smiled. "Quicksilver," she said. "You're awake, and I must say that you look none the worse for almost dying just a few hours ago."

"Physically, I feel great. Mentally . . ."

"Something bothering you?"

"Bad dreams," he said. "But you didn't call me this early just to hear about my nightmares, did you?"

"No. I just got word that Hamilton Asylum has been breached."

"Is that where they took Burnout's body?"

"Yes."

"He's escaped?"

"No, but someone just broke in. I think they might be after him." Jane's icon smiled. "I thought you'd want to know."

"Thanks," Ryan said. "I did want to talk to Lethe."

Lethe was a powerful spirit who had alternately helped and hindered Ryan's efforts concerning the Dragon Heart. But ultimately, Ryan believed the spirit wanted the same thing he did: to deliver the Heart to Thayla.

Lethe has seen Thayla. He's spoken with her, and despite past differences, he might be willing to help.

Lethe was trapped inside Burnout, who by all accounts should be dead. The cyberzombie had not only taken a high-caliber sniper round through the chest, but he had been caught in the middle of the arboretum during the oxygen explosion.

Lethe may have had a hand in keeping Burnout from stepping beyond the pale, but whatever the case, the cyberzombie had not succumbed to the final sleep. He had slipped into a comatose state, but all his vital signs were normal.

If Burnout does escape, or is taken away, Lethe goes with him. I can't let that happen.

"Jane, I'm going there right now. Where's Dhin?"

"I took the liberty of waking him; he's enroute to you. Flying the Draco Foundation's new Hughes Airstar."

Ryan smiled. "Remind me to kiss you next time I see you in the flesh. What's his ETA?"

"Two minutes."

"Perfect," Ryan said. "I'll be prepped and ready to roll."

He punched the Disconnect and turned to lift the Dragon Heart from the velvet pillow on which it rested. The Heart was large, the size of a child's head and shaped more like a real four-chambered heart than an idealized valentine. Made from pure orichalcum, the color of bronze-tinted gold, and enchanted by some unknown magic, the Dragon Heart was the most powerful object Ryan had ever encountered.

Mana seemed to flow through it like a lens, channeled from astral space and focused wherever the Heart's wielder wished. Ryan had used its magic to accentuate and increase his own abilities, but he would no longer try to keep it for himself, no matter how much its power enticed him. It had another destiny.

Ryan placed the Dragon Heart into a pouch that he attached to a broad sash tied around his waist. When it was secure, he dug through the closet for his running gear. He found his flexible Kevlar III-slatted light body armor, which he pulled over his nightsuit.

He gathered up his carry bag and moved out, angling toward the helipad behind the house. He moved quickly out into the hall and down past the library. He walked along in silence, looking to avoid encounters with security agents or mansion personnel.

He didn't want anyone to notice his departure. Not right away. If someone saw him, Nadja would find out. Ryan didn't know if Nadja was awake or not, but even though he desperately wanted to see her, he couldn't take the time to tell her goodbye. Hopefully, he'd be back before she realized he was gone.

Nadja Daviar was an elven woman of considerable power and beauty. She had been Dunkelzahn's translator and aide and was now the head of the Draco Foundation. She was also nominated to become the new vice president of the United Canadian and American States.

Ryan was in love with her.

By the time he had made his way through the mansion and out the rear entrance to the helicopter pad, he could hear the deep *thwup thwup* of the Hughes Airstar approaching. The craft descended in a rush of wind and bone-shaking thunder.

Ryan saw Dhin through the foreshield, a huge grin on the big ork's tusked face. As soon as the helo's runners touched tarmac, Ryan ran over it and climbed in next to Dhin. "We're on a tight schedule," he yelled over the roar of the rotors.

Dhin turned and nodded. "Got the whole scan from Jane," he said, simultaneously lifting the chopper into the air. "We should make Hamilton in three minutes."

"Good."

Dhin sat in the pilot's seat. He wore a loose-fitting black jumpsuit and a crash helmet over his bony skull. A thin fiber-optic cable plugged into the datajack behind his right ear. The cable's other end disappeared into the control console in front of him.

Ryan noticed the glaze of sleep in Dhin's bloodshot eyes. He'd obviously been awakened from a deep snooze. Dhin saw Ryan's look and grinned again, a good-natured gesture that showed friendship and genuine affection. "It's great to see you up and about, Bossman. I thought you were crisped in that explosion last night."

Ryan clasped the ork's shoulder. "I got lucky," he said. "Lethe intervened somehow and pushed me into the water spray at the last second."

As he talked, Ryan strapped on the Ingram smartgun and

its holster, then checked to make sure the clip was full. It held armor-piercing rounds. Nice. He tucked the extra clips into their slots in the holster strap.

Ryan looked over at Dhin. "I think the spirit's back on our side. He trusts me now, and I could really use his help. I don't want anyone making off with him."

Dhin nodded. "Almost there," he said. "Jane has us cleared with their security, but it looks like the helipad has been taken by the runners. Also, there're two birds in the air. All Aztechnology Aguilar-EX military-grade hoop-fraggers. Gonna have to do some serious maneuvering to get past them, or to avoid being blown out of the sky if they decide to target us."

Ryan slid on his bandoleer of narcotic throwing darts and his grenade pistol with six-round clip. The dart needles were hollow and filled with a tiny amount of a rare drug called xenoketamine—an anesthetic that acted on the brain in less than a heartbeat, causing loss of consciousness followed by wild hallucinations.

"Sounds like our old amigo, General Dentado," Ryan said. "He must have finally tracked down the cyber-zombie." Ryan and Dhin had come across Dentado a few days earlier at the Assets, Incorporated compound in Hells Canyon.

Ryan donned a portable Phillips Tacticom headset, tucking the tiny earphone into his right ear and affixing the pinhead microphone to his throat with mimetic tape. Outside, the first rays of dawn filtered through the blood-brown haze of the city, lightening the blue glass corporate arcologies and the duracrete government high-rises.

The helo pivoted under the whirling blades, angling across the polluted Potomac and toward Hamilton Asylum. Ryan could see the federal facility now with his magically enhanced vision—a squat eight-story hospital of dingy concrete and opaque white windows covered with steel bars and electrified mesh, sitting on the edge of the down-town cluster. Five-meter cyclone fencing topped with spools of monowire encircled the high-security structure.

A military helicopter perched on the helipad like a giant wasp, poised to sting. Ryan could tell from its posture and the speed of its blades that it was ready to go wheels up at any moment. Ryan scanned the surrounding airspace for the other two birds Dhin had mentioned, but he could see only one—hovering a half-klick off to the south.

Jane-in-the-box came on over the helo's internal speakers. "According to the sec-cam images, the runners have taken Burnout. I lost them a minute ago, though, when they went invisible."

"Thanks, Jane," he said. "They'll probably head for the . . ."

Suddenly, the helo lifted off the pad, taking to the air in a rush. "We're too late," he said into his mike. "They're out already." Ryan turned to Dhin. "Can you get me close?"

The ork shrugged. "Can't promise anything," he said. "But I'll work my miracles, if you work yours."

Just then a third helicopter emerged from behind the asylum, looming up over the edge of the structure like an angry hornet. Facing them.

"Drek!" Dhin yelled.

The floor tilted beneath Ryan as Dhin banked hard left, just as a barrage of bullets sprayed the space where they had been moments before. Ryan watched as the enemy chopper swiveled toward them, approaching rapidly.

"Frag me, Bossman. This bird wasn't made for air-to-air combat. We've got a recessed minigun, but nothing harder. No missiles, no cannons."

"Get that minigun online, pronto."

Dhin nodded. "It's ready to spit lead," he said. "Not that it'll do us much good against these chummers."

Ryan saw a missile launch from the Aguilar, spitting fire as it flashed toward them. "You got any antimissile defenses?"

Dhin just shook his head. "Null chance. This was the only bird available, and nobody told me we were going into a combat zone."

"Take us up and out over the water," Ryan said. "As far away from any roads and buildings as you can."

Dhin flashed him a look of disbelief. "We're about to be blown to bits, and you're thinking of civilian casualties, Bossman?"

They banked right and climbed as Ryan touched the Dragon Heart with his power. He focused his telekinetic strike through the Heart, building mana as the missile rocketed up toward them. When it was nearly on them, he released his power in a massive push.

He felt the magic wave hit the missile with amazing force, backed by the Dragon Heart. The missile stopped dead for a nanosecond, then exploded. Shrapnel and fire shook the air, rocking the helo in the wake of the blast behind them.

Dhin looked at Ryan. "Miss Daviar's going to have my eyeballs for dinner if I scratch her helo," he said.

"Quicksilver, are you all right?" Jane's voice. "Please copy, Quicksilver."

Ryan spoke into his mike. "Shaken, Jane. But not stirred." Ryan smiled. "At least not yet."

The sound of Jane's sigh reached Ryan's ears. "There are UCAS fighter jets coming down on your location. I've been told that the military has taken charge of the situation. You are to back off."

"We'll be out of here in less than five," Ryan said. Then he turned to Dhin. "Take us as close as you can without provoking another missile attack."

Dhin glanced over at him, shaking his big warty head. "You're the boss, though sometimes I wonder why."

Ryan laughed. "I haven't gotten us killed yet."

"That's right," Dhin said. *"Yet."*

"Just get us as close as you can."

Dhin nodded, then angled the helo forward and kicked in the jets, pressing Ryan into his seat. In response to the oncoming UCAS fighters, the three Azzie choppers had turned and made for the Confederate American States border. Ryan couldn't see the fighters, but he knew the Azzies would have picked them up on radar by now.

Again Ryan focused his mana through the Dragon Heart. He didn't know if he'd be able to pull off what he was attempting, but it was worth a try. He shifted his awareness into astral space, using the power of the Heart to amplify his astral senses.

Material objects blurred, the dull gray of the physical images giving way to the colored landscape of the astral. Life force gave off light in the astral plane—auras that were unique to each creature and object.

The astral sky was a flat violet color here as Ryan searched out the auras of those inside the flying machines ahead. He couldn't move his spirit from his body, but his sight was keen, and the Dragon Heart made it even sharper, magnifying his senses.

Yet, even with the enhanced mana from the Heart, the aura of Burnout and Lethe was at the limit of Ryan's perception. It was so faint at this distance, he could barely see it through the side window of one of the retreating helicopters.

Lethe, Ryan projected his thoughts toward the aura. *Lethe, respond if you can hear me.*

"Ryan Mercury, is that you?" came the response. "We are trapped."

I am behind you, Lethe. I am trying to stop your captors.

"I am not important," Lethe said. "You must not waste your effort. You must find a way to take the Dragon Heart across to the metaplanes and give it to Thayla. She needs it. I thought you were committed to this."

I am committed. It is now my singular goal. But, Lethe, I'd like you to help me.

"You don't need my help," Lethe said. "I do not know how to get the Heart across the barrier and into the metaplanes. Besides, I am trapped inside this body now. Intertwined with this spirit. You must accomplish this mission on your own."

A fighter jet slashed past on Ryan's left, a red and black streak against the neutral gray sky of the astral.

"Ryan Mercury," Lethe continued, "you are everything you need. I am sorry that—"

A missile exploded close, shaking the air around the helo, and Dhin vectored away from it. A string of expletives came from Dhin.

Ryan pulled his senses back into the physical and looked over at the ork rigger. "What was that?"

"One of the UCAS jets fired a missile that nearly blew us out of the sky," Dhin said. "Fragging amateurs."

"Not exactly," Jane's voice rumbled through the speakers. "That was a warning shot, Ryan. A deal has been made between the Azzies and UCAS. You'd better back off."

Another explosion rocked the helo, rattling Ryan's teeth with its force. "They paid someone off? I hope it wasn't that easy."

Jane's voice was filled with frustration. "Nobody was paid off. The Azzies claimed that Burnout was the property of Aztechnology Corporation, that he had been stolen by a renegade faction that the UCAS was aiding and abetting by holding it in a Federal facility. The corporation promised serious retaliatory measures if they weren't allowed to take their 'experimental cybernetic organism' back."

Dhin's voice was harsh. "Excuse my fragging Sperethiel, but what a load of smelly dragon drek!"

"Dhin," Ryan said, "take us back to the mansion. Jane, see what you can do to track where they take Burnout."

"You got it," came Jane's response as Dhin gladly throttled back on the jets and banked right.

Ryan focused on the astral again, trying to use the Dragon Heart to regain contact. *Lethe . . . Lethe, if you can hear me . . . thank you. Thank you for saving my life.*

No response came; the enemy chopper was too far.

Frag, Ryan thought. He'd been hoping to get some help from Lethe.

Ever since the spirit had saved his life, throwing him

clear of the explosion, Ryan thought he would need Lethe.
In the echoing recesses of his mind, he knew that without
the spirit trapped inside Burnout, his mission would be a
lot harder.

Perhaps impossible.

2

Nadja Daviar stood on the balcony of the Watergate Hotel's penthouse suite, feeling the morning heat rise up to greet her like a cloying damp cloth. Washington FDC's downtown cluster promised to be a sauna again today. Since last night's explosion at Dunkelzahn's Georgetown mansion, Nadja had decided to use the suite for her Draco Foundation business.

Too many security guards and police and construction workers at the house. She couldn't work there.

Yet she knew there was more to it than work. Nadja had come down to the site of Dunkelzahn's assassination at least once a day for the last two weeks since the explosion. She had come to remember, to hold that moment in her mind until it became as much a part of her as her own heart.

She had taken out a long-term lease on the penthouse suite.

Nadja wore a smartly cut business suit, a deep green color, almost black. Her frame was elven—slender and just over two meters tall, with square shoulders and long legs and arms. Her raven-black hair shone in the sunlight as she looked down at Virginia Avenue below. At the prismatic cloud hovering over the gaping hole in the street where Dunkelzahn had been murdered.

Rainbow colors shimmered and danced in the cloud, what her mages called a manastorm. Around the edge of the crater stood masses of people, pressing up close to the hurricane fencing that prevented them from being pulled into the manastorm. Several people had disappeared into the phenomenon already.

Her experts had told her that it was a puncture—a tear in the fabric that separated physical space and the meta-planes, left by the destruction of Dunkelzahn's spirit.

Nadja took a slow breath as images of the explosion rushed into her mind. She remembered inauguration night, two weeks ago. The party in this very hotel, downstairs in the Grand Ballroom. She had danced with Dunkelzahn, a splendid, perfect moment as they tangoed across the floor, adored by the crowd.

The onlookers were admiring their new president—Dunkelzahn, in his human form, a young man with beauti-ful proportions like Michelangelo's David—flawless olive skin and curly brown hair. Only his eyes betrayed his supernatural origin—metallic blue and silver with pupils that were unnaturally black, like pinpoint windows into a deep void.

He moved with grace and poise on the parquet floor, leading Nadja, the woman who was known as his transla-tor. His voice. She was his aide and campaign manager. His friend and closest ally.

Their dance entranced the crowd, watching in awe and satisfaction. They were the center of the universe for a sublime moment. A breath-holding instant of pure beauty.

Their dance was interrupted by Carla Brooks, the tall black security chief, who informed Dunkelzahn of a cru-cial phone call. Urgent.

Dunkelzahn had quickly made his excuses and retired to an anteroom to take the call. It wasn't until later that Nadja learned that it had been Ryan Mercury on the line.

When Dunkelzahn returned to the dance floor, Nadja had felt his thoughts touch her. *I must take my leave of you, Nadjaruska.* The dragon's thoughts passed over her like a static charge, and she understood them, not as words, but as an extension of her conscious mind.

That had been the last time she'd heard the dragon's thoughts in her head, and she missed them. It felt like a

part of her had died with Dunkelzahn, like a bit of her
spirit had fled.

Now, Nadja gripped the railing and became entranced
by the hypnotic patterns in the manastorm below. Images
of the explosion flashed through her mind, like a battering
of hailstones. Dunkelzahn's limousine pulling out from the
hotel's circular drive. The explosion ripping through the
night, vaporizing the limo in an instantaneous fiery blast as
Nadja stood on the curb and spoke with Carla Brooks. The
sleek black Mitsubishi Nightsky engulfed by a spiked
sphere of plasma and searing orange heat.

Cars in front and behind Dunkelzahn's limousine flew
up into the air. Trees burst into flames, and Dunkelzahn
bellowed in pain, a telepathic scream exploding inside her
head before the physical sound reached her ears.

Out of the explosion, Nadja saw him emerge in dragon
form, his body a ghostly white behind the flash spot on her
retina. A transparent specter, the detailed scalloped ridge
of each scale glimmered with white fire, but there was no
solidity to him. Only the outline of him left, writhing in
desperate agony as his ancient flesh disintegrated.

Then he was gone and the blast wave hit her, a wall of
fire and kinetic thunder, lifting her off her feet and hurling
her backward through the glass doors. She landed on the
plush carpeting, the shattered glass cutting her in a thousand places, and somehow she was still alive. Still in one
piece even though she knew that was impossible. The explosion should have killed her.

Now, standing at the balcony's railing, Nadja shook her
head to clear away the memories. She wiped tears from
her face with a handkerchief and stood up straight. Carla
hadn't been able to explain why the explosive blast had
been contained, had stopped and reversed itself. That was
the only reason that Nadja had survived at all. Carla had
found no magical barrier. Nothing simple like that. The
best Carla had come up with was that somehow, when the
manastorm had been created, the blast energy had been

sucked back into the vortex and had vented into astral space and the metaplanes.

Perhaps it was a lucky accident that Nadja was still alive while Dunkelzahn—the creature who had been her master, her benefactor, and teacher—had been vaporized. Or perhaps whoever had killed Dunkelzahn had wanted to protect those at the inaugural ball—the many powerful people inside the Watergate Hotel.

Now, Nadja became aware of Gordon Wu's presence at her side and slightly behind her. Gordon was her aide, extremely reliable, with a perfect sense of etiquette. He waited without sound for Nadja to acknowledge his presence.

Nadja hardened her will, and turned toward him. Gordon was a short human of Asian heritage outfitted with a simsense rig that recorded everything he experienced while on duty. He also had a separate headcamera as a backup; it could record full-motion video or stills, if necessary.

Nadja nodded for him to speak.

"There are two elves here to see you," Gordon said. "They do not have an appointment, but when I told them this, one of them laughed and the other got angry. They persisted until I promised to announce them. I am supposed to tell you that Aina is here."

Nadja felt a thrill of excitement. Aina was in Dunkelzahn's will and was to be offered a position on the Draco Foundation's board of directors. Among the various secret documents that had come into Nadja's possession after Dunkelzahn's death was a statement regarding Aina, a warning that while her participation in the Draco Foundation was crucial, she would most likely be reluctant to join.

Nadja had tried to contact Aina many times since the reading of the will, but none of her telecom messages had been answered. Until now.

Nadja gave Gordon a smile and indicated for him to lead on. She followed him through the double glass doors and into the living room where two elves waited. One stood by the tall windows, and there was a coldness to her stance. Distance.

She wore comfortable blue jeans and a white t-shirt, and her features were striking. Her skin was deep black in tone, her hair shockingly white and very straight, cropped close her skull. She wore no make-up, but her elven features needed no emphasis to enhance their sharpness.

This is Aina, Nadja thought.

Aina studied Nadja intently as she walked in, seeming to scrutinize Nadja's aura as well as her physical body. Aina did not smile; there was a sadness to her expression. Which was to be expected; she had just lost a dear friend in Dunkelzahn.

The elf sitting on the blond leather couch was a man. Also quite striking, he wore his long auburn hair pulled straight back into a pony tail. His face was painted clown-white and there were diamond shapes done in red make-up over each eye and a smile painted on his face. Like a jester at court.

Under the make-up, his face seemed weathered and quite handsome, bearing no scars except perhaps the faintest hint of one just next to his left ear. He wore tight-fitting black jeans that were humorously about ten years out of fashion, a Maria Mercurial shirt, and a black leather jacket festooned with assorted pins. Despite the outside heat, he did not seem to be perspiring.

He smiled at Nadja as she entered the room. "Miss Daviar, so good of you to see us. My name is Harlequin and this is Aina."

Nadja returned the smile, then turned to Aina. "I'm glad you came. I've been wanting to talk to you about joining the Draco Foundation."

"You can talk," Aina said. "And I might even listen. But like all the other grave-robbers, we're merely here to collect our booty from the dragon's hoard." She gave a sarcastic laugh. "I'm here for my hope."

Nadja shivered a little inside at the woman's tone, though she tried not to show it. One of the entries in

Dunkelzahn's Last Will and Testament was directed at Aina. The old wyrm had expressed sorrow at the great suffering that had plagued Aina, and he had left her the one most valuable thing he had to offer—hope.

Dunkelzahn had intended that by joining the Draco Foundation, Aina would gain hope as she learned of the power of his far-reaching plans. Nadja felt that Aina needed her as much as she needed Aina. But the black elf's blasé attitude toward Dunkelzahn's offer of hope was far from encouraging.

"And I'll do my best to make sure you get your hope," Nadja said, her tone completely serious. "It was Dunkelzahn's wish that you be informed of the inner workings of the Draco Foundation and help in the long-term guidance and development of the plans he laid out."

The elf called Harlequin chuckled. "Just your style," he said to Aina. "Sitting behind a big corporate conference table and pushing papers."

Sarcasm seemed to be the sauce of the day.

Nadja ignored Harlequin. "I'd like to discuss this in more detail at your convenience," she told Aina, "but I'm afraid it'll have to be solo."

"You can trust Caimbeul, er, Harlequin."

"I don't mean to be rude, but I'm afraid I can't. Dunkelzahn specified you and you alone. Perhaps Mr. Harlequin can excuse us for a few hours."

Harlequin laughed again. "You've certainly got balls," he said to Nadja. "I'm beginning to see why Dunkelzahn chose you."

Nadja turned toward him. "While I'm afraid that I can't let you check personally, I assure you that I don't have balls, sir. I am quite female."

Harlequin threw his head back in laughter, genuine and deep. Even Aina smiled. Still, Harlequin made no movement to leave. After his laughter had died down, he looked hard at Nadja. "Actually, I have come to claim something from the dragon hoard as well."

Nadja brought her full attention on him. "I remember no mention of a Harlequin in any of Dunkelzahn's papers."

"He rarely referred to me as such," Harlequin said. "He had many other names for me, most of them unspeakable in polite company."

Aina gave a harsh laugh. "As if this qualifies as polite."

Harlequin ignored her and continued. "The second to last item in Dunkelzahn's public will leaves the sword Excalibur and King Richard the Lionheart's suit of armor to the Last Knight of the Crying Spire." He gave himself a self-indulgently cute smile. "That's me."

Nadja frowned, imperceptibly. *I have made a serious error in judgment.* She had made the mistake of assuming that this pompous, painted elf was merely an annoying friend or lackey of Aina's acquaintance.

I cannot afford such misjudgments, she thought. *Not in my position.*

"I'm very sorry for not recognizing you," she said. "Dunkelzahn didn't leave me a key to the identities of everyone to whom he willed items."

"Actually, I'm a little hurt that he didn't tell you about me," Harlequin said. "We were close."

Aina looked at the painted elf. "I'm sure he did it as a purposeful slight," she said. "Just a last little insult that you can't return. It's brilliant actually."

Harlequin flashed a harsh glare at Aina, but when he spoke, his tone was light. "Perhaps, but I tend to think that he just wanted to protect my identity. You can see that he intended to put you in the spotlight."

Nadja jumped in. "That's not true! He merely hoped that Aina would join in the long-term goals of the Draco Foundation. It does not necessitate public exposure. I can handle most of that."

Aina moved away from the window and sat down next to Harlequin. "I can vouch for his claim to be the Last Night of the Crying Spire," she said.

Nadja nodded. "All right, let me get the official forms." She nodded to Gordon Wu, who brought over a small computer and handed it to her. Nadja punched up the instructions Dunkelzahn had left for her, and read off the first of four questions. "Who sits at the bridge, protecting us from the Enemy?"

Harlequin nearly jumped in his seat. "What?"

"These questions were left by Dunkelzahn to judge the veracity of someone's claim."

His composure returned instantly. "Thayla," he said.

Nadja made a mental note. *This elf knows about Thayla. I should tell Ryan about him.*

She read the next question. "Whose daughter have you taken on as pupil? Or, is that concubine?"

Harlequin narrowed his eyes.

Aina gave a harsh laugh. "Score one for the wyrm."

Nadja simply waited, trying to keep her composure.

Finally, Harlequin answered, "Ehran the Scribe's daughter, and I'm teaching her."

"Two down," Nadja said. "Two to go. The next is: how old are you?"

Harlequin looked at Aina.

As response, she shrugged.

Seconds ticked by as Harlequin pondered what to say.

Nadja shifted in her seat. The answer on the screen was difficult to believe, and there was a note saying that the true Knight of the Crying Spire would be unwilling to divulge the information. The instructions said to make him sweat to see what he would say, then ask him the last question.

"I'm a few years younger than her," he said, indicating Aina.

Nadja simply stared at him. "That's not an answer."

"A lot younger than Dunkelzahn or Lofwyr, and far older than you."

Nadja crossed her arms and waited.

Aina looked at Harlequin.

Harlequin began to sweat.

"It says here," Nadja said, "that . . ." She hesitated.

"What does it say?"

"It says you're over three hundred years old."

Harlequin breathed a sigh. "I've aged well," he said.

Nadja knew, of course, that elves were long-lived, and she was aware of the rumors concerning the immortals, but she'd never given any of it much credence before now. She took a slow breath. "Last question: what was the original name of the Crying Spire?"

Without hesitation. "The Crimson Spire."

Nadja nodded. "Congratulations, your claim is officially valid. You can take possession of the armor today, or I can ship it to you. I'm sorry to say that the sword Excaliber is currently lost. We're looking for it."

"You can send the armor to my place in France, Château d'If."

"Very well." Then she turned to Aina, who had stood up again, looking like she was ready to leave. "And what about you? Will you join the Draco Foundation?"

Aina gave her a sad look. "Dunkelzahn was a very close friend," she said. "And for that reason only, I will think about it." Then she pulled on Harlequin's ponytail. "Come on, Caimbeul, let's go."

"When will I hear from you?"

Aina stopped by the door. "When I've decided." Then she turned and walked out into the hall.

Harlequin paused as he passed Nadja. "I'm impressed, Miss Daviar. She didn't tell you to frag off. You should consider this a victory."

Nadja smiled at him as he turned to leave. It didn't feel like a victory. Aina's help was crucial to the long-term plan Dunkelzahn had left in his documents. Without her, the whole future of the world could suffer.

3

The fragments of Ryan's nightmare fluttered in the recesses of his consciousness as Dhin brought the helo down onto the helipad behind Dunkelzahn's mansion. Ryan said goodbye to the ork and stepped out of the helicopter and into the wind and heat. He ducked, walking across the duracrete toward the door.

Four security agents met him there, and made him look into a portable retinal scanner. The guards knew him and were expecting his return, but security had been tightened in the aftermath of Burnout's forced entry last night.

As Ryan waited for the scanner to check his retinal image against the datastore and give him clearance to enter, Dhin lifted the bird into the air behind him. The ork would return the helicopter to National Airport for a full systems check and any necessary repairs.

The retinal scanner beeped. The guards smiled at Ryan and waved him through. He headed for his recovery room, trying to keep the recurring images of his dream at bay. His wristphone sounded as he passed into the west wing.

He punched the Connect and found himself looking at the most beautiful face he'd ever known. She had cut her hair again, probably to get rid of the parts burned in the explosion. "Nadja, my sweet, it is so lovely to see you."

Nadja smiled, her green eyes bright. "Likewise, dear. How are you feeling?"

"I'm completely recovered." Ryan decided not to discuss his nightmare, which had come back to plague him with visions. "I'm worried about you."

"I came through without a scratch," Nadja said. "Burn-out didn't hurt me. There's still some ringing in my ears from the explosion, but I've got an appointment with a snake shaman to see if that can be fixed."

Ryan smiled. "I'm sorry I pulled you into this."

"Don't speak nonsense, Ryan. Burnout kidnapped me. Anyone else would have been stopped by security. You had nothing to do with it."

"Yeah, well, I'm sorry anyway."

Nadja smiled. "Stubborn slot."

Ryan removed his guns and his bandoleer. "That's me."

"Do you feel up to having lunch with me?" Nadja said.

"Always."

"I don't have time to leave the hotel, but I'd love to see you here. Can you make noon?"

"Yes."

"Good." She disconnected.

Ryan finished removing his running gear and decided to make his way to the arboretum to dance some katas. He needed to think, to sort out some things. Was getting Lethe back important enough to plan a run into Aztlan? Or would that simply divert his attention when it should be focused on his mission?

The Silent Way will help me.

Wearing his black plycra unibody with the Dragon Heart still strapped around his waist, Ryan walked through the house to the arboretum. When he reached the shattered double glass doors, he stepped beyond the yellow hazard tape and into the room where he and Burnout had fought just the night before.

In the center of the room, Ryan began his katas, moving in slow motion, dancing in morning sunshine. Mana came to him through the physical contraction and stretching of his muscles. The power came, bringing focus with it. Concentration into his mind.

All around him were the remnants of the burned arboretum. Scorched plants and blackened marble trees stood beneath open sky. Most of the broken macroglass had been removed, cleaned in the hours since the explosion. Since Ryan had used his distance strike to make Burnout pull the trigger on his Colt Manhunter, and in so doing trigger a massive oxygen explosion.

Miraculously, they had both survived.

Now, the morning air blew cool through the skeletal stone trees of the destroyed arboretum, bringing the smell of cherry blossoms and azaleas from the mansion gardens outside. Dunkelzahn's estate boasted some of the most impressive grounds in all of the Washington FDC sprawl. Even so, Ryan could still smell the acrid tinge of burning corpses underneath the aroma of flowers. The stench of death from the sprawl-wide rioting that had followed Dunkelzahn's assassination two weeks earlier.

Ryan danced the moves of the Silent Way, the physical adept path that Dunkelzahn had taught him years ago, concentrating as his body flowed with deliberately slow gestures. He searched inward as he moved, looking with his magic, until he found his core, the solid rock that was his essence, the fountainhead of all his power. He became centered.

Ryan's power grew from his core, expanding outward until it touched the Dragon Heart, resting in its pouch by his gut. He sensed the immense puissance from the item, radiating like white-hot spray of sunfire. He could feel it like a molten orb, a searing ball of slag in his stomach, but he did not tap into its power. He had decided to use it only when absolutely necessary.

As his power brushed over the Dragon Heart, the nightmare dream flooded back through his mind . . .

In the dream, he stands on a cracked plane of rock, a rough and windswept wasteland bathed in a light so brilliant and so lustrous that he cannot bear to look at it.

The light sings to him, beckoning for him to come to her. To help her. And all he can think about is pleasing the light. He wants to protect the joyous voice that sings like a chorus of angels.

When he sees the wedge of darkness growing on the

rock, a vile stain spreading against the light, he tries to move. He tries to run to the light. He can protect her, he can help.

He finds that he cannot move. An invisible membrane surrounds him, like clear latex, and prevents him from going into the light. The membrane stretches and yields when he pushes against it, but it does not break, and the more he tries, the more he finds himself tangled up in it, struggling to breathe.

Suddenly, the voice stops and the light fades. Ryan has failed, and great sadness washes over him as he holds his breath and watches the woman who had been singing. She falls under the onslaught of darkness, her throat ripped out first. Then her heart. Her eyes. Until she is in fleshy tatters, and the light that had radiated from her is blanketed by the stain of blackened blood.

The dream faded from Ryan's awareness, and he remembered to breathe. He knew some of what the dream meant now. The place was a spike of mana in the astral plane, a point where the world was closest to a plane where horrible creatures existed. Dunkelzahn had called these creatures the Enemy in his message to Ryan.

The light was Thayla. She protected the site from those who would use magic to finish the bridge to the plane of the Enemy so that they could come across and destroy the world. But Thayla's song was not impenetrable, and perhaps the dream was telling Ryan that the place had been breached.

Perhaps it's paranoia and means nothing.

Dunkelzahn had given Ryan instructions to take the Dragon Heart to Thayla; she knew how to use it to stop the darkness. If he didn't get the Heart to her soon, it would be too late to stop the war.

Now, in the ruins of Dunkelzahn's arboretum, Ryan drew mana around him as he moved. As he walked the forms of the Silent Way.

Magic built inside him, and he remembered his mission—told to him by a messenger spirit that had been instructed by Dunkelzahn. The messenger had emerged from the shining silver statue of a small dracoform deep inside the dragon's lair.

"I have taught you of the cycles of magic," it said, speaking with Dunkelzahn's voice, "but no one has dared manipulate them as they do now . . . The discovery of a Locus by Darke may be the single most devastating event in all of history. If the metaplanar Chasm is breached before we are ready, we will all suffer. All beings will die.

"*All* beings.

"My fellow dragons are overconfident . . . Technology changes everything. No magic can protect against it. There will be no hiding this time. There will only be war. We must gain the time we need to build up *our* technology so that we have the ability to fight the Enemy when it can cross. But to gain that time we must protect our natural defenses. They must not be allowed to fail, and the Dragon Heart will ensure that they don't. Thayla will know how to use it. Get it to her before it is too late."

Now, in the decimated arboretum, the spirit's voice faded from Ryan's memory as he finished his dance. He stood perfectly still for several seconds, trying to prepare himself mentally for the coming days, and enjoying the fleeting feel of warm sunshine on the freshly healed new skin of his face.

Gone were the insecurities and doubts that had plagued him before he'd defeated Burnout and regained the Dragon Heart. Forgotten were his desires for vengeance on Dunkelzahn's assassin. Out of his mind for the moment. Shelved until the task at hand was successfully accomplished. The task of delivering the Dragon Heart to Thayla.

More words came back to Ryan from the messenger spirit's speech. "In order to complete your task, you must enlist the service of a powerful mage who knows the ritual that can carry you and the Dragon Heart into the metaplanes . . . Harlequin would be my first choice."

Now that I am completely healed, Ryan thought, *I must*

begin the search for the mage, Harlequin. Anything else is but a distraction.

Ryan returned to his room, showered and shaved, then dressed in a comfortable suit and tie, restrapping the Dragon Heart to his waist under his suit coat. The Heart bulged at his abdomen, almost making him look like he had a gut, but Ryan had decided to carry the artifact with him until his mission was complete.

He tucked the Walther PB-100 pistol into a discreet ankle holster and took two extra clips of armor-piercing ammo. Just in case. Then he allowed himself to be chauffeured to the Watergate Hotel. He arrived a little before noon, very hungry for having skipped breakfast.

The crowd around the Watergate was thinner than it had been the past few days, mainly concentrated in the front by the manastorm. Someone had erected a temporary macroplast podium and was addressing the crowd, spouting off about how Dunkelzahn had martyred himself, about how the dragon had been a saint and had been called up to heaven by God.

Ryan had heard of the Church of Dunkelzahn fanatics, and apparently their numbers were spreading worldwide. The limousine driver pulled into the circular drive, newly repaired since the explosion had taken out much of the hotel's facade and the overhanging canopy. The limo stopped by the brand-new revolving glass doors and the driver came around to let Ryan out.

Initially, Ryan had felt a tad conspicuous in corporate attire, but that had lasted only a few minutes. He knew that in this part of the Federal cluster, a suit and tie were almost as effective as an invisibility spell. He stepped inside and up to the elevator.

Nadja greeted him at the door to the penthouse suite, a beaming smile on her lips. And Ryan ran to her, ignoring the defensive looks from the secret servicemen clustered around her. He plunged himself into her arms, pulling her off her feet in a rugged embrace. She smelled sweetly of faint vanilla.

She laughed and kissed his neck. Squeezed his body tightly.

Ryan ran his fingers through her hair. "I'm sorry," he said. "I'm so sorry."

"Shh," she whispered in his ear.

He held her close, her face in the hollow of his neck. His tears threatening to come. He loved her more than he'd loved anyone, and he'd nearly caused her death. Burnout had gone for her because of what she meant to Ryan.

After a minute Nadja pulled back and straightened her suit and skirt, the deep green going perfectly with her eyes and hair. She always did know how to kill in the fashion department. "You hungry?" she asked.

"Famished."

"Come. I've ordered Greek from Aesop's."

Nadja led Ryan into the raised dining area, situated next to the kitchen. A young human male poured him wine and brought a plate of stuffed grape leaves, hummus, and pita bread.

Ryan's stomach rumbled. He took a sip of his wine and helped himself to the food.

"I heard Burnout was taken by the Azzies," Nadja said.

"Yes."

"Any idea where?"

"Not exactly," Ryan said. "Jane is trying to track him."

Nadja nodded and swallowed a piece of pita smothered in hummus. She was so beautiful, so strong. Ryan would do anything for her.

"I was hoping to have Lethe's help, but he and Burnout can't be my main focus right now."

Nadja nodded as though she instinctively understood what Ryan had spent an hour of meditation figuring out. "You have the Dragon Heart."

"Yes, and I need to figure out how to get it to Thayla."

"It's curious," Nadja said. "I met someone else today who knows of Thayla."

Ryan snapped his attention on her. "Who?"

"A strange one. Elf with a painted face. Calls himself Harlequin."

"You met Harlequin? He's the one Dunkelzahn said I should ask for help. Where is he?"

Nadja sat back and delicately wiped her mouth with the corner of her napkin. "I'm sorry to say that he left."

"Do you have an LTG number or a satellite telecom code for him?"

"No . . ."

Ryan held his breath, waiting for Nadja to finish.

"But I do have an address where I'm supposed to deliver his suit of armor."

"Thank the spirits! Where?"

"It's an island in the Mediterranean Sea off the coast of France—Château d'If. It's where the Count of Monte Cristo was held prisoner."

"He owns a castle on an island?"

"An ancient French prison. Have you read Alexandre Dumas?"

"No, but I've chipped the sim."

Nadja chuckled. "You really should try the archaic practice of reading sometime."

Ryan ignored the tease. An idea was taking shape in his mind. A plan forming. "When are you supposed to deliver the armor?" he asked.

"I was planning to send it out tomorrow."

"You'll need more security than usual," Ryan said. "Won't you, considering the inordinate value of the merchandise?"

Nadja narrowed her eyes on him. "What are you scheming?"

Ryan smiled. "I plan to be on the plane with that armor," he said. "And I've got a few friends I'd like to invite along."

Nadja sighed. "I supposed as much. As far as I'm concerned, you and Assets can take charge of delivering the package. Just be careful. I have a funny feeling about Harlequin. He's been around a long, long time it seems. He could be extremely powerful, and he's possibly known Dunkelzahn far longer than either of us. We can't be sure that their relationship has always been on good terms."

"What are you suggesting?" Ryan asked. "Do you think he could have been involved in the assassination?"

Nadja sipped her wine, deliberately hesitating before she answered. "I'm not suggesting anything, Ryan. I'm just saying that he's got a known history with our master, and we don't know whether they were friends or enemies."

Ryan steepled his fingers in front of his face, contemplating. "Why would Dunkelzahn want me to contact an enemy for help? It doesn't make sense."

"When did Dunkelzahn's plans make sense?"

"Good point," Ryan said. "But I still need to contact Harlequin. It's very important."

Nadja leaned across the table and took Ryan's hand. "I know," she said, her hands warm around his. "I just don't want anything to happen to you."

Ryan looked into her eyes. "I'll be careful," he said.

Nadja narrowed her gaze on him. "You'd better be." Her stare hardened, though a smile played over her lips. "If you're not, I'll kill you myself."

4

The touch of pure evil resonated inside Lucero and brought shudders to her body. It had been mere hours since she'd passed out from the overwhelming sense of dread and horror that had seized her on the metaplanes, at the site of the dark wedge.

Now she stood in the physical world, high up in the San Marcos *teocalli,* looking out the window of the step pyramid structure, gazing at the growing masses of people outside. The hot Texas sun beat down on her, bathing her in its searing radiation. She didn't mind, however; she enjoyed it. This physical existence, however uncomfortable, was a blessing after her extended stay in the metaplanes with Señor Oscuro.

The valley before her and the plain beyond was filled with people, drawn from the farthest reaches of Aztlan by the Locus—the chiseled obsidian rock ensconced in the lake bed below the temple. Security fences had been set up in a broad perimeter to protect the stone from the huge crowd. Thousands and thousands of metahumans stretched off into the distance, chanting and celebrating the end of the Aztec Fifth Sun.

Which she knew, meant the coming of the *tzitzimine*—demons who would devour the world. A shiver passed through her. Had she seen those demons across the Chasm? Had she felt their touch in her heart?

People were drawn to the Locus, she supposed, or perhaps Señor Oscuro was luring them magically. Their presence made Lucero uneasy, though she wasn't sure why that should be. They were only citizens and common folk, camping out under tents and makeshift shelters.

Perhaps they are merely as entranced by the power of the Locus as I am.

Lucero found herself hypnotized by the allure of the huge black stone. Its glossy surface was cut perfectly flat, like chiseled onyx or black diamond. It seemed to absorb all light around it. A fine tracery of gold lines ran through it, tiny threads of orichalcum barely visible from up here.

The lake was mostly dry now, only the deepest section still holding water. The rest of it was captured by huge pipes and channeled downstream. Lucero could see the needle reflection of the observation tower in the silvery water—an old amusement park structure where people used to ride up high on a cylindrical metal tower to get a better view of the area in the revolving observatory at the top. The observation platform had long rusted to the column and had not moved in the years since Lucero had visited San Marcos.

There was a soft knock behind her, followed by the whisper of the door opening. Lucero turned to see three acolytes dressed in white linen. One of them, a boy of about seventeen with brown skin and black eyes, carried a gray robe for Lucero. He unfolded it and offered it to her.

"Señor Oscuro has requested your presence at the new altar," the boy said. "We will escort you."

Lucero nodded. "Thank you. I will be ready shortly." Modesty was an unusual trait at the temple, but Lucero was an extremely special case. The acolytes took the hint and stepped outside.

Lucero breathed a heavy sigh. She could not disobey her master, but she dreaded what he might ask her to do. The last time they had traveled to the metaplanes together, he had used her as the focus for his blood magic. Because of her, Oscuro had been able to build his wedge against the goddess of light and song who guarded the metaplanar bridge.

Lucero slipped out of her nightshirt, and stepped to the

mirror with her gray robe in hand. She stared at the full-
length reflection of her naked body. She had once been
quite beautiful, but that had been long ago, before the scarring. Before her addiction to the blood, her slavery to the
dark stain on her soul.

Her head was bald—dark brown skin shaved smooth.
The shape of her skull was delicate. It was fragile and unmarred like her face. She had large eyes, the color of worn
leather, faded from time but resilient and strong. Her narrow nose was elegant and her mouth full.

Below the neck, her brown skin was a tapestry of scars.
Deep-etched runes, like embossed tattoos bled of their ink.
They were the runes of ritual blood magic, runes of the
Blood Mage Gestalt, and they covered her arms and shoulders, her breasts and stomach, back and buttocks, thighs
and legs. Such mutilation was a hideous and unnatural
thing.

For the briefest of moments, Lucero saw past the scars,
saw the woman she had been before Oscuro had perverted
her, before he had fostered her addiction to the life energy
in metahuman blood. She could see the bright, intelligent
eyes, the smooth, young skin stretched tight across her
stomach. Unblemished and supple. She tried to remember
what it had felt like to sense the delicate touch of an inti-
mate friend. To be desired.

A gentle knock on the door brought her out of her
reverie. *He will take me across again,* she thought as she
slipped into the gray robe. *He will take me to the dark circle, that place which was once radiant with light and
beautiful music.*

Lucero loved the song and the light; she knew it was her
only chance for salvation. Señor Oscuro had cut a sharp
wedge of his own darkness into the beauty, and she knew
that he planned to destroy the light completely. She also
knew that, for some reason, he needed her help.

I will hinder him this time, she vowed.

She opened the door and followed the three acolytes
down the stairs and outside into the oppressive heat. They

led her across the grass, which felt dry and brittle against her bare feet, then down the recently built wooden ramp into the dry lake bed and across to the small gathering around the Locus.

The power emanating from the chiseled black stone penetrated her and drew her. It was like a dark sun of mana, a magical focus of such unprecedented force that it made her mind reel. The air seemed to grow heavy as she approached, making it harder to go ahead even as the stone's hypnotic enchantment made her desire nothing more than to touch it.

Just when she thought she could walk no further, Señor Oscuro stepped out of the gathering of people and smiled at Lucero, his handsome face adorned with a black beard and mustache. His expression was warm, and it reassured her. His teeth showed in his smile, perfectly straight and white, almost gleaming.

Oscuro wore the tan robe of ancient Aztec magic, embroidered with profiles of the old gods. Around his neck hung a ceremonial collar of gold and dragon feathers. The feathers were deep blue and crimson, brilliant green and yellow. They had been encased in enamel and their edges rimmed with gold.

Oscuro's skin glowed with life, shedding hope on her, giving her the strength to continue. But his eyes were darkly framed holes of blackness, and underneath their false sparkle, they cut her up like a surgical laser. They betrayed his true nature.

Oscuro reached to her with a pale hand, the back of it sprouting hundreds of individual black hairs. "My child," he said. "We are close to victory." He gave her a secretive smile. "The bridge is nearly ours."

She put her warm hand into his, cold as damp fish, and allowed him to lead her into the crowd. They passed medical technicians and Jaguar Guards brandishing automatic weapons as Oscuro guided her toward the short wooden stairs that led up onto the stone itself. The power of the

Locus thickened the air around her until it seemed almost solid.

Then they stepped through the line of guards, and Lucero saw it up close. The partially excavated stone was faceted, each face like a sheet of black glass fifteen meters across. Its surface was unnaturally smooth, unmarred and perfect as though it had been polished. The threads of orichalcum formed fractal patterns over the surface, and Lucero felt a pulse of mana coming from them like the beats of an animal's heart. The Locus was obviously created by man or some other sentience before being buried here long ago.

The Blood Mage Gestalt sat in a circle on the surface of the stone, preparing to begin a ritual. The ten mages stood and looked at Lucero and her master as they came up the steps. They were all human, their skin a mosaic of tattoos and runic scars just like hers. There were thick needle track marks on their necks.

When Lucero saw the dark emptiness of their gaze, she felt a swelling pity for the acolytes who had escorted her; more than likely they would be sacrificed to power the blood magic. The blood mages wore the traditional crimson robes and had catheters in their necks that allowed them to share their blood with each other during the ritual.

Lucero had been a member of the Gestalt herself and had participated in the blood spilling, in the blood sharing many, many times. But since she had been touched by the light, this seemed evil to her, a perversion of magic. To use life energy for such purposes was highly addictive and Lucero had succumbed to the lure of it. Only by hearing the beauty of the song, by witnessing the sheer goodness of the light had Lucero been able to see her own inner evil, the shadow on her heart that made her destroy innocent lives in order to achieve power and domination.

"It is important for you to remain strong, my child. The one who blocks the bridge is on the verge of defeat now that we've breached to the tip, and our allies across the

Chasm have lent us their influence. This will be our final battle."

Lucero shuddered.

When her bare foot touched the surface of the Locus, Lucero froze. Her knees buckled as a wave of electricity passed up through her until every nerve in her body exploded. She felt her consciousness sink into the stone, swallowed up by the geometric black hole. For a moment she thought she could sense the whole earth at once, a split second of perfect godlike awareness—she was part of a huge network of power, manalines and other Loci that spanned the planet.

Then it was gone, and Señor Oscuro was helping her to her feet. Her skin tingled as she entered the circle formed by the Gestalt members. "Lie down, my child," said Oscuro. "Soon we will be together on the metaplanes."

Lucero lay with her back against the cold, hard surface of the Locus and opened her robe as the Gestalt mages encircled her. Oscuro appeared above her with an acolyte in tow—the boy who had spoken to her earlier. There was a look of distracted satisfaction on the boy's face—he was under magical hypnosis.

The boy's look changed momentarily as Oscuro produced an obsidian knife and drew it across the boy's throat in a well-practiced slash. Then he was dead, his warm, thick blood spilling over Lucero's naked body, and his eyes going glassy in the far-off stare that she had seen too many times.

Oscuro threw the boy's body aside and knelt down in the pool of blood. As the iron smell of it overwhelmed Lucero, she gritted her teeth and fought down the urge to taste it. Oscuro traced patterns over Lucero's flesh and spoke under his breath in a language she didn't know.

Then the sun was gone, replaced by the flat light of the astral sky. Lucero saw the Gestalt entity forming around them for an instant before Oscuro spoke again and they rode the column of power rising out of the Locus.

"Stand up, my child." Oscuro's voice held a tone of authority now.

Lucero stood up and looked around, nearly panicking from the sense of overwhelming horror that filled the area. It was a raver's madness, a rapist's glee that penetrated to the marrow of her bones.

The cold ground brought shivers to her, a mean, hard chill that dug into her and wouldn't let go. The cracked rock beneath her feet was part of a giant outcropping that extended over a bottomless canyon. She could see the other side of the Chasm now, an impossible distance away. And she could sense the creatures there, moving in slow motion as they constructed an outcropping of their own. An arch that extended toward her.

They want to come across. If they are the tzitzimine, *they will ravage the world. They bring apocalypse.*

Lucero listened. She ached to hear what she knew must be there.

So faint was the music that she barely made it out over the sound of dead bodies coming to life as Oscuro waved his hand over them. Then she heard it, a song of such pure beauty that it either purged ugliness or destroyed it.

Help me, she prayed to the music. To the light that shone from the singer. Pure white brilliance that barely penetrated the wedge of blood and corpses that Oscuro had erected. It was the light that made the creatures move in slow motion.

Some of the zombie-corpses around her began to transform. Huge sharp bristles of spiny black hair popped out of their skin. Their legs and arms changed into furry tentacles, multiplying until they were four on either side of their now-hideous bodies. Their heads flattened and massive insect mandibles jutted from the base of their jaws as their eyes split and divided.

They cannot move when he is not here, Lucero realized. *And he cannot be here without me.*

Oscuro laughed. "We are ready to begin the final assault."

If only I could leave so that he would have to stop.

Suddenly the sky around her darkened, and Lucero felt a slippery chill slide over her spirit. An intense trepidation gripped her, and she could not move. She could not think. There were eels in her mind.

Annihilation. Eternal suffering.

The song filtered through to her, the dim rays of light from the outside. Holding her sanity in brittle fingers. Balanced on the fragile edge. . . .

5

Ryan sat cross-legged in the garden courtyard behind Dunkelzahn's mansion, relishing the scent of roses and freshly turned earth that filled the air around him. The heat of the sun against his closed eyelids. He still wore the corporate-style suit from his lunch with Nadja; he had made plans for dinner with her, but didn't know whether she'd make it back in time. She was swamped with work.

His wristphone beeped, and he opened his eyes. It was Jane-in-the-box. He punched the Connect and her bubble blonde icon appeared, a big ruby smile on her lips.

"Hoi, Jane."

"Quicksilver, I just worked out the final details with Nadja and Black Angel."

Black Angel was the code name for Carla Brooks, former head of security of Dunkelzahn and current security chief for the Draco Foundation. "Good," Ryan said. "Spill it."

"Black Angel has put together a security team to take the suit of armor from Lake Louise to Washington, at which point, Assets Incorporated will take charge. The change of responsibility will take place at approximately 0500 tomorrow at National Airport. Assets will then transport the armor to the elf Harlequin at Château d'If."

"Prime work, friend," Ryan said.

"Dhin and Grind will bring a chopper to pick you up at 0330, which should give you enough time to load equipment and gear onto the jet. I've contacted Axler at Hells Canyon, and she's flying up to Lake Louise. She'll be on the plane with the merchandise when it arrives."

"Any news on getting a new mage?"

Jane's blonde head nodded. "I've made contact with a good one, but he's cautious. I'm still waiting on final word from him."

Ryan remembered Miranda, the mage who had died in the assault against Burnout on Pony Mountain. It seemed like months ago even though it had been only two days. Miranda had been a good mage and a friend.

He looked at Jane. "Tell me about this mage."

Jane laughed. "You worried we're hiring another redshirt?"

"Assets hasn't had the best of luck with magical backup."

"His name is Talon, and he's been doing runs for me through a Seattle fixer named Spanner. He's very competent and will make a good addition to Assets." Jane paused. "If we can keep him alive."

Ryan chuckled. "He'll have to attend to that himself," he said. "When can I meet him?"

"With luck, he'll come with Axler. You can meet him then, and get to know him better on the flight to France."

Ryan sighed. He hated bringing runners in at the last minute, though he supposed it couldn't be helped this time. They needed a mage, especially since they'd be dealing with Harlequin, rumored to be a powerful master of arcane energies.

We need a good magician, he thought. *And a lot of luck.*

"Thanks, Jane," Ryan said. "I am in awe of your abilities."

Jane smiled, her Matrix icon's hand waving at her face in a mock attempt at cooling off. "Flattery will get you anything you want, big boy," she said. Then she thrust her breasts forward—huge, gravity-defying flesh barely contained in a lacy black bra.

Ryan laughed and cut the connection.

Nadja didn't make it back in time for dinner, which saddened Ryan a bit even though he knew she was carrying on the truly important long-term plans Dunkelzahn had left behind. Ryan didn't know what those plans were, and didn't much want to know. He was a soldier and a spy, not a general or an administrator.

Ryan ate alone and went to bed early.

He woke from a dream about Nadja to find her climbing into bed with him. Into his arms. Naked and flushed. She kissed him, her dark, soft hair falling over his chest as she ran her lips along his body. As she worked her way up to his mouth.

In the dim light of the moon coming through the slats of the miniblinds, she nibbled on his lower lip. She tasted faintly of mint. He drank in the warm smell of her, gazed into the glistening darkness of her eyes as she straddled him.

They made love, long and slow. Unwilling to let go of each other.

Until finally Nadja collapsed from exhaustion and release. She fell into a deep sleep.

The clock read 0315. Dhin and Grind would arrive in fifteen minutes.

Ryan slipped out of bed and dressed in the dark, utterly quiet so as not to wake Nadja.

He kissed her cheek. "Goodbye, my love," he said. Then he picked up his gear bag and stepped out into the night.

6

Jane-in-the-box stood up from her decking recliner and stretched, massaging the back of her head where the fiber-optic lines had rubbed a callus. Jane's six datajacks at the base of her skull were covered with a retractable plastic static window, but the input cords still chafed the skin around the area when she was jacked in for long periods of time.

Jane spent most of her existence in virtual reality. It was a necessary element of her profession as decker for the now-deceased great dragon. Jane missed the wyrm even though she'd been mortally afraid of him. During Matrix runs, she'd had to resign herself to the telepathic link with Dunkelzahn. It was a level of surrender she'd never liked.

Jane hated being out of control.

Still, Dunkelzahn had been very good to her. He had personally pulled her from her duties in the VisionQuest programming think tank, and had given her a lab in the lair with a huge budget. He had fostered her interest in Matrix hardware and had allowed her to build her own private network of decks and hosts right here in Cyberlair, as she called it. Working for an ultra-rich great dragon had its bennies, especially when the dragon was a technology freak.

Now she stretched again and stepped away from her console. Cyberlair was a huge cavern of cut stone situated under the Canadian Rockies near Lake Louise in the Athabaskan Council. The massive doors at one end had made it possible for the dragon to enter from the adjoining corridor without changing shape. The decks and hosts around Jane's console sat on a low marble dais opposite the main entrance.

The cavern was illuminated with track lighting bolted to the stone walls and ceiling high above. It was a dull-looking place compared to the Matrix. Perhaps Jane would have some art brought in, ask Nadja if she could commission some remodeling.

She noticed that Enrico, the lair's troll chef, had left a soybeef sandwich au jus on the small table adjacent to her console. She was sure it was cold by now, but the smell of it permeated the room and made her stomach grumble. Too often, she forgot to eat.

She sat down and bit into the sandwich just as her deck beeped to indicate an incoming telecom call. She looked over to the terminal screen and saw that the call came from the Assets system and showed Axler's decryption code. *Finally,* she thought. *It's about time.*

Jane took another quick bite and stood. She stepped back over to her console and eased into her chair, snapping the six-jack multi-plug into the six datajacks at the back of her skull. The cavern dissipated as the virtual space of the command center materialized in her awareness.

A square-shaped room with riveted stainless steel walls surrounded her. Six sides of computer-generated reality, each face representing one of her datajacks. Each representing a connection, a channel to another world to which she could instantly switch. A die-shaped virtual gateway created by her network of cyberdecks and hosts.

The feeling in her physical body gave way to the imposed signals from her box, provided by her MPCP— Master Persona Control Program.

During runs, five of the steel faces displayed head-camera images and statistical data, four of them live feeds from members of Assets Incorporated—Axler, Dhin, Grind, and Ryan Mercury. No headcam image came from Ryan, but Jane got real-time vital stats through his wrist-phone. The fifth face, below her, took the form of a shining gold door, the gateway from her private virtual space to the Matrix—the electronic universe of the world-spanning computer network.

Jane popped into her blonde-bimbo persona and plunged through the gateway and into the Matrix, activating a routine trace as she answered the incoming telecom call. Just to double-check that the Assets anti-trace evasion utility was working properly.

Axler's face hovered in cyberspace, her thin blonde hair framing a pale visage. Doe brown eyes that could be so soft, if she would let them. Her stare was as purposely cold and hard as always.

"I'm here," said Jane.

Axler regarded Jane's ridiculous persona without expression. "The new mage, Talon, has arrived," she said. "We're ready for your briefing."

Jane nodded. "Very well."

With a quick motion, Jane activated her Assets command-room-linkage, which set up a highly secure communications protocol between them both. It manifested in her virtual reality as a bleb of cyberspace that was a Matrix replica of the command room.

The Assets compound was physically located on the eastern rim of Hells Canyon, but the holographic cameras in the command room fed data to Jane's hosts and gave her a nearly complete picture. The room was a large cavern with a massive oval table in the center that had seating for fifty. Only two chairs were taken, one occupied by Axler, her toned body in an erect posture, ready to move. She was a combat expert, an accomplished mercenary of the highest caliber.

In the other chair sat a young human male with shoulder-length brown hair and white skin. He was of average height and build, though his brown eyes held a glimmer of intelligence. This was Talon, by reputation a man of far better-than-average skill with the arcane.

Unbeknownst to Talon, Jane had hired him for several runs. She had followed his progress and he had performed excellently. Very professional, if somewhat smart-hooped. Just enough edge to stay alive in the shadows for quite awhile. He was as ready for induction into Assets as any mage she knew.

The hologenerators came to life, and Jane's persona appeared in one of the chairs. "Welcome to Assets Incorporated, Talon. I am called Jane-in-the-box."

"Good to meet you, Jane-in-the-box."

"You can call me Jane."

"Okay, Jane. I've flown out here, wherever it is, in the middle of the night because my fixer assured me you could be trusted. He said I would want to work with you. That it would be lucrative."

"Talon, all that is true. Allow me to explain."

Talon inclined his head.

"Assets is a corporation of shadowrunners. We screen those who join very carefully so that we can place some amount of trust in them."

"Is there any trust left in the world? I've seen slotting little of it, especially among shadowrunners."

Jane laughed. "True," she said. "We are different. We have independent funding so we don't have to work for Mister Johnsons. We don't take runs from corporations. Or should I say, we work for only one corporation, but we have a lot of say about which runs are done and how."

"Which corporation?"

"You've heard of the Draco Foundation?"

Talon sucked air through his teeth. "Who hasn't?"

"Those who run with Assets run for no one else. We take good care of our own. We run because we want to change the world for the better. We're trying to restore the balance. Idealistic drek, neh?"

"No," Talon said. "I read Dunkelzahn's Will. I think the Draco Foundation might be able to make a difference. *If* it's guided by plans that were left by Dunkelzahn."

"We'd like you to do one run with us," Jane said. "It pays well, but it will take several days, requires you to leave the country, and could be very dangerous."

"What's the scan?"

"Axler will fill you in on the way. Basically, the job is security for an item being delivered. You and Axler will pick up the item and the first security force, then travel with them to Washington FDC, where the rest of the Assets team will replace the sec force. Axler is in charge until then, at which point command will be transferred to Quicksilver."

Talon shifted in his chair. "Who?"

"Quicksilver is a physical adept," Jane said. "He inherited Assets, Inc. from Dunkelzahn and is one of the best undercover ops in the world."

Axler swung her new cyberarm to exercise it. She had lost her arm a few days ago in the fight with Burnout and a powerful bear shaman on Pony Mountain. "Time is short, Talon. Are you in?"

Talon shrugged. "I'm intrigued," he said. "Enough to do this run with you. If, after that, you want me and I want you, I'll join Assets."

Jane laughed. "Well said, Mister Cautious. Well said."

"Welcome aboard," Axler said. "Now, here's how we operate. We have a standard military-style command structure. It may not be what you're used to, but it works. We use top-of-the-line equipment and armament, all provided by Assets."

Jane interrupted. "You need to leave ASAP," she said. "In order to make it to Lake Louise on time."

"Copy," Axler said. "We'll be there."

Jane nodded. "I'll be monitoring you. Talon, I'd like you to wear a microcam and transmitter. It'll make it a lot easier to keep track of you."

"I'll wear one," Talon said. "As long as you guarantee that no one else will be able to pinpoint me with it."

"Not while it's on my system," Jane said. "The Phillips tacticom units we use route through the temporary LTGs and teleporting System Access Nodes I've set up in the Matrix. So far nobody's even tapped into our communications, let alone deciphered the encryption."

Talon gave her an open-jawed stare, then snapped back to his faked nonchalance. "I guess that'll do," he said, acting like this sort of offer came his way every day.

"Excellent," she said, then she faded her icon out and moved out of the Matrix and into the brushed steel space of her box. Talon was online. Jane liked him; liked his caution and dry wit. She just hoped he could handle the magical tasks of this run.

Frag, she thought, *we're going into the home of an old and powerful associate of Dunkelzahn. If Harlequin decides to fry us, no street mage born in this world will be able to stop him.*

24 August 2057

7

Ryan felt the take-off acceleration push him back against the cushions of the Draco Foundation Lear-Cessna Platinum III jet as it lifted off the National Airport runway. He took several calming breaths and touched the Dragon Heart strapped to his gut just to reassure himself that it was still there.

The transfer of security had passed smoothly as Ryan, Dhin, and Grind had replaced three of the Draco Foundation sec personnel assigned to the jet by Carla Brooks. Axler and the new mage, Talon, had stayed aboard.

Ryan's plan was a testament to simplicity and having friends in the right places. And so far it had worked brilliantly.

So far.

Seeing Harlequin was a gamble, Ryan knew. If the elf was as powerful as Dunkelzahn's messenger spirit had implied, the elf might simply take the heart from Ryan. *What could I do to stop him?*

Ryan looked over at Talon, who sat facing him. With his brown hair and plain brown eyes, the human was perhaps the least striking mage Ryan had worked with. He looked like a mundane, which, Ryan suspected, worked to Talon's advantage.

"Talon," Ryan said. "How much has Axler told you of our mission?"

Talon regarded Ryan with cautious scrutiny. His skin was very white, in sharp contrast to the cobalt blue Draco Foundation uniform he wore over his flexible body armor, and his shoulder-length hair was pulled into a ponytail. "Some," he said. "But not enough. I expected to be fully briefed enroute."

Ryan shifted in his own body armor and uniform, flexing his neck to work out some kinks. "As soon as Dhin gets us up to cruising altitude," he said, "we'll get Jane-in-the-box online, and discuss the run."

Next to Talon, sat a black dwarf named Grind. The dwarf had two cyberarms made of a matte gray-black composite—light and extremely strong. Ryan knew Grind also had a third articulated arm, hidden under the heavy uniform coat, which extended from the dwarf's chest.

Grind watched the exchange between Ryan and Talon with mild interest, nodding at Ryan's last statement. Grind would speak up later during the discussion of tactics or security. He was a experienced mercenary and could handle nearly any weapon that wasn't too big for his stature.

Axler sat on Ryan's right. She was his lieutenant, second-in-command for Assets and the finest field commander for this kind of small team, special-forces type combat that he'd had the pleasure of working with.

On the surface, Axler looked like blonde sweetmeat with frag-me doe brown eyes—a real mantrap. Underneath, though, she was a deadly blend of cyber and flesh; none of her cyberware showed, except perhaps in her ultra-chill demeanor. Axler could be frostier than anyone Ryan had met.

His Assets team was all present—Grind, Axler, Dhin in the cockpit, and Jane in the Matrix. Ryan hoped the new mage lasted longer than the previous two. Assets didn't have a good track record keeping spellworms alive.

"Talon," Ryan said. "You scanned my aura when we met back at the airport?"

The mage nodded.

"What did you see?"

"A mundane human," Talon said. "I know that you're a physical adept, so I assume you're masking your aura to make yourself look mundane."

Ryan nodded. "What else?"

"You're carrying some sort of power focus that you can't mask completely."

"The Dragon Heart," Ryan said.

"I've never known any physads who could use a power focus," Talon said.

"This item is unique."

Talon nodded. "Still, it may make you and the team vulnerable to astral attacks."

"Perhaps, but I doubt it. The Heart has its own protection." Ryan paused, giving Talon a moment to ponder. "As you might have surmised, our mission doesn't involve the suit of armor we loaded into the cargo hold. That is only peripheral to our goal."

"What then?"

"Our true mission involves the Dragon Heart," Ryan said. "I want to enlist the help of the elf mage—Harlequin. He knows the ritual that will take me and the Heart across to the metaplanes."

Talon looked dubious. "I didn't think it was possible for a non-initiate mage to cross into the metaplanes."

"Dunkelzahn believed it was."

"Yes," Talon said. "And maybe he could have done it, but unless you plan on asking Lofwyr—"

"I don't think Lofwyr would agree to help us," Ryan said.

"I was kidding."

Ryan smiled. "So was I," he said. "But the fact remains that Dunkelzahn told me that Harlequin could perform the necessary magic. If he is willing to help, it may be as simple as explaining the situation to him. If not, we might have to pay or convince him somehow. In either case, it will be up to me.

"The problem will arise if he decides not to help, and that he wants the Dragon Heart for himself. He's rumored to be extremely powerful. I'm not sure I can keep the Dragon Heart from him."

"And you want me to think of something," Talon said.

Ryan nodded. "Jane said you were good."

Talon laughed. "I'm not sure I'm glad she thinks so."

Ryan joined in the laughter. He liked this mage.

Dhin's voice came over the speakers. "We've reached our cruising altitude of seven thousand meters," he said. "Feel free to move about the cabin, but remember to avoid using firearms or high-explosives during the flight." The ork's chuckle sounded eerie through the electronic modulation of the rigger interface. "Such devices may cause a sudden change in cabin pressure."

Ryan stood up immediately and stretched his muscles. "Jane, you online?"

"I'm here," came her bubbly voice. "And I come bearing gifts—schematics and data."

"My hero," said Ryan.

Grind and Axler stood and paced about the small cabin, working out the kinks. "Anyone want soykaf?" came Grind's gruff voice.

Everyone did, so he made an entire pot. Ten minutes later, when the entire crew was ready, Ryan started the briefing.

"Jane," he said, "give me the satellite images of Château d'If."

A flat screen in a dividing wall powered up, showing an aerial view of a small island. The image was out of focus and distorted. "There's some sort of permanent shimmer that keeps fragging up the resolution," Jane said. "This is the best I can do."

Tan-colored rock formed a wall around the entire isle so that any sort of assault from the sea would be nigh to impossible. There was no beach, only sheer walls jutting fifteen meters straight up from the pounding surf. The only boat landing was a narrow wooden dock that led into a small cave in the rock.

Ryan noticed what looked like a helipad sitting next to a few squat buildings. About thirty meters from the helipad was the old prison itself—a huge stone structure consisting of three cylindrical towers of different diameters. The towers were connected by high walls, forming a courtyard inside. This part of the building was covered with what appeared to be modern macroglass, and shielded with a mirror coating so that the sat image couldn't show the inside.

Another rock wall, three meters high this time, cut across the island, separating the castle from the rest of the buildings. The rear of the old prison shared the outer seawall with the perimeter. Ryan couldn't see enough detail to tell if Harlequin had installed any sort of modern defense system.

"Jane, you got any data on security—cameras, track drones, that sort of drek?"

"Unfortunately not, Quicksilver. I think he's got some of that, but it might be isolated from the Matrix."

"Frag," said Grind. "I'd hate to have to assault this place."

Ryan smiled. "That's why we're taking the easy way in. We'll come over from Marseilles in a chopper. Harlequin is expecting a delivery, and he has to sign for his inheritance. If all goes well, I'll simply talk to him then. We only need to prepare for his response.

"If he decides to help us, then all this prep will have been only for practice. But it's just possible that Mister H was involved in the assassination of Dunkelzahn, and he could perceive us as a threat. If he decides to waste us, we need a plan of escape. And we need a way to keep him from taking the Dragon Heart. Any suggestions?"

Axler stepped up to the screen. "We should conduct all negotiations in this area, outside the castle walls. And we should have a second mode of transport, perhaps a boat or a scuba sled."

Ryan nodded. "Good thinking. Jane, can you arrange for scuba gear and three scuba sleds?"

"Consider it *fait accompli*."

"Nice French."

"Merci."

Ryan looked at the dwarf samurai. "Grind, you and Axler will pilot the sleds to this location with the extra gear for Talon and Dhin and me. Plan Beta will involve es-

cape over the side and under water. We'll also need a boat
or a T-bird to pick us up."

"I'll get a safe house set up in Marseilles," Jane said.

"Great," Ryan said. "Now let's go over the details again."

The flight went quickly as they worked the plan over
and over. Ryan was satisfied, his confidence high as they
began their descent into Marseilles. And it stayed that way
as they transferred the cargo to the waiting helicopter.

Ryan put on his Phillips tacticom unit, sliding the tiny ear
piece into his right ear and taping the thin wire microphone
to his throat with mimetic tape. Axler and Grind went off to
gather the scuba equipment and begin the underwater trip
out to the island of Château d'If. It would take them a couple of hours to get there. That gave Ryan and the others
plenty of time to prepare for meeting Harlequin.

Too much time perhaps. Idle time to think about the
consequences of failure.

*The fate of the world rests on my ability to convince this
elf to help me. I cannot fail.*

8

The spirit Lethe looked at the astral images of the technicians and mages hovering over Billy's cybernetic body. Billy was asleep; they had done that with their drugs and machines. But they couldn't put Lethe to sleep.

Billy's body was flat on its back again, paralyzed and strapped to another operating table, this one at a cybermancy clinic somewhere in the heart of Aztlan. Lethe knew of cybermancy from Billy. Cybermancy had created Burnout—the creature who Billy Madson had become after his magic was lost and his body had been replaced by synthetic materials, hydraulic muscles, and electronic nerves. All that remained of the original Billy was part of his brain and spinal cord.

Cybermancy is also what had trapped Lethe. Intricate blood magic had been used on Burnout to prevent his spirit from leaving his body. Powerful spells had been quickened to make them permanent. These spells formed a mesh of magic that held spirits in, and when Lethe had taken possession of Burnout to prevent him from harming the Dragon Heart, he discovered that he could not escape. Soon after, his spirit had become intertwined with that of the cyberzombie.

Burnout, however, was gone. Lethe wanted to believe that he had influenced the change in the cyberzombie, but he had to admit that Burnout's change into Billy had occurred when Ryan Mercury had nearly killed them both. Unable to escape, Burnout's spirit had suffered severe trauma, leaving only the naive Billy.

Lethe liked the change. Billy was young and full of hope. Lethe's natural state was pure spirit, but he had grown accustomed to inhabiting Billy's body. It was as though the cyberzombie's body belonged just as much to Lethe as it did to Billy—a physical manifestation that they shared.

Technicians worked diligently to fix and replace their damaged parts. New skin was being grown and applied; a new articulated arm had been attached to replace the one Ryan Mercury had broken. Burnout's extendible fingers were replaced, his integrated gyromount. Everything was being made new.

Everything physical that is. The mages couldn't seem to figure out what had happened to the cyberzombie's spirit.

Two mages examined him in astral space, scrutinizing his aura, which Lethe had tried to mask to look like a mundane human with lots of cyberware. These were sophisticated mages, however, and they saw through some of Lethe's masking. He was sure they could tell that Burnout was not a typical cyberzombie.

"What do you make of it, Meyer?" asked one. In astral space, Lethe understood the meaning of their words, though he couldn't actually hear what they were saying. Billy's ears had been deactivated.

The one called Meyer was an elf with the aura of a powerful initiate. "It is beyond my experience," he said. "All the cybermantic magic is fused with his spirit, and . . ." Lethe noticed recognition dawning in the elf. "I think he can see us, Vendic."

"What?" Vendic said. "That's impossible. He's unconscious."

"I mean astrally."

Vendic laughed. "You've been working too hard, Meyer. Even if he were awake, cyberzombies can't use magic."

Meyer glared at Vendic. "Something has happened to this one. I want to—"

"Sir," said a technician, entering the room. "You have a telecom call."

Meyer nodded to her. "Thank you. I'll take it here." The elf walked over to a device on the wall and touched it.

"Mister Roxborough," Meyer said. "What can I do for you?"

Lethe couldn't make out the reply. Being electronic in nature, it did not register in astral space.

"A security breach?" Meyer said. "I was not aware of anything since the Ryan Mercury escape."

The mage paused while the other spoke.

"Certainly, Mister Roxborough," Meyer said with a heavy sigh. "I will check the datastore immediately, but I don't see how it could have been wiped. The spirit-transfer material was protected by the best ice we have."

Pause. Meyer shook his head in irritation, but his voice gave nothing away.

"Of course I know about Reise's transfer, sir. You authorized it yourself. Frankly, I thought it a bit rash. She is the only scientist who can perform the viral memory reconstruction. It'll take years to replace her. I—"

Meyer was interrupted. He stood rigid, anger building inside him, though Lethe saw a hint of amusement there as well.

"No, sir, I don't know any Alice. I'm afraid I don't understand what you're talking about."

Lethe tried to use Billy's ears to hear what Roxborough was saying, but he failed. Even Billy's connection to his senses seemed to be severed.

"Yes, Mister Roxborough," Meyer said. "I will begin an investigation, and I am sorry about what you have gone through, but there is a more immediate problem concerning the recovered cyberzombie, Burnout."

Pause.

"Yes, the techs have repaired the damage done to him. Physically he's like new, perhaps better than before, but he's been through something. His aura is disturbingly human, too much so for a cyberzombie. He's not exhibiting the polluting effects normally associated with cybermancy."

Meyer listened.

"I suppose it's good, but I don't have an explanation for it yet. I don't like it when I can't explain what's happening. Makes me nervous."

Pause.

"I don't know how much time. Perhaps a day, perhaps a—"

Interruption. Meyer waited, listening carefully. Then, "Very well. I will travel to San Marcos with the cyberzombie. I've always wanted to meet the mysterious Señor Oscuro. We'll figure this out together." He punched the Disconnect.

Lethe watched Meyer turn and look at him, scrutinizing his aura. "I know you're watching," he said. "But soon, with Darke's help, I will dissect you. Carve you up astrally until I've got you under control again."

Lethe said nothing, merely watched the mage intently, and hoped that Billy would soon awaken. He missed Billy. For the first time in as long as he could remember, Lethe felt very, very much alone.

9

Ryan stood on the tarmac of the small airfield where they had landed, just outside Marseilles. He smelled the clean salt Mediterranean air, and leaned against the open door of the rented helicopter, double-checking his gear. His cobalt blue Draco Foundation uniform with its integrated body armor fit him snugly, though it was a little hot in the summer sun. His bandoleer of narcotic darts and his two guns rested in their proper positions. The Dragon Heart was nestled snugly in its sash.

He was as ready as he could be.

Jane's voice sounded in Ryan's ear piece. "Axler and Grind have made excellent progress with the scuba sleds. They're five minutes from the island. No problems so far."

"Copy, Jane," Ryan subvocalized into his tacticom mic. He climbed into the copilot's seat and strapped himself in. The Hughes Aerospace Airstar 2057 chopper was brand-new and in excellent condition, but it was more of a commuter vehicle for corporate executives than an attack copter.

Ryan looked back to make sure Talon was ready, then he glanced at Dhin in the pilot's seat. "Take us up," he said.

The whine of the rotors grew in pitch as the helo took flight, and soon they were skimming out across the blue Mediterranean, heading for the small prison island. Château d'If loomed up before them like an ancient Alcatraz. A castle of old, brown masonry rising directly from the surf.

Ryan saw the image waver as though he was seeing it through a heat haze. "I guess that's the permanent shimmer

Jane was talking about," he said. "Talon, what do you make of it?"

Talon pushed his head up into the front. "There's a magic barrier of some sort surrounding the island," he said. "I've never seen anything like it."

Ryan shifted his perception to the astral, and looked at the island. He could make out a translucent haze dome around the château. "It looks somewhat like the veil around Tir na nÓg," he said. "We're expected. We should be able to pass through."

Talon gave him a doubting look. "You hope," he said.

"You disagree?"

"I just don't share your level of confidence."

Dhin gave a harsh laugh. "Well, chummers, either way, we're almost to the island."

Ryan felt a slight lurch as they passed through the astral barrier and swung up over the rim of the island's wall. He surveyed the structure as Dhin brought the chopper into a low hover, preparing to drop onto the wide flagstone piazza. Ryan saw the narrow wooden dock, jutting like a toothpick from the far edge of the island. The sleek form of a yacht was moored to it—a Harland and Wolff Classique, very expensive and luxurious.

Axler and Grind would be under the dock by now, waiting to disable the boat in case Plan Beta was activated. Ryan touched the Dragon Heart at his waist and hoped it wouldn't come to that.

As the helo's runners touched the flagstones, Ryan saw a woman in a summer dress of mauve cotton. She stood quite tall for a human, with flowing white hair that cascaded down her back.

Ryan gave her aura a once-over as he stepped out of the helicopter with Talon just behind. *She's not a human,* he realized, *but an elf, and more than likely a mage.* She was masking her aura, but with the help of the Dragon Heart, Ryan could see through it.

She stepped up to meet them, extending her hand. "My

name's Jane Foster," she said, yelling above the scream of the blades.

Ryan noticed an ornate ring on her finger, platinum in the shape of a coiled dragon. "I'm Ryan Mercury," he said, shaking her hand. "And this is Nolan Falcor." Ryan motioned toward Talon. "We've brought the package from the Draco Foundation."

Foster nodded. "Please tell your pilot to shut down and step out of the helicopter."

At the command, Ryan's awareness grew hypersensitive as he turned and signaled to Dhin. He subvocalized, "Cut the engines and show your handsome face to the lady."

When Dhin was out of the helicopter, Foster gave Ryan a smile. "Thank you, Mister Mercury. Now if you'll show me the suit of armor and your authentication papers."

"Certainly," Ryan said. "Is Mister Harlequin here? He has to sign the papers."

Foster threw her head back in laughter. "*Mister* Harlequin," she said. "That's a good one."

Ryan opened the side door of the helicopter to reveal the three wooden crates that held the suit of armor. Then he pulled a suitcase from under one of the seats. "Regardless of what he likes to be called, I need a signature."

"I can sign," said Foster.

"I'm afraid not."

Foster gave Ryan an icy stare. "Harlequin will not want to be disturbed with this," she said. "I will sign for him."

"That's simply not acceptable. Besides, I have other business with him."

"Concerning what?"

"It's a private matter."

Foster froze him with that stare again. "Just who do you think you are, Mister Mercury?" Then she was stepping away from him and examining his aura, no doubt trying to figure out what his abilities were. He had masked the Dragon Heart, but he wasn't sure if it could hold up under scrutiny.

"I am perhaps more than I appear to be," he said. "But

my mission here is simple. I agreed to deliver the armor to the elf mage, Harlequin, as per Nadja Daviar's instructions. Plus I have another errand, given to me by Dunkelzahn, but I can speak of it only with Harlequin."

Foster backed away until she reached the narrow archway that led to the main castle. Her face was a mask of anger. "Harlequin was not expecting you," she said. "I shall have to prepare—"

Talon's shout seemed to come from far away. "She's casting!"

Ryan yawned suddenly, and watched as Dhin and Talon dropped to the ground next to him. Sleep and fatigue clawed at his consciousness, desperate to drag him under.

In his disorientation, a force slammed into him—a mana bolt that stung through his body. The impact snapped him out of the effects of the sleep spell.

Ryan's awareness returned, and he focused on his magic. He felt the power of the Silent Way come to him and his outline blurred. He masked his physical appearance, using his stealth magic to become harder to see as he bolted toward Foster. He crossed the distance between them in seconds, taking the elf by surprise. He brought the power of the Dragon Heart to bear and hit her with a telekinetic strike, right in the chest.

The blow never hit, impacting instead on her magical barrier and dissipating. But it disrupted the barrier; the next strike would land home without interference. Ryan didn't think that he'd need another distance strike; he was already on top of her.

A spirit manifested in front of him as he sprang toward Foster, ready to hit that cluster of nerves that would drop her into unconsciousness. The spirit burned itself into existence, a molten shape, like living lava, burning with incredible heat that seared Ryan's flesh.

Frag me!

"Be gone, elemental!" Ryan yelled, channeling his vehemence toward the spirit. At the same time, he pummeled the creature with his fists. It slotted him off that he was giving Foster more time to cast another spell.

Suddenly the spirit was gone, disrupted from the impact of his attacks, and Ryan stood face to face with Foster. Tiny droplets of sweat prickled on her immaculate forehead, but she seemed frozen. Her mouth set in an unmoving scowl.

Ryan tried to lunge for her; he wanted to complete his nerve cluster strike before she could get her spell off. But his legs wouldn't respond, and a heavy weight grew in his chest as he tried to move. He, too, was frozen.

"Children, children," came a voice. "You will kiss and make up, or I will be forced to punish you."

Suddenly the pressure abated and Ryan fell to his knees, gasping for air. He was marginally satisfied to discover that Foster was in the same condition. He focused himself quickly and leaped to his feet.

The elf walking toward him could be none other than Harlequin. Despite the heat, he was dressed all in black— jeans and leather jacket. His auburn hair was nearly the same color as Ryan's, though the elf's was much longer and pulled back against his head in a ponytail. His face was painted clown white with red diamonds over both eyes, which themselves sparkled green in the sunlight.

In the astral, Harlequin's aura was unmasked and frightening. *What have I gotten myself into?* Ryan thought. *This elf's power is immense.*

"Harlequin," Ryan said. "I am Ryan Mercury, and it is imperative that I speak with you."

The elf laughed. "Ryan Mercury? No wonder you bested Frosty here."

"He did not best me," Foster said.

Harlequin gave her a condescending smile. "I stand corrected. He was *about to* best you." He laughed again.

She gave him a withering glare, then turned to Ryan. "My apologies, Mister Mercury. I was instructed to incapacitate you if anything out of the ordinary occurred. When you insisted on seeing Harlequin and started going on about Dunkelzahn, I judged you a threat. It was his idea." She pointed to Harlequin as she stood. "Not mine."

"I had to test you against a real security force," Harlequin said to Foster. "And if Mister Mercury hadn't been along, you'd have handled them well enough." Harlequin turned to Ryan. "I must admit I'm impressed. Even after all I've heard about you—trained by Dunkelzahn himself and all that—I never expected the banishment."

"What?"

"You banished that fire elemental, my friend." Harlequin chuckled. "Frag, you don't even know what you can do."

"I can't banish elementals," Ryan said. "I simply disrupted it with the force of my blows."

"If you say so," Harlequin said, then his tone changed. "Now, tell me why you are here."

Ryan nodded. *Here goes,* he thought. *If he decides he wants the Dragon Heart, I'll have to run for it.* Ryan doubted he could put up much resistance to the mage, but he would try.

"Dunkelzahn gave this to me," Ryan said, as he pulled the Dragon Heart from its pouch at his waist. The orichalcum artifact glowed bright yellow in the sun. "With instructions to give it to Thayla so that she could prevent the Enemy from crossing over."

Harlequin drew close. "Let's go inside to discuss this. I'd like a closer look."

"Certainly," Ryan said. "But I can't just leave my team stunned and unconscious on the ground."

"Frosty will attend to them," Harlequin said. It was a statement of fact. An order to comply with his instructions, not subject to debate by either Ryan or Foster.

Ryan nodded.

Foster groaned.

"Let me know when everyone's awake, and you have unloaded the armor," Harlequin said.

Foster snorted. "Yes, your highness."

Harlequin laughed. Then to Ryan, "You'll have to remove your communication headgear."

Ryan considered objecting, but decided against it. This elf's cooperation was crucial to the success of his mission. He had no choice. He pulled the tacticom out of his ear, and peeled the mic from his throat, then nodded to Harlequin.

Ryan followed the elf through the archway and into the ancient prison, passing into a broad courtyard, complete with French gardens, sculptured hedges, immaculately trimmed trees, and a variety of blooming flowers. The rich fragrance of roses filled the air.

Harlequin led Ryan along the central flagstone path and through a set of huge wooden doors, recently varnished, but scarred and ancient-looking. Just inside was a veran-dah with a high arched ceiling, stone walls covered with tapestries. Pristine suits of armor and medieval weapons from a wide variety of cultures were displayed on either side of the hall as they walked through.

The verandah led to a huge central room that used to be an interior courtyard, but was now covered with a macroglass ceiling three stories up. Balconies on each level gave a view of the room, which was furnished with ornate wooden Renaissance chairs and tables. A massive hearth dominated one end of the room, though no fire burned in it.

Harlequin led Ryan up onto the raised parquet flooring, around what looked like a study area dominated by a mas-sive cherrywood desk and a small cyberdeck, and over to the hearth. Harlequin indicated that Ryan should take a seat in one of the Louis XIV chairs.

"Talk," Harlequin said as he returned, sitting in the op-posite chair. "I'm listening."

Ryan nodded. "Let me tell you a story," he began. And Ryan did. For better or worse, he unfolded the story of his quest to Harlequin. He opened himself up to this elf. He explained about his mission to Aztlan, about discovering the Locus, reporting it to Dunkelzahn just before getting caught.

Ryan brushed over his experience with Thomas Rox-borough's personality transfer, skimming to his escape from Aztlan, his discovery that Dunkelzahn was dead, that his new mission required him to take the Dragon Heart to Thayla. Dunkelzahn thought Thayla was vulnerable, that she needed the Heart to stop the Enemy.

Ryan went on to tell how the Dragon Heart was stolen by the Atlantean Foundation. He told of how he had met the spirit Lethe and how they had regained the Heart. He recounted the events of the past weeks to Harlequin, mentioning the cyberzombie Burnout and how he had taken the Heart from Ryan.

"I have just recovered the Dragon Heart and so I come to you as Dunkelzahn advised," Ryan said. "I come seeking your help."

Harlequin listened to Ryan's story, total attention on his painted face, forefingers steepled over his mouth. Then he was silent for a long moment, thinking.

"First of all," he said. "I was responsible for putting Thayla at the bridge. Me and some others. But when Dunkelzahn learned of it, he came to me here, extremely pissed . . . er, slotted off, as you say now.

"Fragging dragon nearly forced a showdown. Made me angry that he didn't appreciate what I had done." Harlequin stared at Ryan with an intensity Ryan had never seen. A look that chilled his core. "I had saved the world from the . . . the . . . Enemy. You think I wanted to? You think I volunteered to be a fucking hero?"

Harlequin stood up and began pacing in a wide circle. "But I did it anyway. I knew no one else would. And I succeeded! I accomplished a stalemate." The elf heaved a deep breath. "Then Dunkelzahn comes to me and rants about my incompetence. Trying to tell me that Thayla is vulnerable, that her song had been breached before and it would be again.

"Dunkelzahn told me that he suspected Aztechnology was creating an elaborate map of their astral space. Connecting the auras of all their *teocalli* so that they could measure changes in mana across their entire country. He thought they were doing this in search of something. Something they obviously found. A *Mel'thelem*—a Locus."

"What exactly is a Locus?"

Harlequin shot a hard look at Ryan. "It's best not to ask too many questions," he said.

Ryan bristled. Harlequin might be powerful and most unusual for an elf, but he still had that arrogant attitude that made Ryan want to slap him. "I'm Dunkelzahn's operative," he said. "I know all about the cycles of magic and that drek. Just tell me."

Harlequin smiled. "All I can tell you is that the *Mel'thelem* are now part of the Sixth World as they were of the Fourth. They were created long ago to be magical reservoirs, like batteries that have now gone dead during the low mana. But if activated, they can be used to store, enhance, and focus magical power on a massive scale."

"In the wrong hands—"

"They could mean disaster," Harlequin interrupted. "Dunkelzahn tried to warn us, me and others, but we did not act quickly enough. We never suspected that they would find one so soon." A sad look crossed Harlequin's face. "Because of this, Dunkelzahn and I parted in anger," he said. "And that was the last I saw of the old wyrm."

"When was that?" Ryan asked.

"About a week before the assassination." Harlequin gave Ryan a queer glance. "No, I didn't kill him if that's what you're thinking. Oh, I've wanted to several times over the years, in flashes of anger. And this last time, when he challenged my methods of stopping the Enemy, implying that I took the easy way out. Believe me, I was supremely pissed at him. But even if I'd actually had the guts to try to kill him, I could never have pulled it off alone. I'm not strong enough."

Harlequin sighed. "But I didn't try. Because when you strip away all the layers of jockeying and posturing, all the painted faces and illusions—" he raked his nails over his make-up, gouging it away in lines—"underneath it all, we were after the same thing. We were friends."

He sounds sincere, Ryan thought. *Either he's telling the truth, or he's the most convincing liar I've ever met.*

"Now," Harlequin said, "let me have a look at this Dragon Heart of yours."

Ryan shivered and clamped down on his trepidation. He slowly lifted the Dragon Heart and held it out to the elf.

10

Lucero steadied herself, trying to remain focused as she stood in the wedge of darkness on the cracked outcropping of rock. She took shallow breaths, wincing at the stench of bloody corpses. She strained to hear the song, widened her eyes in the direction of the light.

I must not succumb completely, she thought. *I cannot let the darkness control my thoughts.*

The light filtered dimly through the barrier of blood and corpses, into the stained wedge. And as she moved toward the edge of the stain, Señor Oscuro's forces advanced beside her. Decapitated corpses and crawling spider creatures and fat, toad-like monsters that dripped with slime.

Oscuro himself stood behind his troops, sacrificing acolyte after acolyte and spraying the fresh blood over his creatures like a protective coating. Armor against the light.

The first wave slammed into the barrier of beauty and music, disappearing in a flash. Screams of agony ripped through the dark sky as the creatures disintegrated. But when they were gone, Lucero noticed that the darkness had advanced several meters.

He's slowly extinguishing the light. Soon the song will be silenced.

I can't let that happen. The light is my only salvation.

Lucero remembered a time before. A time when the light penetrated her heart completely and nearly erased her desire for the blood power. She remembered the instant of elation she had felt, the sensation that her own inner beauty had returned once again.

How she longed for that sensation. She would give up the blood addiction for it. She would give up anything for it.

Lucero crept slowly toward the light, watching it grow brighter and brighter. Hearing the aching beauty of the song in her heart. Just a few more steps, and she'd belong to the light again.

Lucero breathed slowly, feeling the anticipation. Her salvation neared step by little step as she moved. Oscuro could bleed himself dry and she wouldn't stop now.

Almost there.

"Lucero, my child." His voice blew across the short distance between them like a chill wind, freezing her. "What do you think you're doing?"

11

Ryan leaned forward in the Louis XIV chair and handed the Dragon Heart to Harlequin. Ryan felt naked without his tacticom gear, isolated without his connection to Jane and the others. This was his show now, and his actions alone would make or break his mission.

I must convince Harlequin to help me.

The Dragon Heart felt heavy in his hands as he passed it into those of the painted elf. It was as though it were reluctant to part from Ryan. Or perhaps he imagined it.

Harlequin's hands looked delicate as he took the Heart, but their appearance belied a hidden strength. Ryan knew that Harlequin had the ability to mask his aura, to disguise the extent of his power and mastery of magic and other things. The elf seemed to have dispensed with masking, however, because what Ryan saw as he used his astral perception to look at Harlequin was a complex and nearly incomprehensible creature.

Somehow, his aura was still elven at the very core, but like no elf Ryan had ever seen. Harlequin glowed like a sun going nova, sending out a shower of astral flares like volcanic spew into the flat light of the astral. Ryan marveled at the obvious power of this elf.

Harlequin pulled the Dragon Heart to him and placed it in his lap. Then he looked up at Ryan. "This is certainly a strange item," he said.

The Dragon Heart's aura flared for a second as Harlequin refocused his attention on it. "It was made by a dragon, that much is certain. And it seems to be fairly new.

I don't think it has held power more than a year, perhaps far less. It has little history."

Harlequin sat up suddenly and peered at Ryan. "What bothers me," he said, "is that it's too powerful. It has been imbued with more power than should be possible at this time."

"What do you mean?"

"Did Dunkelzahn tell you everything about the cycles of magic?"

"I think so," Ryan said. Magic came and went from the world in tides that lasted thousands of years. The magic had just returned, forty or so years earlier, and would continue to rise for several thousand years before peaking. Then it would slowly ebb away over a similar length of time.

"Well," Harlequin said, "to explain it in modern terms, the mana level is too low to fashion an item of this power." He held up the Heart. "But it is too new to have been made in the last cycle of high magic. Frankly, I'm impressed. Dunkelzahn must have made this recently, but unless his magic is far greater than we thought, I don't know how he could have created it."

"I don't understand."

"Then listen! The very existence of the Dragon Heart is anomalous. It seems to be a lens for manipulating mana, for channeling it. But it operates on a scale far above what should be possible for anything created so early in the cycle."

Harlequin stood up and began pacing again, holding the Dragon Heart in his hands. He sighed. "Even if it were ancient," he went on, "it wouldn't be fully powered until the mana rose sufficiently high."

Ryan focused on the Dragon Heart, reaching out to maintain his connection with it just in case Harlequin decided not to help him. Ryan didn't think he could prevent the elf from taking it for his own, but he wouldn't give it up without a fight.

"Are you going to help me?" Ryan asked.

Harlequin looked up at him in surprise, as though he had forgotten Ryan's presence. Then he tossed the Dragon Heart into Ryan's lap. "Depends," he said.

Ryan breathed a sigh of relief as he clutched the Heart in his hands. "Depends on what?"

Harlequin stared at Ryan. "Why are you doing this?"

Ryan was surprised by the question. "That should be obvious. I'm going to use it to save metahumanity from annihilation."

Harlequin smiled behind his ruined make-up. "Just as long as you're not blindly following the dragon's orders."

A smirk formed on Ryan's face. "I'd like to think I'm beyond that," he said.

"Good."

Foster entered the room then, striding with purpose, the hem of her mauve dress fluttering around her calves. "The crates have been unloaded, oh-painted-one," she said.

Talon entered the room just behind her. The Assets mage looked a little haggard from his magically induced slumber, and like Ryan, his tacticom unit had been removed. He examined Ryan's aura briefly, and when he was satisfied that Ryan was unharmed, he merely stood and waited.

Ryan tucked the Dragon Heart back into its sash over his gut, and spoke to Talon. "What's the status with Dhin?"

"He's up and seems one hundred percent. Standing by for us to come back out."

"Good."

Harlequin turned toward Foster. "Where did you put the crates, my dear?"

"They're in the courtyard."

"Good work. Have Terrish unpack the contents, and tell him that we'll be indisposed for a while."

"What's going on?" Foster said with a heavy sigh. "It's not another one of your save-the-world adventures, I hope."

Harlequin gave her a guilty shrug.

"Frag!" she said. "All right, I'll be ready in an hour." She turned from the room.

Harlequin laughed.

"So you're going to help?"

"Like you," he said, "I am willing to play the hero, if reluctantly. My motivations are a little different, however. I am partially responsible for Thayla being where she is, and if she's in trouble, I want to help her. I can take us over from here, but we'll need guards to watch our bodies while we're on the metaplanes."

"I can contact a couple of street samurai right away," Ryan said. "Plus we have Dhin and Talon."

Harlequin gave Ryan a shrewd stare. "I doubt there's going to be any opposition," he said. "Thayla should be just where I left her. But if something has happened, I'm pretty sure I know who'd be responsible."

"Who?"

"A maniac called Darke, an agent of Aztechnology."

Ryan blinked. "Do you think they'd send troops after us?"

"It's possible."

"Do you want me to get more security forces here?"

Harlequin stopped at the archway and turned. "Yes," he said. "Retrieve your communications equipment and make any plans necessary."

Ryan nodded and walked up into the verandah.

"Okay," Ryan said, "I'll contact my decker. If anyone can get reliable, dependable help on short notice, she can."

Harlequin smiled at him. "I need some time to prepare," he said, walking to the edge of the parquet flooring toward a low archway at the far end of the room. "We'll perform the ritual downstairs. Normally I'd have to go to the physical location of the Great Ghost Dance to be able to take someone with me to the metaplanes, but you're a very high-level initiate. I should be able to do it from here."

Ryan nodded and turned to walk outside. He didn't know what Harlequin meant about him being a high-level initiate, but this was no time to argue the fine points.

"And Ryan?"

He stopped, pivoting around to look at Harlequin.

"Get your two runners out of the water." The elf gave a little laugh. "Nasty creatures have been known to prowl around my island—water elementals, gorgons, storm dolphins. I'd hate to have your friends fall prey to something. The guilt on me would be unbearable."

Ryan couldn't help but laugh. "I'll bring them out immediately," he said.

"Good, we'll proceed when everyone's ready."

Ryan nodded, trying not to let himself feel the excitement that was building inside him. *Harlequin has agreed to help! Now it's only a matter of time before I can get the Dragon Heart to Thayla.*

"You know, it's ironic," Harlequin said. "Dunkelzahn and I are finally working together on something." There was a touch of sadness to his voice. "It's too bad it took his death to make it happen."

12

Jane-in-the-box watched the different faces of her virtual cube. The riveted stainless steel box rotated around her as she shifted points of view in order to keep track of the runners. She alternated between Axler's headcamera, showing the view through her scuba mask—the blue depths of the Mediterranean disappearing below—and Dhin's awareness in the helo. The inputs from Ryan and Talon were blank since they had removed their tacticom units and entered the château.

As far as runs go, Jane thought, *this one has been a major cluster frag.*

"Hold position, Axler," Jane said.

"Copy," said Axler. "Grind and I will wait."

"We'll give them five minutes," Jane said. "Then we're going in."

"I don't know, Jane," came Dhin's husky voice. "I don't trust that mage slitch, Foster." The ork was standing next to the cooling helo, looking toward the archway where Talon and Foster had disappeared five minutes earlier.

Jane laughed. "Stay sharp, Dhin. Just 'cause she took you out, doesn't mean she's the enemy. I think she was being tested by Harlequin, and we were the test."

"I just don't like being out of communication."

"Me neither," said Jane. "Me neither."

Through Dhin's eyes, Jane watched Talon emerge from the archway, followed by Ryan who still had the Dragon Heart tucked inside the sash around his waist. Dhin walked up to them. "Good to see you, Bossman."

Ryan smiled, looking pleased for the first time since the whole Dragon Heart mission began. His voice filtered through Dhin's electronics. "Good to be seen," he said. Then, "Better make yourself comfortable. We're staying for a while."

Ryan donned his tacticom headgear and activated it. "Jane," came Ryan's voice out of the darkness. "Copy, Jane."

"I'm here, Quicksilver, what's your status?"

"Talon and I are alive and well," said Ryan. "I've got Harlequin online. He's agreed to perform the ritual that will take me and the Heart across to the metaplanes. We'll need the others topside."

"You got that, Axler? Grind?"

In her video link, Jane saw Axler hold out her gloved hand and make a fist with thumb extended upward.

"They're coming out now, Quicksilver," Jane said.

"Good, I'll meet them down by the dock," Ryan said. "Also, we're going to need more runners to provide security in the physical world just in case the Azzies decide to come after us."

"The Azzies?"

"You heard right. Harlequin thinks they're the ones who'd come after us."

"Fragging great."

"That's what I thought."

Jane started thinking. She knew a team who was based out of Marseilles, runners who had previously worked with Carla Brooks and had an excellent rep. But she didn't know if they'd be available on such short notice. "I'll contact one of the teams I know who work this area," she said. "They did freelance sec-work for Black Angel on the night of the assassination."

"Uh, Jane," Ryan said.

"What?"

"They must not have done a very good job," Ryan said, his tone deadpan.

Jane paused for a second, not sure if Ryan was joking or

serious. "They were the best," she said finally. "Black Angel will vouch for them."

Ryan laughed. "I trust you, Jane. I was kidding."

"Frag you!"

"You name the time and place."

"No, forget it. Nadja would kill me."

"Me too."

Jane laughed, and had her system load the telecom number for the team's fixer into her virtual reality. Most shadowrunning teams didn't know Jane, except perhaps as a decker for Assets, Inc. They didn't know she used to act as an über-fixer for Dunkelzahn or do his decking. That was just the way she wanted it, so she always worked through other fixers.

"I'll be out of touch for a few cycles," she told Ryan.

"Copy."

The fixer was a free spirit called Cinnamon who worked out of Los Angeles, but handled contracts everywhere. She did most of the biz for the team Jane wanted to hire. Jane dove down through her Matrix gate and pulsed across the electronic skies and into Cinnamon's LTG—Local Telecommunications Grid.

Jane engaged her sophisticated relocate utility in case of trace ice and rang the telecom.

The fixer picked up almost instantly. She appeared as a beautiful human woman with golden blonde hair that fell straight around her shoulders. Her blue eyes widened as they recognized Jane's icon. "Hello, Jane-in-the-box," Cinnamon said. "What can I do for you?"

"I need a team of runners for some security work," Jane said. "Cluster's group, if they're back in the Marseilles area."

"You think they stayed in Washington after the assassination? Black Angel cleared them of blame, but Cluster didn't want to hang around to take any fallout."

Jane kept her tone extremely serious. "I wouldn't be contacting you if I didn't trust them."

Cinnamon picked up on the tone. "I think I can arrange for their services. What are the details?"

Jane smiled. "I think you'll like this one," she said. "Extremely urgent, but very, very lucrative."

Cinnamon's face lit up. "Good."

"Your team will meet with my runners at Château d'If as soon as possible. I need someone within two hours so if it's going to be longer, we'll have to go with another team."

Cinnamon allowed a slight downward curve to touch the corners of her mouth. "That's really tight," she said. "But I think they can do it."

"They'll be responsible for guarding the island for a few days at most. They should bring their own supplies and equipment, even though some minimal resources may be available to them. You'll be paid one hundred thousand nuyen per runner per day for as long as they're needed. You can skim whatever you want from that, of course."

"I'll set it up," Cinnamon said without hesitation.

Jane laughed. "Excellent," she said, and disconnected.

13

Ryan tried to put the upcoming ritual out of his mind as he and Talon found the stairs that would take them to meet Axler and Grind. The stairs led down from inside one of the small outlying buildings and had been cut into the rock itself.

Harlequin had given Ryan a set of keys and free rein over the island. The elf was busy inside the château, preparing himself for the ritual.

Excitement built inside Ryan, anticipation at the prospect that his mission might nearly be complete. He was amazed that Harlequin had agreed to help. With a little luck, it would soon be all over.

They took the stairs down and Ryan felt the cool spray of the sea, heard the roar of the waves as they came to the bottom. The stairs opened into a cave of sorts—a massive chamber with hewn floor and walls. The floor dropped sharply halfway through the chamber, and the ocean lapped against a short sea wall.

The far end of the chamber was open to the water, and the wooden dock extended from the stone floor out of the cave opening. A pair of Suzuki Watersports floated just inside the cave, tied to the dock. Through the opening Ryan could see the Harland and Wolff Classique yacht moored at the end of the dock.

The rest of the chamber was filled with equipment lockers and scuba driving gear. Weapons and an array of what seemed to be magical talismana lay helter-skelter, with no seeming regard for their value or well-being.

Axler and Grind poked their heads out of the water and climbed up a short ladder. Ryan helped them haul the three scuba sleds up onto the dock. As they removed their wetsuits and gear, he briefed them.

"I want you two to help me deploy the new runners. Cluster is the name of their leader."

"I know him," Grind said. "He's a minotaur, a metahuman similar to a troll, but from the Middle East. He was an excellent merc back in the late forties."

"Good, let's go. They'll be here soon, and I want to have the whole island scoped out before that."

Soon, Ryan and Talon had explored the island. The sunset painted the sky in brilliant red streaks, the clouds floating like hot coals in a darkening blue sky. Axler and Grind were dry and geared up. Dhin was jacked into the helo's console, remote-rigging the two drones that had come with the team. One was an Aerodesign Systems Condor II that floated in the air high above the island and gave Dhin an array of tools for surveillance. The other drone was a Commonwealth Aerospace Wandjina—one of the most effective combat drones made.

Talon had been paying particular attention to patrolling the island's astral space and studying the arcane defenses. "It's going to take an army to get onto this island," Talon said. "Besides the veil around the island, Harlequin's got spirits patrolling everywhere. I don't see anyone getting through."

"I wouldn't be surprised if Aztechnology did send an army," Ryan said.

"Great."

"Bossman," came Dhin's voice over the tacticom, "we got company. Motorboat coming fast from the city."

"It's Cluster and his team," said Jane-in-the-box, also over the 'com.

"We'll meet them at the dock."

The team consisted of six runners, and Ryan assensed them as they approached. The rigger—a black dwarf like

Grind—nestled the GMC Riverine up against the dock opposite Harlequin's yacht. There were two physical adepts like Ryan, a white elf in ninja silks and a Latino woman wearing light combat armor. There was also a mage and a heavily cybered street samurai.

The team leader disembarked first—a huge troll-like individual with white skin and wearing a tuxedo over body armor. "Greetings," he said. "I am called Cluster. We are here to secure the island."

"Thank you for coming on such short notice." Ryan had never seen a minotaur before. Cluster was about the same size as a typical troll, but his head was shaped more like a bull. He had a snout instead of a nose and his horns jutted from either side of his head and curved up to a sharp point. Despite his appearance, Cluster spoke in elegant, German-accented English.

"I'm Quicksilver," Ryan said.

"It's an honor to finally meet the infamous Quicksilver," Cluster said.

Ryan silently acknowledged the compliment. He gestured to his own team. "This is Axler, my lieutenant. And this is Talon. I believe you've already met Grind."

"Yes, Grind and I did a Desert War tour together."

The Latino physad stepped up next to Cluster, giving Ryan a challenging look. "Quicksilver, maybe you and I can go hand-to-hand sometime? Just to see who's the—"

Cluster cut her off. "Starfish, cut the drek!"

Ryan laughed. "Perhaps so," he said. "But now, we're in a bit of rush. Your job is to guard the island perimeter. My rigger, Dhin, has two drones in the air. He and Grind will assist you. The others and I will be indisposed inside the château."

"Very well," Cluster said. "Let's go."

Ryan and Cluster made a full walk around the perimeter wall, discussing the positioning of Cluster's team. The man's tactical skill reassured Ryan that Jane had chosen well. He learned the names of each of the other runners as they set up the defense. The dwarf rigger was called Bingo. Raven was the samurai; Slider was the elf ninja, and the mage was called Radar.

Ryan wanted to touch base with everyone, examine their auras, and generally keep his mind off the upcoming ritual. Ryan had never been to the metaplanes, and he was sure the trek would not be easy. He had heard stories about the difficulties of traveling there—passing the dweller on the threshold, meeting strange and powerful spirits. Many of his mage friends had spoken of their quests as though they had gone on an inner journey, had delved more into their own spirits than traveled abroad.

I have nothing to fear.

Ryan shook his head, and focused his attention on the details of setting up an impenetrable defense. He asked Dhin if Bingo, the dwarf rigger, could jack into the chopper's hitcher port. Bingo wanted to use the surveillance drone to scan the area.

Starfish, the hothead physical adept who wanted to spar with Ryan, was assigned to the point of the island farthest from the château. Then Cluster set up the rest of his team to monitor the island with overlapping fields of fire.

As they were finishing, the last red light of the dying sun waned in the west. Harlequin and Foster emerged from the château, walking hand in hand as they approached. They advanced slowly toward where Ryan stood on the sea wall, their faces serious. Determined.

Ryan turned to Grind and Cluster. "You got it under control?"

They both nodded.

"Good." Ryan then turned to meet Harlequin and Foster, who were making their way up the short stairs to the walkway that ran along the top of the wall.

"Ryan," Harlequin said. "It's time."

Ryan nodded. He subvocalized into this tacticom mike.

"Axler, Talon," he said. "Meet us at the entrance to the château. You're coming inside with me."

When they had all gathered at the main entrance, Harlequin turned and led them inside. "Let's get this over with," he said. "The ritual chamber awaits."

14

Strapped to a table, Lethe looked around at the abandoned restaurant. The astral background smelled old and musty here, almost stagnant. Chairs and tables lay like discarded toys, scattered pell-mell. A giant aquarium built into a wall a hundred years earlier was host only to thick dust and grime-smeared glass.

The auras of several metahumans stood around Lethe, different from those who had transported him in the jet from Panama. Here, two guards flanked each of the two entrances. Four total, and at least two of them were magically adept.

A human technician stood above Lethe, above the cyborg body that held Lethe's spirit. He was beginning to consider Billy's body his own. The boy's spirit was growing more and more enmeshed with Lethe as they spent time together. They were growing interdependent.

"He's coming around," said the technician, referring to Billy. "Alert Meyer. He's out by the Locus."

"Sí, señor." One of the guards left the room.

Lethe could feel Billy's spirit awaken as the effects of the drug wore off. His systems clicked on one by one. First Lethe felt sensory data come in through Billy's cybereyes, ears, and nose. Billy blinked as the smell of mold and dust hit him.

The feeling in his head and shoulders came on with a click. Next were his chest, arms, and hands. Billy opened his eyes and tried to sit up. The straps held him in place and he relaxed.

Spirit, are you with me?

"I am here, Billy." Lethe could hear his own thoughts channeled through Billy's Invoked Memory Stimulator and become words in the cyberzombie's mind. It was an odd sensation.

Where are we?

"I think we have been brought to a place called San Marcos, to see a man named Oscuro or Darke."

I know this place. I have been here before, long ago, it seems. A different lifetime. But I remember it, I remember walking outside, seeing the lake, the stone underneath. Feeling the power.

"I have felt it," Lethe said through the IMS. And he could still sense it even through the walls of the old restaurant—an immense subliminal power. "It is the magic that draws all those people outside."

People? Billy flexed his hands, checking his cybernetic systems with internal diagnostics. Most everything was on-line—his cyberspurs, his telescoping fingers, his wrist gyromount, and magnetic palms. And internally, his headgear seemed to be functioning normally as well. His GPS showed their exact location, his homing signal had been repaired, his eyes and ears checked out perfectly with all their augmentation intact.

"Yes, all around this place, thousands of people have gathered. They have been drawn by the Locus—the stone that you see in your memory."

Feeling clicked on in his legs and feet, and Billy continued his diagnostic cycle. His internal air tank was operating, as was his move-by-wire system and his power supply. Everything was as good as new—heel spikes and hydraulic jack—except his articulated arm, which didn't show up.

"They replaced your third arm and the gun," Lethe said. "I saw them do it."

Must be locked out. Maybe you can access it, Lethe.

"I'll try, but I doubt I'll have any success." Lethe exerted his will over Billy's articulated arm, seeing if he could nudge it.

Nothing.

Lethe could see where Billy's access to it had been cut, but the operation of the arm was tied into the cybernetic part of Billy's brain. Maybe they could get past it by merging the metal with spirit. That might be impossible, but Lethe didn't know.

"Sorry, Billy."

Don't fret it. We can get out of here without it.

"I'm ready when you are," Lethe said.

The technician standing above them spoke. Lethe could see him physically now, a dark-haired human with brown eyes and bronze skin. He wore a jumpsuit with a Jaguar Guard flash patch on his shoulder. "How do you feel, Burnout?"

Billy smiled up at him. "Never better. I'm good as new."

"Good," said the tech. "Now, please relax. I'm going to be running a series of—"

He never got to finish his sentence. Billy's cyberspurs snapped out of his forearm with a barely audible *snick*, their brand new monoblades slicing cleanly through the restraints. One of them caught the technician's wrist as he was reaching down to touch the access panel in Billy's torso.

"Ahh!" screamed the tech as Billy cut away the rest of the restraints.

Lethe drew mana around them, using his power to make them nearly invisible.

"¡Qué!" yelled one of the guards, bringing a machine gun to bear.

Another guard followed suit.

Billy leaped up to his feet, tossing the bleeding body of the technician to the side like a rag doll.

The rattle of automatic gunfire exploded into the room as two guards unloaded weapons into the body of the technician. Billy had disappeared. Lethe's masking was working.

Billy closed the distance to the guards in a flash. He was

even faster now, with all his equipment repaired. His monoblades retracted and he leveled a blow into one guard's skull, just over the cerebellum.

The other turned just as Billy snatched the weapon from the guard crumbling to the ground. His eyes widened for a second as they managed to focus on Billy. Too late. Billy's extendible fingers shot out and coiled around the guard's throat, and with a jerk he snapped the man's neck.

The two guards near the opposite wall scanned the room rapidly, one trying to see Billy with his astral sight. To no avail. Lethe had masked that as well, making them very difficult to pinpoint. The guards sprayed the room with gunfire, erratic and desperate.

Billy picked one off with a burst from the SMG. The other broke and ran, sounding the alarm.

"Now let's find a ride out of here," Billy said aloud.

Lethe gave his silent consent, and they stepped out into the heat and light.

In an instant, Billy scanned the area, looking for transportation. The glass door led to a cement plaza of sorts, bounded on one side by the restaurant and a parking lot crowded with people, and on the other side by the edge of what must have been the lake. Before it had been drained.

Now the cement led up to a five-meter drop onto a rocky lake bed covered sporadically with brown reeds and river plants. Across the lake bed stood the *teocalli,* a step-pyramid replica of an ancient Aztec temple. And behind that, more people, and an *ollamaliztli* stadium in the distance.

The smell of rotting plants filled the air, causing Billy to squint as he scanned toward the parking lot. While he was cataloguing the various vehicles, Lethe felt the immense pull of the Locus, sitting at the bottom of the dry lake bed.

Lethe focused his attention on the faceted stone, ignoring the gathering of people around and on top of it. Its awesome power enticed him, like a candle flame draws a moth. It was beautiful, magnificent.

Abruptly, a sick sensation slicked through Lethe, dread on a massive scale, and he knew that something was wrong here. Something was terribly wrong.

Billy hadn't moved from his position at the door of the restaurant. He, too, was drawn by the Locus.

Lethe began to notice the mages and guards on and around the stone. He saw the blood sacrifices, and he focused on the ring of mages linked by their life energy to become one perverted creature in astral space. He saw how the stone's power was being used.

Two people lay on the hard surface of the stone. Their bodies were there, but their spirits had left to travel to the metaplanes.

Lethe called on the Locus to hone his vision. He was stuck inside this machine-man, but he could still manipulate mana, and perhaps he could tap into the stone's reservoir of power.

Energy rushed into him, and Lethe could barely make out a dim wispy tendril, a resonating echo in astral space left by the two people. One was a human man with an aura as black and tainted as any Lethe had ever seen. The other was a human woman whose aura flickered on the edge of darkness and light.

Lethe had seen the effects of this woman's aura before. Long ago it seemed, when he had been bathed in light from the goddess, Thayla. When she had showed him the dark spot, the flaw in her song.

Realization hit him. *This is where the darkness that threatens Thayla is originating. This is how they plan to destroy her and take the bridge.*

"Billy," Lethe said, through the IMS. "I need to tell you something."

"I saw it all, Lethe," Billy said. "Don't ask me how, but I saw it in your mind."

"We need to stop them before they destroy Thayla."

Lethe saw images in Billy's mind; he was thinking about the beauty of the song she sang. The painful perfection of the blinding brilliance that issued from her soul as her voice rang out over the Chasm.

Billy checked the clip on the submachine gun and the integrated grenade launcher. "Let's do it," he said, then started toward the lake bed.

15

Ryan followed Harlequin into the château and through the central room. The elf led him into a side corridor and down a set of tight-winding stone stairs into the dungeon of the ancient fortress. The air grew cool and humid as they descended, the walls glistening slightly under the yellow light of torches.

Behind them came Jane Foster, Axler, and Talon. Foster was giving Axler and Talon instructions. "You two will stay with me outside the ritual circle. We will watch over the bodies, and defend them if any nasties come through from the astral or the metaplanes."

Axler stared coldly at Foster. "I'm ready."

Talon merely nodded, his full concentration on the elven woman.

Harlequin led them into a low-ceilinged chamber with walls of thick masonry. The wide space smelled of the tallow candles that were the sole illumination. The room was nearly circular, about ten meters across. Over the walls hung tapestries and murals the like of which Ryan had never seen. They depicted beautiful and terrifying scenes—a battle in a city of spires, a sword duel at dawn, and the one that caught Ryan's eyes most strongly—a likeness of Dunkelzahn crouched in a cave, speaking to two tiny dragons.

"Do you like it?" Harlequin asked, sweeping his arms to indicate the whole room. "I've haven't shown it to anyone in millen . . . a long time."

"Wow, Harlequin, this is totally amazing. I've never seen anything like it."

"Don't patronize me!" Harlequin turned suddenly. Swiftly and with a dangerous look in his eye.

Ryan had been completely serious. "I didn't mean—"

"You must know that I could destroy you with a thought," Harlequin said. "I could destroy you all and take the Dragon Heart."

The chill edge of adrenaline scissored up Ryan's vertebrae. "What?"

"I am powerful," the elf said. "You've only seen a fraction of it. And the Dragon Heart is . . ." Sounds of satisfaction came from Harlequin's throat. "Divine."

Ryan focused himself. It was hard to believe that the elf was going to try to take the Heart now, after all this, but if he did, Ryan would fight him.

"I could take it for myself. It would have many uses against those who believe I am but a jester between courts." Harlequin's face showed nothing but seriousness.

Ryan narrowed his eyes on Harlequin. "Frag off," he said. "You aren't going to destroy me. You don't want the Dragon Heart."

They stared at each other in a silence that stretched. Ryan did not waver in the slightest. He prepared to use his stealth magic to escape.

Finally Harlequin smiled. "You are right, of course, Ryan. I have no reason to take action against you. We want the same thing."

Ryan breathed a sigh of relief, but he felt anger smoldering. "I've indulged your little game. Shall we get on with the ritual?"

Harlequin walked to a small chest that sat on the floor next to the wall. "Don't be too hasty," he said. "The metaplanes should not be traveled lightly, especially by a first-timer." He opened the chest and removed a long blue candle that was inlaid with a coppery gold metal.

In the astral, the entire room burned like a sun that it almost hurt to look at. The candle flared in the astral as Harlequin lit it, the metal veins sparking flares of mana as the elf mage paced around the chamber, making patterns with the dripping candle.

Ryan waited while the elf moved around, using the time to reflect on the last exchange with Harlequin. *The fragging sonofaslitch!* Ryan thought. *He taunted me purposely.*

Ryan watched Harlequin carefully, fascinated by the elf's hands. They had an unnaturalness to them, gaunt and chalk-white. They appeared fragile, yet the tendons, which stood out like cords, crisscrossed by veins of deep purple under the pale skin, held a strength that Ryan had never seen before.

An undying vitality.

After a few minutes, Harlequin stopped dripping candle wax. The circle had been made complete, the tracery of patterns intricate and beautiful. The painted elf extinguished the flame and set the candle down. Then he beckoned to Ryan.

Ryan nodded, awaiting instructions.

"Please step to the middle of the circle," Harlequin said. "Place the Dragon Heart in the exact center. I've marked it."

Ryan nodded, then carefully removed the Heart from his wide cloth sash. He set the artifact on the blue spot in the center of the room.

"The Heart will be the tricky part," Harlequin said. "While the physical components of you and me will remain here in the physical world, the entire make-up of the Dragon Heart has to be carried into the astral and the metaplanes."

Ryan nodded his understanding.

Harlequin dripped orichalcum wax from the smoking candle in his hand onto the Dragon Heart until the whole artifact was covered. "We're almost ready," he said, taking his free hand and filling his palm with hot liquid wax from the candle. He brushed Ryan's forehead with it, then his own.

"One more thing, Ryan Mercury."

"Yes?"

"The metaplanes are a mirror of the soul. Across the threshold, truth is always shown in metaphor—nothing is as it seems. Everything is both hidden and revealed."

"I have heard stories."

Harlequin gripped Ryan by the shoulders, iron-tight and unshakable. His piercing green eyes flashed with impatience. "I don't know what Dunkelzahn did to you, but you're more than you seem."

Ryan did not flinch; he held Harlequin's stare. "In all sincerity, I don't know what you mean."

"Then you're more than you know," Harlequin said. "I think you should be prepared, because in the metaplanes, you might learn the truth. And in my experience, the truth has the nasty habit of fucking up a perfectly good fantasy."

Ryan held his breath. He wasn't sure what Harlequin was talking about, and he just wanted to get on with the mission.

Harlequin released his grip on Ryan. "I'm only telling you this because you've never traveled the netherworlds. When truth hits you, which it will sooner or later, I don't want you to freeze up. At the wrong moment, it could mean death."

"I don't think I have any secrets," Ryan said.

Harlequin smiled. "Everybody does."

Ryan grinned. "Even you?"

"I have more than most," Harlequin said. "Maybe even more than you."

Ryan thought about that. What secrets did he have? Since defeating Roxborough's personality transfer and recovering the Dragon Heart, Ryan knew what he had to do. He knew who he was. Or at least he *thought* he knew.

"You're ready," Harlequin said. Then he began pacing along the interior of the wax circle, gesturing for Ryan to follow suit.

Ryan stepped in behind him and soon the world around them changed.

16

Señor Oscuro's words echoed in Lucero's ears as she stood poised to step through the dark barrier and into the cleansing white. As she balanced on the verge of salvation.

"What are you doing, my child?"

Lucero did not turn to look at him; she could not afford any doubts now. Could not allow herself any hesitation or Oscuro would control her once again. He would stop her from purifying herself in the beautiful song.

Lucero heard the wondrous voice more clearly now, near the rim of the spreading stain. And the exquisite loveliness of its harmony and strength made her heart ache for more. The song was her salvation. Her rectitude.

I must not stop now.

"Do not be hasty," came Oscuro's words, like hissed ghosts from the darkness behind her. "You will have time enough for frivolity after."

With difficulty, Lucero maintained focus. Time seemed to lengthen as she pushed against the glowing rim of the stain. Her advancement slowed; it was as though the atmosphere around her had grown thick.

Step.

Another onslaught of Oscuro's minions struck the barrier before she could pass through. Corpses and gum toads, hideous crawlers, all bathed in the blood of a new sacrifice, threw themselves into the light. All around Lucero, they shrieked in agony, bursting into flames as they plunged into the searing white. The song drove all the stain from them until there was nothing left but a bubbling black splotch where each one had stood.

Black smoke fouled the air around Lucero as the creatures vaporized. But the blood they carried fused into the ground, advancing the line of darkness. Lucero lost her focus then. Smoke clouded her vision and she could no longer see the light.

The intolerable shrieks from the burning monsters winnowed their way into her brain, and she could no longer hear the song.

Is it gone? Has Oscuro finally extinguished the light? Silenced the song?

Lucero groped through the darkness for a long moment, listening for anything. Any fragment of the song.

Darkness and blood swirled around her. Smoke and screams.

Then it filtered through again, the hint of gray in the night. The perfect tone of the song touching her ears. It sang to her in desperation. And she understood the words.

You are the reason he can be here. You are the balance between good and evil. The yin and the yang.

Lucero squinted against the smoke. The dark wedge took up nearly all of the outcropping now, the stain of blood spanning the entire width of the unfinished bridge.

Your weakness has allowed you to be used. Step into the light and he can use you no more.

Only at the tip, a meter away, did the light still shine. A small area of glowing perfection in a wash of putrid stench.

Embrace the light, and you will be free.

Lucero stepped closer to the tip of the outcropping. She heard the music grow as she neared the new edge. It was obvious that the singer would not last through another onslaught; Lucero must join her now.

Oscuro's hissing voice whistled on the cold wind. "If you step into the light, you will only end up like the others—vaporized and bubbling. You will die."

Step.

One more and . . .

"My child," came the hiss again. "You have been useful to me thus far, but your betrayal pushes even the limits of my patience."

Lucero maintained her focus and started through.

Searing heat flayed the flesh of her right hand and arm as she entered the light. Its beauty bringing intense pain into the parts of her body that had penetrated the barrier of brilliance. Part of her face and torso, her right leg. Purifying patches of her stained soul as the song flowed around her.

Thick tendrils of flesh, like ropy intestines, flew from the eviscerated corpses surrounding Oscuro and latched onto her. Shackles that coiled around her left leg and arm, the two that were still in darkness.

Stopped her mid-step. Half in light, half in dark.

"I cannot allow you to leave me," came the hissing wind to her left ear. She barely heard it, however, as her soul strained under the power of the rift between worlds. Torn asunder by juxtaposition.

Immobilized on the brink of contradiction, Lucero lost all capacity for rational thought.

You must fight him. The goddess spoke to her. Her name was Thayla, and she was the protector of the world. Lucero knew all that now, all about the light and the dark. *You must give yourself wholly to me.*

She knew all, but could not move. She could do nothing.

Oscuro raised another onslaught of corpses and creatures, bathed in blood. She felt them coming, and she knew that when they hit the barrier this time, they would swallow the song. Thayla and the light that came from her was on the verge of extinction.

Lucero's breath caught in her throat as she waited for the end.

17

Ryan floated in an inky black void, silent and odorless. The absence of sensation.

He tried to remain calm; he had heard stories about metaplanar travel. During his undercover stint at Fuchi Industrial Electronics, his friend Miranda had told him about the dweller on the threshold—an entity that guarded the gateway to the metaplanes.

Miranda had told him that the dweller appeared to each traveler in a different incarnation, to test his worthiness. Ryan tried to put the thought of Miranda out of his mind. She'd been part of the Assets, Inc. team for a brief period, and had died in a battle with Burnout. A battle for the Dragon Heart. Ryan still felt partially responsible.

The void took shape around him. Coalescing and brightening until a small dracoform glowed a fiery red in front of Ryan. It stood about two meters high and was similar to the silvery statue holding the spirit of Dunkelzahn that had tasked Ryan his mission. Standing upright on hind legs, its wings spread and radiant, there was an intelligent look in its silver eyes.

"You must pass a test, Ryanthusar," it said, using the name Dunkelzahn always called Ryan. "Before I can let you cross."

Ryan nodded. "Who are you?"

"As you suspect, I am known as the dweller on the threshold," it said. "But for you I take the likeness of a drake—a small dracoform who lived long ago and was just like you are now—a servant of the one you serve."

"Dunkelzahn?"

The drake inclined its scaled head. "He went by a different name then."

"You must know that he is dead," Ryan said.

"I know what you know, no more. No less."

"Then you know that I have no time to waste. I must get the Dragon Heart to Thayla. It was the last mission given to me by Dunkelzahn."

"I know that since you lost your master, you have been through a harrowing search for who you are. I know that since overcoming Roxborough and defeating Burnout, you think you have found your true self, and I know that you are wrong."

"I have no doubts."

"Liar!"

The accusation hit Ryan like a tongue of flame and heat. Suddenly, two other creatures materialized in the dark space around them. Ryan crouched in a defensive stance, turning to assess the situation. One creature shimmered in the air like a heat wave, barely visible. Its presence was a tornado of wind.

An air elemental.

On Ryan's other side was a creature of molten clay. Animated lava, heat rippling out from its glowing red skin.

A fire elemental.

"Ryanthusar, in your master's absence, you have embraced change with reluctance and fear."

The fire elemental struck out with two globular arms, trying to engulf Ryan in fire. Simultaneously, the air elemental fanned the flames and released a billowing stench of smoke.

Ryan focused and struck out, accelerating up to his maximum speed as his blows landed on the fire elemental.

The spirit barely flinched, coming on with limbs of lava, spread wide.

Ryan whirled to get clear, trying not to breathe the noxious gas as he struck again.

His blows landed in rapid succession, but the elemental

seemed unfazed. His hands and arms came away burned, but Ryan channeled the pain away with his magic.

"You must know that you cannot defeat both of them," said the drake. "Using your standard tactics."

Ryan immediately saw that the dweller spoke the truth. These were the most powerful elementals he'd ever faced. Smart and resilient.

"If you do not pass the test, you cannot complete your mission. You will have failed your master."

Ryan tried to ignore the drake's words. He struck again, but the fire elemental wrapped itself around Ryan, engulfing him in searing heat. Pain like he'd never known struck him. His skin melted from his flesh, stripped in burning shreds from his bones. His eyes seemed to pop from the heat.

He tried to use magic to hold himself together. He tried to channel away the pain, but it was too great. He took a deep breath to gather his remaining strength to get free. His lungs seized up as the fumes filled his chest, making him cough and wretch.

I am failing, he thought. *There must be another way. The dweller wouldn't give me an impossible task.*

Ryan remembered defeating the fire elemental that Foster had sent to attack him. He remembered what Harlequin had said afterward. "You banished that fire elemental, my friend." Ryan hadn't believed him for a second; he had never banished a spirit before. Physical adepts couldn't do that.

If he had banished Foster's elemental, it had been the Dragon Heart's doing. He didn't have the Heart now.

No choice, he thought. *I have to try.*

Ryan focused on the fire elemental, studying its aura as he focused his mana. He targeted the spirit with his magic, using his will in an attempt to send it away.

"Be gone, spirit!" he yelled.

The elemental wavered around Ryan, then faded out.

The pain dissipated, and Ryan sank to his knees. He needed to gather his strength to banish the other one.

He looked up to see it all around him, sucking the wind from his lungs. He couldn't speak the words to banish it so he drew power through himself as though he were throwing a telekinetic strike at it. In his mind he willed it to disintegrate, and threw the last of his force.

The air elemental wavered for a second, teetering on the brink of life. Then it fluttered and shredded into nothing.

Gone.

"Congratulations," said the drake. "You passed the test."

Ryan took a deep breath of fresh air. His pain was completely gone, his wounds vanished. He felt whole and strong.

The drake faded in front of him, its words like echoes in a canyon. "Remember, Ryanthusar, your master may be lost to you, but you must continue to grow. You cannot deny your nature."

The dweller vanished, and Ryan floated in the void again. Then a glowing object appeared in the space next to him.

The Dragon Heart.

Harlequin's ritual had worked. It had transported the artifact across. Ryan picked it up and wrapped it in his sash.

"Took you long enough," came a familiar voice, edged with sarcasm.

Ryan found himself looking at Harlequin. "I had a run-in with the dweller on the threshold."

Harlequin smirked under his face paint. "I should've warned you, I suppose."

Ryan finished putting his sash around his waist. "No," he said. "Wouldn't have done any good."

Harlequin nodded. "You ready?"

Before Ryan could answer, the scenery materialized around them. Flat sky of muted rainbow colors. Smell of blood and leaking guts. Ryan recognized the stench of the battlefield.

A feeling of nausea ground inside him as they appeared on the cracked plane of rock. Something was terribly wrong.

Ryan recognized the place from his dream, though the

details were off. The plane of darkened rock was ten meters or so wide here, narrowing to a point about a hundred meters along the outcropping. The edges of the plane dropped away into a bottomless abyss.

A chill wind cored into his skin as it whipped up through the Chasm, but it carried away the stench and lifted Ryan's hopes a little.

"Shit!" Harlequin said, holding his hand to his ear. Listening. "What the fuck happened here? Where's Thayla?" He started running toward the tip, moving faster than Ryan would have thought possible.

Ryan followed close behind, watching for Thayla. Looking for any clues that might tell him what had happened. He heard it then, a distant singing, like a muffled songbird. The music behind the veil touched Ryan's heart and broke it. It was the most beautiful sound he had ever heard.

Suddenly, he was walking over corpses and blood. He looked up to see a line of hideous creatures attacking something at the very tip of the outcropping. Throwing their own lives away in a series of vicious attacks.

The woman who stood at the tip fought them off with her song. Ryan could see a brilliant radiance emanating from her now.

Thayla!

As Ryan watched, pushing past Harlequin in a burst of speed, the creatures overcame her. They were simply too numerous. They crashed into her.

Ryan was too far to reach her.

Thayla staggered back and fell over the edge. She teetered for a second, still singing. Her eyes fell across Ryan and Harlequin, intense sadness cast in her single glance—a look that shattered Ryan's heart.

Ryan dove for her, plowing through the last of the animated corpses and oozing spider creatures to reach the tip of the outcropping.

He was too late.

Thayla stopped singing as she plummeted. "I am lost,"

she called out. "Find the spirit Lethe. I named him and he carries part of me inside. He will know how to wield the Dragon Heart."

Ryan lay on his stomach, watching her disappear into the abyss. Helpless to save her. He had failed after all.

"Get up, Ryan," Harlequin's voice. "Get up now!"

Ryan stood and turned to see a fresh army of blood-let corpses and other creatures coming for them. Ryan momentarily cringed at the cuts in the zombies' pale flesh crawling with tiny maggots. Many of the corpses changed shape before his eyes, some growing tentacles, others pustules of oozing brown and yellow stench.

Behind the advancing guard stood a human woman and a man Ryan had seen before. Seen in a dream, in a distant memory, ordering Ryan to be beaten, tortured for information.

The woman's skin was stark white and smooth on one half of her body, the other half marred by runic scars. She knelt at the man's feet, shackled by ropes made of flesh.

The man had raven-black hair with a matching beard and mustache. He held a sacrificial knife in one hand, a stone bowl in the other, and wore an ancient robe of the Aztec priesthood and a ceremonial collar of enameled feathers. He looked at Ryan and Harlequin with hatred and glee flashing in his black eyes. Pupils like windows to Hell itself.

"Who is that?" Ryan asked.

"That's Darke," said Harlequin. "He's the pawn of the Enemy, and seems to have grown somewhat in power since I last fought him."

"So what do we do?"

"We try to get out alive," Harlequin said as the dark horde closed in around them.

18

Lucero knelt on the hard stone, sticky with drying blood, cowering in the shadow of her master. She had seen everything. Thayla, the goddess of light, thrown into the Chasm by Oscuro's army. The two newcomers, arriving to help Thayla.

Coming too late.

A rush of regret shook Lucero, intense sadness at the fact that she had waited too long to cleanse herself of her addiction. It was too late for that now. Too late.

She put her head in her hands and heaved sobs of despair. The sounds of combat filled the black air around her, but she didn't care anymore. Her life was lost. With Thayla gone, Lucero had abandoned hope.

Soon, these two others would fall before Oscuro's onslaught. Then it was only a matter of time before construction on the bridge would accelerate. *How many innocents would lose their lives for that?* Lucero couldn't comprehend such a number.

My life is forfeit now. The realization hit her like a sledgehammer, sending a ripple of fear through her. She had been necessary for Oscuro to maintain the dark blood circle against Thayla. But now that the goddess was gone, now that the song had been silenced, she was no longer necessary.

Expendable.

The word swirled around inside her head like a leaf on a wind. Faster and faster until she grew dizzy and weak. Her shoulders shook from fright and sadness. Tears came in heaves and sobs, wracking any remaining strength she had.

She realized after a while that Oscuro no longer stood near her. She lifted her head and looked about her.

All around was death and wretched ruin.

Near the tip of the outcropping one of the newcomers fought the zombies and the spider creatures. He was human, handsome and strong with shining auburn hair. His muscular arms and legs struck with incredible speed, his blows deadly and accurate, felling Oscuro's minions with precision and phenomenal power.

His aura glowed with a golden brilliance, and Lucero noticed that he carried an artifact of immense magical strength, that he was using it to focus his energy.

The other fought Oscuro directly, using spells as weapons. This mage was an elf, and his face was painted white with red diamonds over his eyes. His magic was very strong. He was a good match for Oscuro, and perhaps would have handled Oscuro without trouble if the corpses and other creatures hadn't kept interfering.

The zombies grew elongated nails like sharp, blue-black claws that slashed out to tear at the flesh of the newcomers. Their bones and teeth jutted from flesh in barbed cornices, spurs for ripping skin and muscle.

The army kept on coming. Zombies replacing fallen zombies. Crawlers and oozing toads taking the place of their dead counterparts. It was too much, Lucero saw, for the two metahumans. They would soon be destroyed.

Flashes of brilliant white, like lightning, arced from the elf with the painted face, slicing through the minions, and stinging Oscuro. He flinched visibly, and a wound opened up on his chest. Lucero watched as the wound knitted itself closed in the moments that followed, and an identical gash formed on the body of one of the sacrifices.

Oscuro gave a diabolical grin, then he counter-attacked with his own magic.

A spirit formed in the air above Oscuro then. It was huge, perhaps the manifestation of the Blood Mage Gestalt entity on this metaplane, and it took the form of a dragon—a feathered serpent like Quetzalcóatl, except this one was much smaller. The dragon's feathers glimmered blue and yellow, but Lucero noticed that patches of it were blank. Almost transparent.

Inside those patches, something seemed to be moving, like a million tiny snakes writhing in agony. The sight made Lucero shudder.

Lightning flashed from the painted elf to the dragon spirit, but it did not slow the dragon's descent. The spirit crashed down on the elf mage, slamming him to the ground behind the surrounding zombies.

The human with the glowing aura cried out and started to move to help his fallen companion. His path was blocked by Oscuro's minions.

The dragon spirit crashed down again. And again. Gouging flesh from the elf.

Oscuro advanced on the elf, wielding his obsidian knife, looking down over his prone body as the dragon spirit descended again. "I will defeat you finally," said Oscuro.

The mage focused all his power and released it against the feathered serpent. Like a sun flare, the dragon burst into flames and dissipated.

Zombies piled on the elf's arms and legs, pinning him down.

Oscuro smiled and brought the knife down over the elf's chest.

Lucero felt something then—a tug on her aura.

Oscuro stopped, looking at Lucero in surprise. A questioning expression crossed his features. "What?" he said, then glanced around rapidly, searching for something. "No," he said. "Not now." He brought the knife up again, and stabbed down, its tip aimed at the elf's heart.

As the knife slid between the elf's ribs, Lucero and her master watched as the world around them dissipated.

Oscuro screamed, "No!"

The cracked plane of rock and blood-tinged sky swirled into a vortex around them. Oscuro's anger slammed into

Lucero like a palpable blow to her head as they flew back into the physical world. As she plowed into her meat body.

Crying, naked, bathed in blood.

Hands of acolytes helped her to sit up.

"What is the meaning of this?" Oscuro yelled at the startled faces of the mages around him. "Why were we brought out? Why was the ritual stopped?"

In answer, Lucero heard the rattle of an automatic weapon. She looked around. Mages and technicians huddled behind the Jaguar Guards, who formed a tight, protective perimeter around the Locus and everyone on it. The guards had drawn their guns and cannons, searching for the source of the bullets.

"There!" yelled one of the guards, pointing toward a space in the crowd.

At first Lucero saw nothing, but after a second, she caught sight of something, almost invisible as it approached in quick bursts. The creature's aura and his physical being flickered under some masking power, but once she pinpointed him, she got a clear look.

He seemed human, though his proportions were immense. Cyberspurs retracted into his forearm as he rushed toward her, a machine gun in his other hand. He moved faster than should be possible for his size, and there was something inhuman about him—his body too symmetrical, his limbs too long, his bald skull too uniform.

A cyberzombie? Lucero had seen one or two before. They were sometimes used to defend members of the Gestalt. *What is this one doing?* she wondered. They rarely acted on their own.

The cyberzombie's aura was a confusion, but she could read his intent clearly. He wanted to destroy the Locus and those around it. Including her.

Lucero heard a deep *thunk,* then an explosion shook the air, throwing three guards to the ground. Pandemonium ensued as the Jaguar Guards returned fire. Lucero's ears rang, and she breathed shallowly in the acrid air.

Lucero coiled into a fetal position, knowing that death was near. It circled her like a descending vulture.

She rocked herself slowly, holding her hands over her destroyed ears, and waited. *Perhaps I'm already dead,* she thought. *Perhaps I've slipped beyond the pale, and this is Hell.*

19

Pain sliced into Ryan's shoulder as one of the spider creatures bit into it. The monster's jagged mandibles penetrated his armor, and Ryan felt the poison start to paralyze him. Winnowing down his arm with a numbing cold.

"Frag you!" he yelled, spinning toward it. Burying his fist into the largest of its eyes. He penetrated the gooey black ichor and punched through to its brain. He grabbed a handful of dripping soft nervous tissue and yanked it out.

The creature released its bite on Ryan's shoulder and slumped into a quivering heap. Only to be replaced by another of the same kind, fighting to climb over its fallen kin in order to devour Ryan.

Ryan turned to his other side, using his distance strike, amplified by the power of the Dragon Heart to plow back the phalanx of zombies closing in.

I must get to Harlequin.

The elf had fallen under that magical dragon's pounce, and even though he had destroyed it, Ryan knew he was in trouble.

As Ryan turned, time seemed to thicken, like each moment was longer than the next. Each heartbeat spaced a fraction further from its predecessor.

Moments ago, Ryan had seen the dead black of the obsidian knife in Darke's hand. He had seen the arc it had traveled as it fell. He'd watched helplessly as the razor-honed tip of the sacrificial weapon penetrated Harlequin's jacket and shirt, stabbing down into his chest like a jagged hypodermic needle.

Harlequin's back had arched in pain, and he'd cried out in agony as his blood gushed out in a geyser. The elf had started a spell—a powerful volley of magical force— aimed at Darke. But at that exact instant the human had looked up in surprise, abruptly yelling, "No!"

Darke vanished as Harlequin's spell hit.

Now, Ryan yelled, "Harlequin!"

"I live, my friend," came the response. "But that may not be true for long. He has wounded me deeply."

Zombies closed in on Harlequin, though without Darke to direct them, they seemed less effective. Still, the creatures bore their claws and teeth.

"I'm coming to help," Ryan said, struggling to move through the masses around him.

Hands and tentacles groped for a hold, snagging Ryan's legs and arms. Spilling gore and foul-smelling pus over him as he tried to push through to Harlequin.

"No," said Harlequin. "You must go back, Ryan. You heard Thayla. You must find the spirit called Lethe and bring him here."

Ryan ran into a wall of zombies. "What about you?"

"I will try, but I am weak. If I don't make it back, you must contact Aina. She knows the ancient magic and can bring you and the Heart across again."

Ryan tried to move through the zombies, but they blocked his way. Groping with their razor nails to gouge out his eyes. "But—"

"Go!" Harlequin gestured with his arm, and Ryan found himself flying. The world swirled around him, a mass of gray and red and rainbow sky. Cracked earth and darkness. Sick feeling of dread.

Then it was all gone, and Ryan crashed back into his body.

20

Bullets ricocheted off Billy's metal body as Lethe tried to keep them hidden using his masking ability. It became more and more difficult as the guards around the Locus used flash grenades and magic to alter the light conditions.

"They're also using radar," Billy said, diving into a rolling dodge behind a large rock covered with dried river plants. "Our grenades are gone, and we're nearly out of bullets. We're not going to make it. Even I can't take all of them hand to hand."

"Maybe there's a way."

"And that would be?"

"Magic," Lethe said. "Casting spells."

"I can't do that anymore, remember?"

"I know you lost all your power when you became Burnout, but I can manipulate astral energies." Lethe waited for his message to sink in. "But you were a mage once. You still remember the formulae for spells, don't you?"

"I think so, but—"

"What can it hurt to try?"

Billy was shaking his head, firing a quick burst at a group of guards advancing on their position. The gun stopped firing abruptly, and Billy shook it before ducking back behind the boulder. "Frag," he said. "Okay, let's do it. What've we got to lose now?"

"I'll channel the mana through you."

Billy nodded, and Lethe could feel him searching his memory. "All right. Let's keep it simple. Hellblast."

Lethe drew power to him and paid careful attention as Billy reached for it like a groping blind man. He floundered for a second, then seemed to feel it. Lethe showed him astral space, watched as Billy targeted the aura of one of the advancing guards.

The spell coalesced and discharged. The guard exploded in a massive ball of flame that flattened those around him.

"It worked!" Lethe said.

Billy's response came slowly, a labored whisper. "Too strong," he whispered. The magic had drained him, weakened him. Lethe waited helplessly as Billy sank into unconsciousness.

More guards were coming, approaching slowly, wary of magic and any other surprises that Billy might have. Lethe contemplated trying to cast another hellblast spell himself. He could probably accomplish it now that he'd participated in one. How the mana was gathered, focused and released inside the aura of another as fire. But Lethe didn't know how that would effect Billy.

Might even kill him.

He decided to run instead. With Billy passed out, Lethe had a measure of control over the body, but it was jerky and awkward. He stood and tried to run.

Guards swarmed around him, their weapons ready to kill. "Hold your fire," came the order over a bullhorn from the bank of the dried lake.

Lethe looked over as he moved awkwardly toward the water. If he could get into what was left of the lake, perhaps he could swim over the dam and down river, staying under by using his air tank. Perhaps escape was possible after all.

The man who spoke was a dwarf wearing a white technician smock. He slung the bullhorn over his shoulder and leveled a remote signaling device toward Lethe and Billy.

Lethe's legs seized up and he fell. His arms froze in place, clicking off as though they didn't exist. Lethe watched helplessly as he hit the ground and scraped to a stop in loose gravel. Billy's systems shut down one by one. His eyes, ears. All sensory input erased.

Lethe shifted to his normal perception, watching everything from the astral as guards surrounded him. Their auras indicated a mixture of fear, duty, and anger at the death of their comrades.

What will they do now? Lethe wondered.

"Step aside," came a man's voice.

"Sí, señor."

The guards parted to let him through, a human with black hair and a beard. The man wore a tan robe soaked in blood. Around his neck hung an ornate ceremonial collar made of brilliantly colored enamel feathers, rimmed with gold. His aura flickered with blank patches, sections that writhed like a million slithering, transparent worms. Lethe had seen this before; it was like parts of his aura were missing or connected to somewhere else.

A tall elf accompanied the man, an elf Lethe recognized as the mage from the cybertechnology clinic in Panama. "This is your fault, Meyer."

"Believe me, Darke," Meyer said. "I gave strict instructions for Burnout to be kept bound and under heavy guard. We've never seen this sort of behavior from a cyberzombie before."

Darke narrowed his eyes on Lethe, looking into the astral with a level of scrutiny that Lethe had rarely seen. Darke's perception stared directly at Lethe, recognizing his presence inside Billy's body. "I see you, spirit," he said. "I see you, and I will destroy you."

Magic gathered to Darke's aura, a phenomenal reservoir of mana building in the seconds before Lethe realized what was about to happen. Lethe reached out to the Locus for strength as Darke's power smashed into him.

"¡Adios!" Darke yelled. "You are banished!"

Scalpels of magical energy sliced into Lethe, cutting him up, dissecting his very soul as it tried to force him from this world. Light and color spun around him, descending into gray, into black pinpricked with white stars.

Lethe felt his essence disintegrate from the onslaught, the fabric of his existence shred and unravel as he groped to hold his life force together. A mushroom cloud of fire seemed to erupt around him, shrapnel flying out from the explosion. Trees bursting into flames. A recurring nightmare of shattering glass and burning sacrifices.

He screamed, and a rift opened between the physical and the astral. A rainbow portal across the metaplanes as the explosion stripped him of his essence, his life energy.

Lethe's mind touched the Locus then, and he drank power from it like a parched man from a mountain spring. The nightmare dissipated and darkness descended, but Lethe channeled mana through the stone and into the pattern of his being. The astral explosion diffused. Vanished into memory.

When Darke's banishment dwindled, Lethe was still alive. Still firmly ensconced inside Billy's body. Lethe used the Locus to replenish his energy. Ready for another assault.

Darke scowled at Lethe. Then turned to Meyer. "There is a spirit in possession of our cyberzombie," he said. "A very powerful spirit who has insinuated itself in and around Burnout's life force."

Meyer's look was grave. "What do you want me to do?"

"Banish it," Darke said. "I don't have time to waste with this right now. I must complete my ritual."

Meyer nodded. "Of course. I will assemble a team of mages," he said. "Surely, this spirit won't withstand a ritual banishment of that magnitude."

"Good idea."

"It might be difficult to separate the two spirits inside without killing the cyberzombie," Meyer said. "We will try, but I thought you should know the complexities involved."

"I know them," Darke said impatiently. "Proceed with

the banishment. If he dies, so be it. Send the parts back to Roxborough for recycling into another cyberzombie."

Meyer watched Darke turn away and walk back to the Locus. "As you wish."

25 August 2057

21

Ryan bolted upright.

His body hung on his spirit like a heavy weight, like dead flesh on the bones of his soul. His skin tingled, flashing between fire and ice. Yellow light crashed in on him, and the heavy fragrance of burning candles choked in the back of his throat.

"What happened?" asked Foster.

Ryan breathed slowly, trying to adjust to the shock of such an abrupt transition. Slowly he came to feel a semblance of normalcy. He sat in the ritual circle in Harlequin's chamber, and as he took breath in and released it, he no longer choked on the sweet fragrance of candles. He relished them; they washed away the metallic odor of blood and the stench of gutted corpses that drifted in his memory.

"Are you all right, Ryan?" asked Axler.

Ryan held his hand up for patience. "I think so," he said. Then he got slowly to his feet, and looked at the concerned face of Jane Foster. Her blonde curls had been pulled back into a clip. "We ran into trouble," he said. "Harlequin sent me back."

Ryan looked over at the unconscious body of Harlequin, lying on the floor next to him. His aura had not returned. "He may need help," Ryan said. "He was wounded when he sent me back."

Ryan checked the elf's body, but he knew there was nothing he could do. The physical body was in fine shape. Then Ryan looked himself over. He felt exhausted and hungry, and his shoulder was a little numb from the spider creature's venom, but it seemed to be healing already.

The Dragon Heart had returned with him, but it was no longer in the center of the ritual circle. It had come back into the physical on his body, tucked once more into the sash around his waist.

Foster and Talon were examining the ritual circle. "The ritual magic has been disrupted," Foster said, then rushed into the circle to Harlequin's prone body.

Ryan looked at Axler. "How long have I been gone?"

"Nine hours," she said. "It's almost dawn."

Time must move slower there, Ryan thought.

Talon and Axler approached Ryan. The mage had pulled his brown hair into a ponytail, and his eyes narrowed with concern. Ryan could tell that Talon was using his astral perception to examine Ryan's aura.

"You look whole," Talon said.

"Thank you, Talon," Ryan said. "I feel fine now. Please assist Foster. I want Harlequin to make it back alive."

Talon nodded and moved to help.

Axler examined Ryan coldly with her doe brown eyes. She scanned him for physical injuries, then lent him a supporting shoulder to lean on.

"What's the status outside, Axler? Any sign of physical threat?"

She shook her head. "Nothing."

"Good."

Talon looked up, his dark brows knitting. "Foster and I need to search the metaplanes for Harlequin's spirit," he said. "Will you watch over us?"

Axler's angelic face gazed down at them with a cold melancholy. "Of course."

"Do what you must," Ryan said. "Whatever it takes."

Talon laid on his back next to Foster and Harlequin. Foster touched the coiled dragon ring on her finger, then went slack. Talon followed suit.

They looked so peaceful, the three of them. Foster truly

was a beautiful woman, especially without all the posturing and attitude.

Ryan silently wished them luck as he stepped out of the circle and spoke into his tacticom mic. "Jane, you online?"

"I've been following events, Quicksilver. Sounds like you hit some heavy drek."

"Understatement of the millennium, but the gist is right," Ryan said.

"What do you want me to do?"

"We've got to locate Lethe. Thayla was destroyed, but she told us that Lethe would be able to wield the Heart."

There was a pause while Jane contemplated. "Frag," she said. Then, "Lethe should still be with Burnout."

"You got any leads on where they took him?"

Jane sighed. "My smartframes tracked the helos to the Aztechnology arcology in Atlanta, but I haven't had the spare cycles to try and deck into their hosts to see if I can get anything more. My assumption would be that they'd eventually ship him back to the home country, but we're dealing with a megacorp. Anything is possible."

Ryan shook his head. "I guess I should've planned that run into Aztlan."

"I'll find him, Quicksilver. How many spirit-possessed cyberzombies are there? He's hard to hide."

Ryan smiled. "Thanks, Jane. It's more crucial than you know."

"On it now." She disconnected.

Abruptly, Talon sat up and shook his head. Foster did not move.

"I don't think we'll be able to find him," he said. "We went to the bridge. Foster knew the way since she's been there before. But there was no sign of him there, and we were about to be attacked."

Talon shuddered. "That place is evil," he said. "I never thought I'd say that about anything. I'd always thought there was no such thing as good and evil, no such inherent absolutes. But if evil exists, I've felt it now."

"Why isn't Foster awake?" Ryan asked.

"She knows him better than I do. She had little hope, but wanted to search some other places anyway."

Ryan nodded. "Thanks, Talon."

"I'd like to help her," Talon said. "She's desperate to find him."

"No," Ryan said. "I may need you awake in case Aztechnology sends people after us. But I know someone else who might be able to help Harlequin."

Talon nodded, then stood up and stretched.

Ryan lifted his wristphone and punched in Nadja's private LTG number. He touched the Connect and waited a few seconds while it rang on Nadja's end. It was extremely early in the AM in Washington.

When she answered, the video was blanked. "Hello?"

"Sorry to wake you, my love," Ryan said. "But this is of the utmost importance."

"Ryan, are you all right?" The concern in her voice touched a chord in his heart.

"I'm fine, but Harlequin may be on the verge of death. I need you to contact his friend Aina. She may be the only one powerful enough to save him."

The video came to life on the wristphone's tiny flat-screen. Nadja smiled, pushing a strand of hair from her eyes. It was mussed from sleep, a rat's nest of dark strands. "I'll do it immediately," she said.

Ryan nodded. "Thank you."

As she disconnected, Ryan turned to look at Harlequin's lifeless body. *I hope Aina gets here in time,* he thought. *Even if I can find Lethe, it's going to be a lot harder to stop Darke without Harlequin.*

Perhaps impossible.

22

The first pink strands of sunlight brushed the underbellies of the scattered clouds above the San Marcos *teocalli*. Lucero knelt on the hard, electric surface of the Locus and watched the lightening sky. All hope gone. Sapped from her like body heat through a wet blanket.

Leaving her shivering. Feeling desperate and alone, despite the bustle of activity all around her.

Deep, resonant drums sounded in the hillside above the lake now. The musicians in the trees around the old amusement park tower were dressed like jungle natives. Body paints on bare chests, feathers and headdresses. Loin cloths and leather sandals.

The drumbeat formed a musical tapestry to the ritual that Señor Oscuro and the Blood Mage Gestalt performed around her. The ritual drew the crowd of thousands closer, mesmerizing them with magical hypnosis.

They came like sheep.

In the aftermath of the cyberzombie's attack, Oscuro had traveled back to the metaplanes. And he had gone alone this time, for with Thayla gone, he had no need of Lucero. He left her in the custody of Jaguar Guards and was gone for some time before standing again in his physical body, ordering the guards to bring her onto the Locus.

Now she knelt in the center of the Gestalt, Oscuro standing next to her as the thousands pushed in closer and closer. The morning wind was cool against her shaved scalp as she waited for what was about to happen. Death, or perhaps something worse.

Is he putting me on display? she wondered.

"Stand, my child," Oscuro said, his voice barely audible over the loud rhythmic pounding of the drums.

Lucero stood. Her power had grown from the exposure to Thayla's magic, and she knew that she was stronger than she had ever been. She would no longer succumb to the addiction of the blood. Perhaps Thayla had redeemed her after all.

Oscuro's dark eyes bored into her. "You will go down in history," he said. "It is because of you that I was able to penetrate the defenses of those who wish to keep us separated from our rightful destiny. It is because of your balance, your love for beauty, and your desire for power. It is your greatest strength and your most dire weakness."

The crowd around was enthralled by his words, which, Lucero realized, they must be able to hear despite the drums. For their eyes had glazed over, their expressions vacant. Hypnotized.

"And now," Oscuro continued, "You have one final duty." The dark man produced a ceremonial sword from under his robe. A *macauitl*—razor-sharp and designed for ritual sacrifices.

He's going to kill me, she thought. *And he will use my spilled blood to lengthen the bridge. To shorten the gap to the* tzitzimine.

The drums accelerated their pace, echoing like a staccato heartbeat in the valley around her. The Gestalt started to chant, a lamenting praise in long minor tones that sent waves of power up from the Locus and into Lucero's body.

She tried to run, but her feet did not move. Anchored by magic into the giant gemstone.

"You should be proud of your sacrifice, my child. Your spirit will serve me yet."

The blade flashed red in the early morning sun as it arced toward her. Magic forced rigor upon her body, thrusting her chest out, arching her back. The sword came down.

Drums, chanting.

The *macauitl* entered her just below the sternum.

Intense pain.

It sliced through her flesh, cutting her open to the crotch.

A fountain of agony.

Blood and intestines burst from the split in her. Gushing out of her—an eruption of veins and membranes.

Gone were the drums. The crowd. The temple. Everything reddened out from the screaming pain that exploded over her.

She fell onto the stone, landing in a pile of her own innards.

Dead.

The pain followed her beyond the pale. Her spirit writhed in agony as it ascended from her eviscerated body, slipping completely into astral space. The pain coalesced inside her as she hung there, surrounded by the vast astral presence of the Gestalt entity.

The final moment of her life stretched on inside her spirit—a moment of sheer torture. Abject terror and ultimate physical pain. It was all she was now. All she would ever be.

23

Ryan walked the perimeter of the island, trying to think through the situation. He had passed the whole night in the metaplanes, fighting for his life. For Thayla's life. After all that time in the metaplanes, out of his body, he felt disoriented. Out of synch with his physical existence.

Surf pounded the rocks below the wall, sending ocean spray shooting into the air. The noon sun shone through the water droplets, turning each one into a tiny prism. A rainbow hanging momentarily on the interface between water and atmosphere.

At another time, Ryan would have allowed himself to appreciate the beauty of this ancient place. But now. . . .

Now he waited on Jane and Nadja and Foster.

Jane to find Burnout and Lethe. Nadja to contact Aina. Foster to retrieve Harlequin.

Ryan felt confidence return as he focused on his physical nature, the fountainhead of his magic. As he strode the wall, he made brief contact with Raven and Starfish, the two runners who guarded the perimeter. Raven, the black human samurai, merely nodded as Ryan walked past. Starfish was perhaps the opposite. She was the one who had challenged him—a hothead, itching for something to happen, not at all happy to report that there was no sign of activity.

Ryan had half a mind to kick her hoop just to regain his focus. Astral travel was the antithesis of what it meant to be a physical adept, to be in tune with the body. Physicality.

Ryan pushed the temptation from his mind. He couldn't

afford a sparring match now. And he didn't want to disgrace anyone. Both Raven and Starfish held themselves with confidence, and they seemed to know how to handle themselves. According to Jane, Cluster and his team were top-notch, consummate professionals.

His wristphone beeped as he rounded a corner of the sea wall. Ryan stopped a good distance from the others and punched the Connect. "Go ahead."

Jane's huge smile filled the tiny screen. Her ruby lips pouting. "I was right," she said. "They took Burnout to Aztlan. The helos only stopped in Atlanta to refuel."

"Where did they go?"

"Your favorite place—Roxborough's delta clinic in Panama."

Ryan sighed. He did not have fond memories of that place. Thomas Roxborough was a vatcase megalomaniac who had developed a procedure for mapping his personality over someone else's. Ryan had been one of his test subjects, had almost become Roxborough.

"I decked into Rox's system," Jane said, her voice resonant with pride. Ryan knew that was no small accomplishment. "Burnout was only there to be repaired. According to my scan, and the vid I've seen, he's as good as new."

"That shouldn't concern us," Ryan said. "As long as Lethe is still inside him."

Jane's blonde curls dipped forward. "The tech notes I saw explained that they moved last night. There were some anomalies with the cybermantic magic so they transported him to San Marcos, just south of the Aztlan-CAS border."

Ryan shivered. "I've been there."

"At least we know Lethe's probably still inside," Jane said.

"True," Ryan said, feeling the cool salt breeze through his hair. "You got a fix on where they're keeping him?"

Jane nodded.

"Where?" he asked.

"He's being held in the *teocalli*. I haven't decked into the temple's system yet, but I got some vid from the external sec cameras. A few hours ago, he escaped and tried to take on practically the whole Azzie army. He geeked a lot of them before they shut him down and carried him inside."

Ryan steeled himself against the memories of his last time in San Marcos, latched to the ancient amusement park tower. Staring down at the underwater excavation of the Locus, its primal black surface emerging through the silt and mud. "There's a heavily guarded dig there," he said.

He'd reported to Dunkelzahn that night, as ordered. Just before the assassination. His transmission had been picked up somehow by the Azzie security team around the site. Ryan had dropped, sliding the hundred meters down the ladder like a droplet of black oil. Falling along the side of the old rusty needle as the rhythmic thunder of the helo's blades grew louder and louder.

They had captured him, beaten him, and given him to Roxborough for experimentation. *All in all,* Ryan thought, *not one of my most cherished experiences.* He gave a sharp laugh.

"I'm not going to downplay the situation, Quicksilver," Jane said. "If anything, it's gotten worse than when you were there undercover. Something major is going down. I had to do some fancy decking just to get inside their local grid."

"Give me a guess as to what's going down."

"Frag if I know, Quicksilver. Thousands of people have gathered around the *teocalli* and the dig site. One thing's mighty certain. It's not the prime place for a discreet run."

"Noted, Jane," Ryan said. "But we've got no choice. I need Lethe now. He's somehow tied into what's going on at the Locus dig. And so am I. We must get Harlequin, Lethe, and the Dragon Heart all together, and it needs to happen soon or the whole world will suffer."

"Doesn't sound like you, Quicksilver. Talking doom and gloom, end-of-fragging-world drek."

Ryan smiled. "Maybe not, Jane, but Dunkelzahn told me at the beginning that this mission was for the survival of metahumanity. And I know what I felt in the metaplanes—

dread, Jane. Dread and horror like I've never experienced in my life. Fear, too."

"Coming from you, Quicksilver, that scares me."

"It should, Jane. How would you like to live out your days as a tortured corporate citizen of Aztechnology? Perhaps controlled by creatures so alien that they live off pain and suffering."

"I'll put together a composite of the data I've gathered from San Marcos," Jane said. "We can run when you're ready."

"Good. If Harlequin hasn't awakened by tonight, we run without him."

"Is there time to infiltrate undercover?" Jane asked.

"Null chance of that. This has to happen tonight."

"Then what do you propose?"

Ryan considered for a second. He found himself at the junction where the castle wall met the sea wall. He'd come full circle. "We'll need these other runners," he said. "They can cause a distraction for Assets to get in, get Burnout and get out."

"I'll arrange it through their fixer," she said. "It's best if they think it's an unrelated run. Keep them ignorant of our plans in case they're captured and interrogated."

Ryan descended the stone stairs that ran down the inside wall, then headed through the courtyard and into the château. He wanted to check on Harlequin. "It's ironic," Ryan said. "We're planning to rescue the man who I've been trying so hard to kill. Until recently."

Jane laughed. "Yes. The dagger of irony is a sharp one."

Ryan approached Grind, standing guard at the entrance to the ritual chamber. The dwarf's black hair and beard were only slightly darker than his skin. "Hoi, Ryan," Grind said, shifting the heavy machine gun—an Ares Alpha— into the third arm that protruded from his chest.

"Any news?" Ryan asked.

Grind shook his head. "Nada. Harlequin's still out. Axler's in there with Talon and Foster."

"Quicksilver?" came Jane's voice from his wristphone. She hadn't disconnected.

Ryan lifted his hand. "Yes, Jane?"

"Incoming call from Nadja."

"Patch it through."

Jane's face disappeared from the tiny screen, replaced by Nadja's, which had a serious expression.

"Ryan," she said. "Aina is with me. We're enroute to you now."

"You're coming here?"

"It's the best way I can help," she said.

"But . . ."

"Don't worry, Ryan. I have my own security detail."

Ryan took a breath and reprimanded himself. He loved Nadja and would worry about her no matter what, but he knew she could take care of herself. "Sorry," he said. "How soon will you arrive?"

"Four hours," she said.

Ryan clutched his heart. "That's an eternity."

Nadja gave him a beautiful smile. Then she said, "Aina wants to talk to you."

"Of course."

The image on Ryan's wristphone shifted to show a female elf with dark brown skin. Her white hair was cut close to her skull, giving her a severe look. "I've heard about you, Ryan Mercury," Aina said. "Most of it good."

"I hope I won't be disappointing in person."

Aina did not smile. "I did not say that to flatter you," she said. "Merely as a reason why I'm talking to you at all. Why I'm coming to help you, instead of to kill you. I presume you had a good reason to leave Harlequin in the metaplanes?"

Ryan bit back his reply. He didn't need this kind of abusive drek, but he did need to remain diplomatic; her help was crucial. "Yes," was all he said.

"Tell me what happened," Aina said.

Ryan unfolded the whole story to her, deciding that he had no other choice but to trust her. He told her of the ritual, bringing the Dragon Heart across to the bridge. He recounted the story of Thayla's fall into the Chasm, the fight with Darke, the zombies and the spider creatures. How Harlequin had flung him back into his body.

When he had finished, Aina's expression had changed slightly. A tiny bit more respectful. "What I've heard about you is true then," she said.

"Can you help?"

Aina considered. "If he's alive and wandering the metaplanes, I can search for him," she said. "I have known him a long, long time and will have a much better chance of bringing him back than . . ." Aina stopped herself, biting back her words. "Than that child, Foster. But if Caimbeul's dead . . ."

Ryan nodded, stepping into the ritual chamber and looking around. Axler and Talon glanced at him briefly. Foster and Harlequin lay side by side, her blonde hair mixing with his auburn ponytail. Both faces slack.

"I hope you make it in time," he said.

"I'll start looking now," Aina said, then she disconnected and Nadja's face filled the screen again.

"Ryan?" Nadja said. "We'll see you in a few hours."

Ryan looked down at Harlequin's face again. The man had been out of his body for over twelve hours now. When Ryan looked at his aura, he saw no sign of spirit left.

"Hurry," he said, and disconnected.

24

Lucero rose from her eviscerated body, her spirit finally free of Oscuro's oppressive manipulation. Pain wracked through her, like an explosion of agony that pulsed through her over and over. Never stopping, never letting her scream subside.

Am I to live out my last moment forever? Is that my atonement?

The Gestalt entity warped astral space around her. The aura of the ten members coalesced into one, swirling and twisting over her fleeing spirit as she rose up above the Locus. The stone's power radiated like a dark sun. Even now, her body lying dead below her, she felt the draw of the chiseled gemstone, and some distant part of her desired to stay.

Perhaps it could take away the pain. Perhaps she could regain her power.

Lucero's spirit stopped rising, encased in the tornado of power created by the Gestalt, swirling green and electric blue above her. She stopped and began to descend again. Back toward her body.

Perhaps I am still alive.

As she fell, she saw her body grow closer and closer. She could not possibly have survived Oscuro's attack with the *macauitl* sword. Her body lay on its side, splayed like a fresh kill, her guts and internal organs a gelatinous heap next to it. Her runic scars rimmed in her own blood one final time. Oscuro's doing.

The cut in her gut was extremely clean, like a precision

surgical incision. Oscuro knelt over her entrails, hands buried to the elbows in the slippery mass of her intestines. Her liver, stomach, kidneys, and lungs had been cut away and set around her disembodied heart, which still beat in sputtering, dry spurts from the aorta.

Oscuro said some words over her corpse, and though Lucero could not hear them, she heard their intent. "I summon you, Lucero Débil. From all that remains, I draw you back."

Lucero's blood flowed backward, the droplets flying through the air from where they had landed. The spray reversed itself, a condensation of life energy that coalesced over the mound of internal organs.

What is he doing to me?

A sickening sensation oozed over her, and she fought to get away. Ignoring the severe pain, she struggled to push up through the tapestry of mana that the Gestalt had woven above her. She pushed with all she had left.

It was not enough.

Her spirit sank slowly, inexorably, back into the blood and guts that had once been part of her. As her spirit appeared in the physical world, shackled into this manifestation by Oscuro's horrid magic, she smelled herself. Stench and vile repugnance, like vomit and sewage and death combined.

He means to keep me as a blood spirit.

She stood there in front of Oscuro. Seething. Wanting to tear him apart.

He was her summoner, however, and he controlled her with his magic. She was bound to him, and forced to obey.

The crowd had gathered to watch, and now Lucero saw their spirits, their auras instead of their bodies. She saw them all hypnotized in front of her. Vacancy in their intent. Vapid resignation.

Lambs, the lot of them. Waiting for slaughter.

Hatred flooded her. The agony of her death had dwindled a bit, though her nerves still held a persistent edge of pain as though someone had flayed all the skin from her body. And when she looked down at herself, she saw that she had no skin. She was merely a mass of coagulated blood, intermixed with leaking intestines and internal organs that floated inside her like chunks of meat in an animated stew.

"You are now bound to me, Lucero Débil. My ally." Oscuro's expression was pure glee. "My slave."

Lucero could not deny the power and authority of his words. She knew them to be true. She was his slave, now and until his death. As she thought this through, she grew more and more angry.

Snatched from the gates of freedom to this existence of servitude. What she was repulsed her. How could she exist like this?

Lucero lashed out in anger, suddenly and with awesome force. She could not harm Oscuro, but she could kill others. They would pay for their happy, petty existences. Their pathetic lives of simplicity.

Her attack manifested as a huge arm of blood that threw six people into the air and smashed them down onto the Locus. *Kill them,* she thought. *Kill them because they mindlessly obey the will of Oscuro. Kill them because they are not in pain. Kill them because they are not me.*

Kill them all.

Lucero lashed out again and again, slaughtering dozens of innocent, pathetic metahumans. Spilling their blood on the Locus, adding life energy to it. She knew what Oscuro was doing now. The blood mana would channel into the metaplanes and lengthen the bridge. With the Locus and the Gestalt and the thousands of metahuman sacrifices who were gathered around, the end would soon be here.

She hated everything now. She hated what she had become. She hated what she was doing, despised that she had failed to reach Thayla's light and absolve herself. She hated that she was helping bring the *tzitzimine*.

Her hatred drove her to kill. Which she did with abandon. And when she was exhausted and could spill no more blood, her hatred festered inside. But around her, the killing continued to the heavy beat of drums.

An organized mass genocide.

25

Ryan carried the exhausted body of Jane Foster up the circular stone stairs into the central room. Grind had asked the cook to prepare something, and the smell of it filled the château and made Ryan's stomach grumble. Garlic and mushrooms and hot bread, perhaps pasta. Ryan couldn't tell exactly what it was, but it smelled fragging good.

Foster had awakened for a minute, announcing her failure to find Harlequin just before collapsing into a heap. Talon had examined her aura, had cast a heal spell on her and had declared her stabilized. That she would be all right after she slept for a while.

Ryan set her down on a burgundy sofa that faced the fireplace, then propped her head up on a pillow. "Sleep well," he whispered to her. "You are a tough fragger."

The elf in ninja silks came running into the room. His name, Ryan recalled, was Slider. "A helicopter is approaching from Marseilles," he said.

Ryan held up his finger, indicating for Slider to wait. He subvocalized into his throat mike. "Jane, is that Nadja and Aina?"

"Yes, Quicksilver."

Ryan looked at Slider. "We're expecting them," he said. "Please tell Cluster to let them land. I'll be out in a moment."

Slider nodded and was gone again.

A few minutes later Nadja and Aina, along with a contingent of eight secret servicemen, disembarked from a Hughes Airstar that had landed just adjacent to Dhin's craft.

Nadja rushed into Ryan's arms, her black hair blowing in the fierce wind from the helicopter blades.

He held her tight, drinking in the smell of her.

Aina came behind her, tall and well-muscled, of indeterminate age. There was something about her physical presence that had been absent over the telecom, a subtle difference that sent a shiver of fear through Ryan. He rarely felt afraid.

What is it?

She was no doubt a powerful mage like Harlequin, though that was hard to tell from her aura. Her power didn't affect him, however; it was something else. An element to her aura that Ryan had seen before somewhere.

"Ryan," Nadja said. "This is Aina."

Nadja's tone snapped Ryan back. "Thank you for coming," he said.

"Studying auras can be unhealthy," Aina said. "But just so you know, I have dealt with Corruption and its ilk before. I may know them better than anyone still alive."

This woman has been exposed to the Enemy. And survived.

"Now, I want to help my friend," she said. "I've searched a few places with no luck. I'm hoping that I'll be able to pick up the trail from here."

"Come this way," Ryan said, leading the way into the château and down to the ritual chamber underneath.

Axler and Talon greeted them at the door. Axler was calm, if a little edgy from the lack of action. Talon's face showed lines of fatigue and strain. He was obviously distressed that he had been unable to help Harlequin.

Aina entered the room, probing the chamber with all her senses. Assensing. "Please leave me," she said. "I have work to do."

"Of course," Ryan said. "But you should know that we will be departing the island soon. We have to try to contact the spirit Lethe, then repeat the ritual of bringing the Dragon Heart to the bridge. Nadja and the guards will remain."

Aina stepped into the ritual circle and knelt beside Harlequin. She did not look up as she spoke. "Very well."

Ryan gestured for Axler and Talon to vacate the chamber, which they did. Talon first, carrying a small pouch of talismana, followed by Axler and the arsenal she carried.

Aina reached down and ran her finger tips along Harlequin's skin, and she sang in a soft voice that sent a prickle wave over Ryan's skin when he heard it.

Ryan followed Nadja into the stairwell and up. "Thank you for bringing her," he said. "I hope this doesn't strain your chances of getting her on the Draco Foundation Board."

Nadja took his hand in hers as they walked back up toward the main room. "The DF Board is meaningless if this doesn't work," she said. "Besides, when I told her what happened she insisted on coming."

When they stepped into the huge glass-covered living room, the smell of dinner nearly overwhelmed Ryan. In an adjacent room, the servants had set out a sumptuous meal. Ryan followed his nose to the dining table—a massive hunk of furniture made from a solid piece of red marble. It was laid out for ten with elegant settings of polished antique silver.

Grind met them just inside. "We're almost prepped to eat," he said. "Foster is still sleeping, but everyone else is famished."

Ryan subvocalized into his throat mic. "I want a strategy meeting over dinner," he said. "Jane, you ready?"

Jane's voice sounded in Ryan's ear piece. "I'm go."

"Axler, Dhin, Talon?"

Three affirmative responses came over the tacticom.

"Good, let's get this done."

Nadja squeezed Ryan's hand. "I'll let you do your work," she said. "I need to make a few calls of my own, track down a few people." She leaned into his embrace, kissed him softly.

"I'll come and see you before we head out," he said.

"I know you will; you have to see me. You have no choice," she said.

Ryan smiled, giving her a sidelong look. "How do you know? It's true, of course, but how did you know?"

Her dark lips curved into a smile. "It's a woman thing." Then she laughed and turned away, followed by her group of secret servicemen.

Two minutes later, Talon, Axler, and Dhin had joined Ryan and Grind in the dining chamber. Through the tacticom, Jane was virtually with them as well. The appetizer course consisted of escargots and baguettes. It was followed by lamb and potatoes exquisitely seasoned with garlic and basil.

As they ate, Ryan spoke to them. "We have an extremely dangerous run coming up. Perhaps the riskiest we've ever undertaken."

Ryan paused to chew another bite of food. "Talon, this concerns you especially, because you need to decide if you want to continue with us. Everyone else is in, I assume." He looked around the table at the attentive faces of his team. And as he came to each, he got a nod of assent.

Talon put his fork down. "Not knowing anything about this run," he said. "It's hard to know if I want to go or not, but I do know one thing; you are the finest team I have ever worked with. I like what you are doing. I like why you are doing it, and I believe I belong here."

"I hope so," said Dhin, "cause the last couple of spell-slingers bit the big bullet."

Grind laughed. "Yeah, we haven't had the best of luck with magic types."

Ryan quickly interrupted. "I won't drek you, Talon. Assets uses its magical talent to the fullest. You will occasionally be in danger of losing your life. But this is true for everyone here. We've all come close to death. With that said, however, we'll always be watching out for you. We take care of our own."

Talon smiled. "Count me in."

"Good," Ryan took a few bites of his lamb before

continuing. Then he spoke to them about San Marcos, about the Locus and the masses of people. He told them of the tight security and the heavy mojo going down around the Locus and the step pyramid temple.

"Jane is working on finding out exactly which room Lethe is being kept in," he said. "But meanwhile we have a number of problems to overcome. One, we have to get over the border and into Aztlan. Two, we have to infiltrate the San Marcos site. Three, once we find the target, we have get back out alive, across the border, and onto safe ground."

Jane's voice sounded in Ryan's ear. "I just finished making the arrangements with Cluster's fixer."

"Excellent."

"They've agreed to do a run into Aztlan. I'm releasing them from your location now. They'll travel to Houston, CAS and wait for instructions."

Grind looked over at Ryan. "It sounds like you've already got a plan."

Ryan nodded. "Just a tentative sketch, but it's something to work with."

"Let's hear it," said the dwarf.

Ryan took a sip from his water glass. "The idea is that two teams come in separately. Cluster and chummers blow something up and generally wreak havoc while we secure Burnout. That way we keep one step ahead of the security forces, keep them turning around in circles, trying to figure out what's going on."

Axler pushed her plate away and looked at Ryan. "I've got an idea for getting in," she said.

"Yes?"

"Night drop. Military style, HALO—high-altitude low opening. It's silent, stealthy, and will be more effective in getting us over the border and inside security. Problem will come with getting out."

Talon looked up. "Nightgliders," he said. "We can use ultralights to fly back out."

Ryan nodded, taking the last bite of his food. "Could work."

Axler gave Talon a cold look. "Can you handle a night drop and a flight out in enemy territory?"

Talon nodded. "I love skydiving, and have logged a lot of flight time in ultralights. As far as enemy territory goes, you should remember that I live in Seattle."

Axler's ice broke, and she smiled. "Touché."

"Jane," Ryan said. "Can you get us the equipment we'd need? Dhin can help you with a list."

"Where should we base our assault?"

"Someplace with an airstrip but no people. An old, deserted USA military base on the CAS side would be ideal. What about Carswell Air Force Base?"

Jane's voice came back enthusiastic. "I like that idea. It's run as a smuggling operation, but I've got contacts there. I'll see what I can turn up."

"Good." Ryan pushed his chair back and stood. "We'll prepare here. I want everyone ready to roll in two hours. I want to drop tonight. The time differential gives us about four extra hours, but even so we're running out of darkness. We go even if Harlequin hasn't recovered by departure time. We need Lethe, and we'll come back here with him."

The others stood as he walked out. Ryan stepped across the large central chamber and through the vestibule. He crossed the courtyard garden, intent on seeing Nadja before it was time to go. The sky grew yellow and orange overhead as he reached Nadja's helicopter.

One of the secret servicemen standing guard turned and knocked on the door as Ryan approached. Nadja's face appeared in the window, then she opened the door and climbed out.

"Take a walk with me?" Ryan asked.

Her smile was all the answer he needed.

He offered his arm to her, and she slipped hers through it, allowing him to escort her across the flagstones, tinted rose from the dying sun.

Ryan led her up a short set of stairs and onto the masonry wall that ran the perimeter of the small island. The sea wind blew cool and clean through her hair, and she gave a sigh of relief as she walked up ahead of him.

It nearly broke Ryan's heart that he had come to say goodbye once again.

The setting sun came into full view as they walked around the east curve of the island, farthest from the château. A huge disc of the deepest orange, burning the clouds crimson.

Ryan stood with his hands wrapped around Nadja's slender frame. Her arms hugged his chest, her hands clasped behind his back.

The red light flushed her face as the sun dipped into the silver-blue water of the Mediterranean Sea. He put his lips against hers, soft and wet, a warm kiss. She blinked, a slow-motion flutter of eyelashes, her emerald eyes staring longingly into his.

He lost himself to the embrace, letting the sensation of her body against his wash over him. He never wanted to forget this moment. He wanted it to last, forever unchanging.

Then the last arc of the sun sank into the sea, its orange rays flickering to green for a split second. Gone, the sky fading from red to the deep blue of night that followed the sun inexorably to its watery grave.

Nadja was running her hands up and down Ryan's body now, his back, his chest, his abdomen. Moving down toward his crotch. She stopped as her hands passed over the bulge of the Dragon Heart, tucked into its sash.

She gave a little laugh as she rubbed it. She leaned in, putting her lips next to his ear. Whispering, "Is that a Dragon Heart in your pocket, or are you just glad to see me?"

Ryan could hold back no longer. He kissed her neck, his hands traveling down her back, running over her slender hips. So tight. His fingertips following the natural curves of her body. Onto her front, smooth skin of her belly and up over the gentle swell of her breasts inside her blouse. Soft, sensitive.

In the growing darkness, her hand brushed his crotch. Her lips sealed over his.

He wanted her.

She pulled back slightly. "How long until you have to go?"

"I wish I didn't have to," he said.

"How long?"

"About an hour before I have to start serious preparations."

She smiled, her tongue running over her teeth. "Plenty of time," she said. "Come on, there's got to be a guest bedroom in this place somewhere."

Ryan laughed, then adjusted his pants so he could follow without too much discomfort.

26

The ritual chamber in the basement of the San Marcos *teo-calli* flickered in the torch light as Lethe watched the elf mage, Meyer, and two others prepare for the ritual magic that would banish him. Lethe could almost smell the magic forming in the thick air, like soapy incense.

Meyer dribbled blood from a tiny bladder covered in animal skin, tracing an elaborate circle around Billy's body, which had been shackled into the stone floor with titanium straps. The other mages inscribed runes and symbols into the blood circle. One was a human woman with dark skin and black hair. She wore a temple robe, and looked to be a priestess of Quetzalcóatl. The other was an ork man, who drew symbols with chalk, hulking down awkwardly in his corporate suit and tie.

Lethe didn't know exactly what would happen if these mages succeeded in forcing him from Billy's body, but his spirit was intertwined with Billy's now.

The magic will probably kill us both.

Lethe reached out for the Locus, trying to use it to stabilize him. But it was distant, his connection to it weak. His access was blocked by the barrier at the perimeter of the ritual circle and the magical background, the polluted astral space that came from all the corrupt magic that had been performed inside the temple over the years.

The woman and the ork let Meyer trace the primary lines, but they continued to add touches to the circle, chalked words and splashes of paint. Gathering their power in song and art as they prepared to focus it upon

Lethe. He knew what was coming, and merely hoped he'd be strong enough.

As the power of the spell grew around him, he struggled to move Billy's body, to pull it free of his restraints. He exerted all of his will, but the arms and legs would not budge. Billy was unconscious again, due to a drug injection, which would normally have allowed Lethe some measure of control over the body. But all Billy's cybernetic parts had been deactivated by the dwarf technician with the remote control. The tech stood just outside the ritual circle, watching the proceedings with disinterest. Even if Billy had been awake, they'd be unable to move.

Time for a little magical attack, Lethe thought. He'd learned how to do telekinetic magic by watching Ryan Mercury, and he'd even used it once when Billy had had the Dragon Heart. Lethe had thrown Ryan Mercury's body several meters into the fire sprinklers, saving the human's life.

Can I do it without the Dragon Heart?

With a thought Lethe flung mana at Meyer, focusing the energy into a telekinetic thrust. The thrust hit Meyer, but it was much weaker than Lethe expected. His imprisonment inside Billy had weakened him immeasurably. The blow merely knocked Meyer's hand and made him flinch slightly.

"Frag!" Meyer yelled. "Who did that?" His vision went astral and he looked directly at Lethe. "I see you now, my meddling spirit. And I will get rid of you." The elf stood up, and with a heavy sigh, he proceeded to redraw the arc of the circle he'd been working on.

It's not much, Lethe thought, *but it is something.* He proceeded to use his telekinetic push on each of the mages, practicing to get better and better at it.

He knocked their hands as they painted, blew out their candles, and was generally a pain in the hoop. He knew he wasn't going to stop them from completing the ritual circle and casting their spell, but he could slow them down.

He could slot them off.

If they got sufficiently angry and distracted, perhaps they'd make a mistake.

Perhaps they would miscast their spell.

It was a small hope, but he clung to it. He kept at it because he knew it was his only chance.

Without it, he would soon be no more than shreds of a tattered spirit blowing on the astral breeze. Dead and disrupted.

26 August 2057

27

Five hours after leaving Nadja and her guards with Jane
Foster and Aina, Ryan and the rest of the Assets team
touched down in Fort Worth. The Texas night air hung hot
and dry around Ryan as he emerged from the Draco Foundation Lear-Cessna Platinum III and looked out across the
tarmac of the abandoned airstrip. Carswell Air Force Base
was generally dead, though smugglers used it as a hub of
operations for refueling and storage, which was the only
reason that ghouls and squatters hadn't taken over.

On the flight from Marseilles, Ryan and Jane had decided to aim for a 2:00 AM local time departure. And now
that hour approached rapidly as Ryan and the team prepared for the run into Aztlan. Night drop. The thought of it
sent chills over Ryan's skin. Anticipation of action was
like a lover's gentle tickle, a prescient thrill.

Nadja had elected to stay behind at Château d'If with
Aina and Jane Foster. She could conduct her business from
there, and she had made an implicit promise not to leave
Aina until it was all over. Aina had taken charge of the
search for Harlequin's spirit.

Ryan hoped the painted elf was alive in a metaplanar
sanctuary of some kind, nursing his wounds. If not, Ryan
didn't know how he'd get Lethe and the Dragon Heart to
the metaplanar bridge.

Time is short. He could feel it closing around him in like
a giant fist. *And growing ever shorter.*

Behind him, Talon and Grind stepped out of the jet and

into the hot night. They carried huge duffels filled with weapons and ammo, communications gear and tools.

All the drek necessary for infiltration.

Dhin and Axler had already gone to the base's rear gate to wait for the smugglers. Everything was ready to go wheels up, except for a plane. They needed a different craft for this job, something that would fly quietly. Everything depended upon stealth. Guile and sleight of hand.

Focused and unexpected force designed to blindside the Azzies.

"Bossman, you copy?" Dhin's voice over the tacticom.

"Go ahead."

"Rodriguez has arrived at the gate."

"On my way." Ryan slung his own duffel over his shoulder and walked toward the gates of the old base. *It's about fragging time,* he thought. Jane had arranged for the meet to happen twenty minutes ago, and the smugglers were late. Ryan wanted to do this run tonight, and every second of delay made the chances of that more difficult.

Ryan gritted his teeth and tried to stifle his anger as he walked, tried to channel the emotion into motivational fuel. He crossed a section of grease-stained concrete, moving toward the rear gate where Axler and Dhin stood with three smugglers.

The lights overhead had been shot out long ago, and the hangars hulked like metal ghosts, giving the airstrip a creepy feel. The smell of oil and gunpowder mingled with the stench of garbage, toxic waste, and urine. As Ryan approached, quietly and quickly, he picked up the muffled rumble of a GMC Bulldog stepvan just beyond the gate, and more faintly, the discreet sound of an automatic weapon's safety sliding off.

Ryan examined the smugglers as he eased up toward them. Two huge trolls flanked a dwarf of Hispanic origin. It was the dwarf who was speaking to Axler. They turned suddenly and walked toward one of the hangars.

Axler's stance was defensive, cool and professional as she walked. Her eyes were on the trolls and the pistols they carried. As they neared the hangar, Dhin glanced in Ryan's direction, peering into the darkness. The big ork waved a warty hand for Ryan to join them.

Ryan reached the door to the hangar at the same time they did, appearing out of the darkness. "I'm Quicksilver," he said.

The trolls turned and scanned him, but said nothing.

The dwarf nodded. "Call me Rodriguez," he said. "I have your plane. In here."

An old fashioned metal key opened the door and Rodriguez stepped inside, switching on the lights. Dhin gave a low whistle as the plane came into view, an old Federated-Boeing Nightowl—a twin prop plane with sound-suppressed engines and a matte black finish over its low-profile curves.

"She's not going to outrun any fighter jets," the dwarf said, "but she's a quiet fragger, and she's hard to see on radar."

"Mind if I check her over?" Dhin said.

"She's yours for the night. Should be fueled up and combat ready."

Dhin walked up and climbed into the plane to scope out all the systems.

Ryan set his duffel down and waited, maintaining his focus on the three smugglers. At his side, Axler held herself at full alert as well. Things were going smoothly so far, but it would only stay that way if strict protocol was maintained.

Dhin's verdict came back a few minutes later. "She looks good," he said. "Let's get the drones and gear loaded."

Ryan held three credsticks out to the dwarf. "Rodriguez," he said, "biz completed."

The dwarf scanned the credsticks on a pocket reader, then looked up at Ryan. A smile spread on his gnarled features. "It's been a pleasure," he said. "If you need anything else, have your fixer contact me."

Ryan nodded. "We'll have the bird back in less than twenty-four hours."

Rodriguez signaled his bodyguards and turned to leave.

Talon and Grind entered the hangar with duffels. Grind looked up at Ryan with a tired expression on his black face. "What's the schedule?" he asked.

"Load and roll," Ryan said. "Wheels up in fifteen."

Talon and Grind nodded.

"Jane?" Ryan said. "You online?"

A moment passed before Jane's voice came over the 'com. "I copy, Quicksilver."

"We'll be airborne in a few. Any specifics on Burnout's location?"

"I was trying to deck into the San Marcos *teocalli* when you called. Our cyberzombie hasn't left the temple that I've seen, but I have to sleaze my way inside and look around. The IC around their system is thick and quick. I don't want to rush it or you'll be minus one decker."

Ryan knew that the ice must be really tough if Jane brought it up. Normally she decked into systems without any mention of difficulty or the possibility of failure. "Take whatever time you need, babe," he said. "If we're on schedule we should be dropping onsite in approximately an hour and thirty-five minutes."

"Copy that, Quicksilver. That's eons in Matrix time. I'll be in touch enroute."

Ryan started loading the Nightowl with their gear. Drones, weapons, ammunition, tools. Everything was black and gray camouflage. There were parachute packs for the assault, which should get them onsite.

Cluster and his team were responsible for stashing five Artemis Nightgliders in a hidden location in the vicinity of the San Marcos temple. The Nightgliders were collapsible ultralights. Once assembled, they would provide Ryan and the others with a silent way back out.

When everything was loaded, Ryan checked himself over before stepping into the plane. His body armor was intact. His bandoleer of narcotic-tipped throwing darts and his Ingram machine pistol in their proper places. He adjusted the Dragon Heart and double-checked his holster for the grenade pistol and the extra-clips of ammo.

"Let's roll this sucker out," Dhin said, opening the big hangar doors.

Ryan and Axler pushed the small plane out onto the tarmac, Dhin closed the doors behind them, and they all climbed into the plane. The cargo area was just large enough for the four of them and their gear.

Ryan sat next to Talon, holding onto a wall eyelet as Dhin lifted them off smoothly and quietly. The plane made almost no noise; Ryan could hear the rush of the night air outside. Through the small windows, the sky was clear as far as he could see.

It is a good night for a dive.

Talon sat with eyes closed, his long dark hair tucked into the black hood of a camouflaged nightsuit that covered light body armor. He carried an Ingram in an armpit holster, and he absently flipped through a small tarot deck.

Across from them sat Axler and Grind. Axler had already applied her face camouflage, irregular spots of gray on a black base. Her blue eyes glinted coldly. She was ready. Next to her, Grind secured his weapons for the drop—an Ares Alpha Combatgun on his back, and a Predator II pistol. Grind also carried an array of grenades.

As they neared the drop zone, Ryan applied his own camouflage makeup and Talon's. The mage stowed the tarot deck inside one of the zippered pockets on his vest, then helped Ryan secure his parachute. When they were all set for the drop, Ryan decided to go over the plan. He laid out a paper map that he had printed out from the composite of the data.

"Where do we land?" asked Grind.

"I'm not exactly—"

Jane's voice sounded in Ryan's ear, panting. "I've located Burnout," she said between breaths. "Nearly got iced, but I found him."

"Where?"

"He's in the basement of the *teocalli*. They're conducting a ritual on him now."

"Good job, Jane," Ryan said. "You all right?"

"Almost got pegged by some of the blackest ice I've ever seen," she said. "But, yeah, I'm wiz now."

Talon spoke. "What kind of ritual?"

"Frag if I know," Jane said. "But it was very bloody."

"Dhin," Ryan said.

"Yes, Bossman?"

"How's our time?"

The ork's voice came husky over the 'com. "Drop zone in fifteen."

"The whole area around the lake bed and the temple is crowded with people," Jane said. "Finding a clear place to touch down might be difficult."

"What about the *ollamaliztli* stadium?" Ryan said, pointing to the arena that sat a few hundred meters behind the *teocalli*. "Is there anyone inside?"

"No," Jane said. "But Cluster was planning to blow it up as a distraction."

Ryan was shaking his head, looking at the map. The stadium was the perfect place to come down, open to the sky. No people. He scanned the area for something else that would provide a good distraction. After a second, he saw it—the dam at the end of the lake. *Perfect.*

"Jane, can you contact Cluster and tell him to blow the dam instead?"

"I'll try," she said. "Hold on."

They waited in silence for a minute until Jane came back online. "Done," she said. "They'll blow the dam instead of the stadium."

"Excellent."

"Is everyone clear on the sequence of events?" Jane asked.

Ryan looked at each member of his team closely as they answered, "Yes." They all looked fairly confident, but he decided to go over the plan once more anyway.

He reminded them of the jump, the landing in the stadium, the infiltration of the *teocalli,* some details of which would have to be determined onsite.

"When it comes to breaching the temple, there are two possibilities for cover entry," Jane said. "The main entrance is watched, but many people go in and out. It's not locked; you could go invisible and try to sneak in with the crowd."

"What's the second option?"

"I've found a rear entrance that's monitored on the sec cameras."

"Which one is closer to Burnout and Lethe?" Ryan said.

"Rear," Jane said. "It comes out lower, perhaps even underground. Once inside, it's just down one level."

"I like that one," Ryan said. "If we can find it."

"Me too," said Axler.

Ryan nodded, then moved on to the next point. He reinforced their objective—to reach Burnout in the basement of the temple and get back out with him, hopefully without triggering an alarm. And lastly, to reach the rendezvous point by the amusement park tower, assemble the Nightgliders, and fly out to safety.

As they discussed the details, it became increasingly clear to Ryan that this was probably the most dangerous run he'd ever attempted. He was working against time, against superior firepower, superior magic, and there was no room to breathe. No room for mistakes of any kind.

Ryan steeled himself. *Then we won't make any mistakes,* he thought.

"Approaching drop zone," came Dhin's voice, pulling Ryan from his introspection. "Get ready to jump."

Ryan stood and pulled open the side door. It was time for action.

Cool wind rushed into the cabin, and the plane canted for a second before Dhin adjusted for the differential drag. The ground was a patchwork of shadows below, the lights of Austin like a scab against the darkness. Ryan picked out the movement of cars and trucks on the old Interstate 35 moving south below them.

"Drop zone," Dhin said. "Go! Go!"

Axler jumped first, then Talon, surprisingly without hesitation. Grind followed, and Ryan went last, tumbling through the vastness of the dark sky. Invisible as individual raindrops.

Plummeting to their fate.

28

Anger boiled inside Lucero. She had become what she most hated—a killer. A demon of blood and entrails who destroyed others in a jealous rage.

The hot, night air pressed around her. The beating of drums making physical existence a thickening, difficult experience for her. The astral atmosphere reeked of foul magic; it suffocated her.

A circle of mages sat on an obsidian black stone, seeming to laugh. Thousands of metahumans crowded around, their auras synched together like puppets. Innocent and mindless.

What has happened to me?

Lucero drew herself up, stopped her rampage. All around her the innocents continued to stare at her with awe. They did not draw back in terror at her hideous form, made from coagulated blood and innards. They did not cringe at the death of their companions, whose mangled bodies lay all around the Locus, their spilled blood collected by acolytes and given to Señor Oscuro who stood and watched, amusement flickering on his features.

The crowd is mesmerized. Their minds lost to Oscuro.

"Well done, my slave," said her master. "You have exceeded all my expectations."

Lucero's own voice came like a gurgling of tar. "I hate you."

Oscuro merely laughed. "Many do," he said. "I have become used to it, a small sacrifice on my part so that the greater power may be served."

Around the Locus, acolytes and workers lifted the dead bodies and tossed them unceremoniously into a flatbed truck that sat at the head of a long line of similar trucks.

"Now let the construction continue as it was planned years ago," Oscuro said. "Before the meddling elf brought his songbird and drove us away." He held out a hand, its white skin prickled with black hairs. "We have the Locus now, and its power will accelerate our progress a thousand fold. Come, my slave. You are needed."

Lucero watched in horror as the crowd filed one by one up onto the wooden steps. Drums beat a rich sculpture in the air as the innocents approached the waiting blood mages. The mages wielded *macauitls,* slicing up the sacrifices as they approached, one by one until blood ran as free as a river, drenching the Locus. They channeled the life energy into the stone, activating it.

Lucero felt the stone awaken beneath her. She sensed it come to life like a giant awakening from hibernation.

Then she was flying through astral space, following Oscuro across the reaches to the metaplanes.

They appeared side by side on the outcropping of stone. So familiar, yet so alien now. The light extinguished. The song silenced forever.

The sky was a textured gray now, like trideo static hanging above a burgundy earth. The thick metallic stench of blood dominated the putrid rot of the zombie corpses that clustered around Oscuro. Lucero saw no sign of the two strangers who had tried to save Thayla earlier. They must be dead or gone.

The outcropping stretched over the bottomless Chasm, reaching for the other side. As Lucero looked out across the space, wind slicing through her like flechettes through paper, she felt the dread again. The incipient horror, growing out from her core. Spreading slowly to take her over, threatening to freeze her solid if she did not wrench her attention away.

Creatures moved over there, writhing like bulbous slugs, amorphous and black. Lucero couldn't make them out. They wanted her to help them. They desperately needed her to finish the bridge so that they could come across and repay her for her exquisite service.

Oh, the rewards they could give. Pleasures beyond her wildest fantasies.

"You will plant the sacrifices as they come," Oscuro said, his words ripping her attention from the *tzitzimine*. Breaking the spell.

Lucero riveted her attention to Oscuro. Pain boiled inside.

"The souls of our devoted metahuman sheep will be coming fast. But you are a blood spirit, my slave. You have the speed and the ability to keep up the tireless construction."

Lucero seethed. She was his ally and must obey. His magic bound her, and she hated him for everything he had done to her. Her hatred bathed her in crimson light, making her vision red.

"Like this," Oscuro stepped to the very tip of the outcropping. The spirits of the dead who were being slaughtered at the Locus began to appear behind him. They were disoriented, lost. Groping in their confusion.

Oscuro took them bodily, one by one, and slammed them into the rocks on the very tip of the outcropping. One by one they sank into the stone, hardened and became stone themselves. The transformation was very fast, and Oscuro moved to the next one. Then the next.

He went faster and faster until the bridge had grown slightly. Moving closer to the other side, where the *tzitzimine* were building an outcropping of their own to meet with this one.

Abruptly, Oscuro stopped. "Now you," he said.

Lucero shuddered and took his place. It seemed like such a long distance to the other side, but the spirits kept coming and coming, an endless supply of corpses to fuel the magic that built the bridge. And Lucero kept planting them into the stone, watching as they calcified and hardened. Then she stepped on the stony remains of their souls, moving along the lengthening bridge.

Soon she would be far out over the abyss.

Eventually the outcroppings would touch.

Lucero shuddered again. *What would happen then?*

Even as the question formed in her mind, she continued her work. Her master had commanded it, and she had no choice but to obey.

29

Ryan fell through the darkness, the warm air blasting his face and hands. Luck had given them a clear night, and he could see the pinpoints of light that indicated San Marcos a good ten klicks south of their position.

"Condition?" he said into the tacticom microphone attached to his throat.

Axler's voice came back first. "Check."

"Check," said Grind.

Talon's voice was last. "I'm okay," he said.

Even though he could hear the others through the tacticom, Ryan couldn't see them. "Pull chutes now," he said. "Our target is that cluster of lights to the south."

The muted sound of chutes opening came to Ryan's sensitive ears, then he pulled his own rip cord. There was a rushing whoosh, followed by rapid deceleration as the harness of his chute dug into his ribs and armpits.

Dhin's voice came over the 'com. "Deploying drones now."

"Copy that."

Somewhere in the dark sky overhead, Dhin released the two drones that would be his eyes, ears, and his muscle during the run. The Condor II would float at high altitude and track the team and any opposition. The Wandjina was a military drone built around a Vindicator minigun. Very fast, very effective in combat situations. With it, Dhin could provide much-needed firepower.

As they floated down through the sky, the San Marcos site came into view far below. It was still some distance away, but its identity was unmistakable. Thousands of people clustered around in tents and makeshift structures, illuminated by portable lamps and barrel fires. There was a lot of activity despite the early morning hour. No one was sleeping; everyone was up and moving around. Dancing.

Around the perimeter, military personnel patrolled in tanks and LAVs. At the limit of Ryan's low-light vision, he could see troop encampments in several locations at a ten-kilometer radius from the *teocalli*. Military choppers patrolled the sky above the temple, circling around the core area, but never flying directly above it.

Huge flood lamps cast harsh shadows on the center-piece of the activity. Nestled into a lake bottom, between an old amusement park and a step-pyramid temple. The crowd was much thicker there, and Ryan could hear the faint rhythmic thumping of drums.

What the frag is going on here?

He remembered the last time he'd been to this place—the night of Dunkelzahn's assassination. He had been alone, high up the amusement park ladder, to get a better view of an excavation Aztechnology was conducting in the lake bed below. He had watched the workers in their scuba gear, seen them uncover the huge stone that Dunkelzahn had called a Locus.

That had been the last time Ryan had spoken to the old wyrm. Dunkelzahn had been vaporized in an explosion in front of the Watergate Hotel less than an hour later.

Ryan shifted to his astral senses, squinting at the inferno coming from the center of the crowd. A huge column of blood-colored fire swirled up from what must be the Locus, stretching like a tornado into the astral sky.

The *teocalli* seemed mute and faint next to it, but Ryan knew that under normal circumstances the temple would itself be a beacon. *There's some major mojo going down,* he thought. *Perhaps this is what Dunkelzahn feared.*

"Talon," Ryan said. "Look into the astral."

"I have," came the reply. "What the frag are you taking us into?"

"Not sure, chummer," Ryan said. "But whatever they're doing down there, I think it's peripheral to our mission. We're here for Lethe. He's in the temple. This ceremony or whatever might even work in our favor."

Axler's voice was cold and analytical. "The sec forces will be focused elsewhere. There'll be way too much confusion for them to do their job effectively."

"If you say so," said Talon. "I'll work on trying to keep the watcher spirits from giving us away. But I've never seen so many in one place before."

"Cluster is right on time," Jane said. "There should be something to occupy everyone's attention very shortly."

Grind's voice growled in Ryan's ear, "Where is the *olla-maliztli* stadium?"

"About six hundred meters behind the temple," Ryan said. The stadium sat in the dim light of surrounding illumination—street lamps and security lights. It was inside the military perimeter, but had not been opened to the public. They wouldn't have to land in a crowd of people.

"I see it," said Grind. "Coming up fast."

As they neared the ground, Ryan began picking out individual teams of armed guards, some occupying stationary positions, others moving through the crowds. "I hope that distraction comes soon," he said. "Otherwise we'll be like glued ducks up here."

"Jane?" Axler's voice.

"Should be any second," came Jane's voice.

A few ticks passed, and Ryan was jockeying his chute to get in position for landing when he saw the flash. A split second before the sound hit, a red and white burst of brightness from the head of the lake. Then a wave of sound crashed over him, ear-splitting and deep. A massive explosion ripping through the dark fabric of night.

Right on time.

Ryan had seen crowds react to explosions before. Close to the explosion, they ran away from the blast, trying to get as far from the destruction as possible. But a few hundred meters farther back, people merely panicked, trying to get out, but not knowing which way to go. Mob hysteria.

As Ryan watched, people ran into each other, trampling the slow and the weak, those who couldn't get out of the way. Military personnel tried to calm them so that they could move through and get to the dam, which now spewed water.

"Look at the center of the crowd," Talon said. "No one is reacting."

As Ryan brought his attention there, he saw that Talon spoke true. The core cluster of people had not moved. It was as though they had not even heard the explosion. Only those outside the lake bed and on the far side of the temple had reacted.

"They're under some sort of enchantment," said Talon.

"It's not important," Ryan said. "The distraction served its purpose. Now concentrate on landing. Can't have you turning an ankle. We need your talents, but I don't want to be carrying you out."

Below him, Grind landed, coming down hard. The dwarf rolled, using the third arm in his chest to tumble into a standing position. He made it look easy. Axler was next, pulling up at the last second to touch down as smooth as polished ice. Talon nearly hit Grind, but his landing, too, was fairly smooth.

Ryan came last, feet hitting, flexing his knees under the impact and running to a halt. "Cut your chutes and hide them," he said. "Won't be needing them."

Jane came on. "Take the south tunnel exit and clip the fencing. I've deactivated the security cameras there, and no one's watching the stadium now. The diversion worked perfectly."

"Copy," Ryan said. "I'm point." He climbed the short stone wall and moved into the tunnel, followed by Grind, Talon, and then Axler bringing up the rear.

Ryan cut the fence and they were through, moving across a parking lot at a rapid pace. The parking lot was covered with trailers and old recreational vehicles. People were running everywhere, confused and scared.

Nobody gave Ryan and the others a second glance.

They crossed a road and a short field of grass as they neared the *teocalli,* which rose from the dark lawn like a mountain of hewn rock. The smell of mana was palpable to Ryan, coming from the temple and the Locus. Like a heavy thickness to the air around them.

The *teocalli* had no perimeter fencing; the first tier of the step-pyramid structure jutted from the grass, seven or eight meters straight up. Ryan picked out the guards and some security cameras on the top of the tier, alert and scanning the crowd. He also noticed recessed weapons mounted inside camouflaged turrets—miniguns and assault canons.

"Okay, Jane," Ryan subvocalized. "Approaching temple. How do we get to the rear entrance you were talking about?"

"It's directly opposite the main entrance. It's at the end of a long corridor, and I'm not exactly sure where it comes out."

Dodging through the crowd, Ryan led the team around the back of the pyramid, the side away from the main entrance and the lake bed where the Locus rested. Ryan scanned the rock of the temple wall, but it was smooth and straight. No sign of a rear entrance.

"It might be masked," Talon said. "Hidden by quickened magic."

Ryan gave a short nod. *And it might not be on the temple at all,* he thought. *Perhaps that corridor is underground, which might mean. . . .*

Ryan scanned the area behind the temple. Live oak and pecan trees clustered here and there in the small grassy field, but there was no sign of a guarded entrance. *Frag.* Further back was an asphalt parking lot, full of cars. Surrounded by a low fence adorned by signs stating that the lot was restricted to *teocalli* personnel only.

No one is camping there.

Still, as he looked, he could see nothing that could be an
entrance. Ryan shifted his perception into the astral plane,
focusing to try to avoid the blinding light of the temple
and the Locus, their auras so close they obscured the nu-
ances of everything in the whole vicinity.

If there was a hidden entrance, Ryan would need to see
details. He drew from the Dragon Heart, its dormant presence a constant reassurance at his gut. And as its power
sharpened his astral vision, something came into view.

In the corner of the parking lot, the aura of a GMC Bulldog stepvan shifted under scrutiny, revealing its true shape
as a small stone building disguised by a sophisticated
masking illusion.

Talon was right! Ryan thought. *There's a fragging guard
house.*

Ryan noticed that the little building was directly behind
the center of the temple. "Come on," he said. "I've found it."

The sound of the drums had not ceased because of the
explosion, but they faded a little behind them, blocked by
the huge structure of the temple. Once he'd broken the
masking, Ryan could see the small stone guard house
clearly.

He could see two guards, one on either side of the wide
stone door. A retinal scanner hung on the wall behind one
of the guards.

"Axler," he said. "Take Talon and Grind around to the
edge of the lot on the far side, nearest to the entrance. I'll
take care of the guards, but have your Supersquirt ready
for anybody we find inside."

Axler's smile stretched the black and white camouflage
patches on her face. She drew her Ares Supersquirt, a
soaker gun filled with gamma scopolamine and DMSO for
skin penetration. Gamma scopolamine was a neurotoxin,
extremely fast-acting. It targeted motor nerves and caused
temporary paralysis instead of death. A few drops on the
skin and even a troll would go down.

"You heard the man," she said. "Let's go."

Ryan waited for a minute while Axler and the others circled around the asphalt lot. Then he took a few deep breaths to center himself. He concentrated his stealth magic, gathering shadows around him, blending his aura into those of the objects nearest him, diffusing his heat signature. All this he did with magic of the Silent Way, the path he had been taught by Dunkelzahn.

When he had disappeared completely, Ryan approached the low fence. Jumped it and moved through the parked vehicles like a whisper on the wind.

The two guards stood alert, probably due to the recent explosion and the thousands of people gathered nearby. They were Aztechnology Leopard soldiers, one troll with a Panther assault cannon, one ork carrying an AK-98 with under-barrel grenade launcher. Both wore tan uniforms over light body armor.

Ryan drew two of his xenoketamine-filled throwing darts.

"In position," came Axler's whisper in Ryan's ear.

Ryan moved, a slight distortion against the background of cars. He fired the darts in succession, the first one nailing the troll in the base of the neck. The second one, off by a centimeter or two, landed just behind the ork's ear.

I'm getting rusty, Ryan thought.

Both guards collapsed to the ground.

Ryan reached them a second later, Axler and Grind and Talon appearing beside him as he checked the guards. Sleeping soundly.

Axler readied her Supersquirt as Ryan lifted the ork's head and placed it against the retinal scanner. With a gentle sigh, the stone door opened.

Axler spun into the space, her soaker dousing the entire area, catching the two interior guards by surprise. They had time to turn, their eyes opening wide with instant realization as they went for their weapons.

Nobody could have reacted fast enough. Axler's spray caught them across the exposed areas, face and hands. They grimaced in pain and went rigid as their muscles

tightened involuntarily. Then they fell, their guns clatter-
ing to the stone.

"There's a watcher spirit," Talon said. "It saw us and is
taking off."

"Banish it!" said Ryan.

Talon focused for a second.

"Grind, can you help me with these guys," Ryan said,
pointing to the outside guards.

Grind nodded.

Talon looked up. "Got it," he said.

"Good work, chummer," Ryan said. "Now, can you do
your invisibility magic on Axler, Grind, and yourself?"

Talon smiled at Ryan. "Ready when you are," he said.

"Anytime," Ryan said, dragging the ork guard by his
booted feet.

Grind lifted the troll's shoulders, nearly as wide as he
was tall, and followed Ryan through the door, pulling the
huge troll body inside with him.

Ryan watched the others fade from view, becoming
harder to see as Talon's magic went to work. Ryan led
them down the stairs and into the underground tunnel.
"We're inside, Jane," he said.

"Good," came her response. "Hurry. I've looped the
camera feeds, but it won't be long before some slot in the
security booth notices that the troll keeps picking his nose
over and over."

Ryan gave an abrupt laugh. "Can you give me an esti-
mate on how long we can expect to be alarm-free?"

"I can give you one," Jane said. "But it'd be wrong.
They've got progs to detect the loop patch. Even with
the sophisticated semi-randomizer I included, their security host will most likely trigger an alarm in less than ten
minutes."

"Copy," said Ryan. The stairs ended in a tunnel, lit by
yellow incandescent bulbs recessed into the stone. Murals
covered the walls, done in the style of the ancient Aztec In-
dians, but Ryan was looking for hidden security cameras
and recessed autofire drones. The invisibility should fool

the cameras, but Ryan was the only one who could move without sound. Microphones could give them away.

"Take a right when the corridor ends," Jane said. "Then another right into the stairwell. Go down a flight."

"Copy."

Ryan caught movement ahead. A group of five meta-humans wearing gray robes crossed in front of the tunnel's open end, moving from right to left. They didn't even glance toward Ryan and the others.

"Quicksilver?" came Jane's voice.

"Go ahead."

"I've lost contact with Cluster and his team."

"Explain." Ryan reached the end of the tunnel and moved into the corridor. This one was more brightly lit, though the theme of ancient Aztec religion pervaded. One wall was covered with a long sinuous painting of a feathered serpent. Quetzalcóatl.

"After they blew the dam," she said. "Cluster made positive contact, but said he was under heavy pursuit. He was confident he and the team would make it to the stashed T-bird, but I can't raise him now."

Moving rapidly and without pause, Ryan led the others into the stairwell on the right. The rust-colored tile steps descended into a flickering darkness.

"Last contact was ten minutes ago," Jane said. "Either they never made it, or communications are out on the Thunderbird."

"Did they have time to plant the Nightgliders for our escape?"

"I don't know."

"Drek!" Ryan whispered, reaching the bottom of the stairs.

Before Jane could respond, alarms started to sound. Loud klaxons in the small space.

"They know you're in there," Jane said, her voice small and tinny in the overwhelming din of the sirens. "Guards are on their way."

30

Lethe watched as the ritual circle was finished, and the spell took shape around him. His telekinetic disruptions had been no more than an annoyance to the elf, Meyer, and the two other mages working with him.

If they succeed, he thought, *both Billy and I will be disrupted, our souls shredded and scattered upon the astral winds.*

Meyer had inscribed an equilateral triangle inside the ritual circle. He and each of his fellow magic-slingers sat at an apex of the triangle. The ritual had caused a barrier to form along the periphery of the circle, a cylinder of mana around him. Lethe could barely make out the dwarf cybertechnician standing against the wall, staring coldly at the proceedings.

Lethe tried one last time to move Billy's arms and legs, bringing his full willpower to the task. To no avail. He managed to budge the body, but it was strapped to the floor with titanium bands. They weren't going anywhere.

"Wha—?" came Billy's thoughts. "What's going on?"

Lethe watched the mana build in the circle as the mages gathered their combined strength. Glowing coldly in astral space, each mage became a swirl of stars. The center of a tiny galaxy, a cluster of comets.

"I'm being destroyed," Lethe said.

The cyberzombie's voice came back dull and hazy. "How?"

"Ritual banishment."

"I can't allow that," Billy said, and he tried to move his

arms and legs. Nothing; his cybernetics had been completely deactivated.

"I hate to be the bearer of bad news," Lethe said, "but I think you'll be killed as well."

Billy chuckled in a jaded way that reminded Lethe of the old Burnout. "Without you, I'd go back to the mindless killing machine I was—Burnout. I'd rather be dead."

Lethe found no response. Billy's admission touched him deeply.

The ritual spell escalated, growing and growing. The mages shone coldly white like stars now. The swirling galaxies of mana grew brighter and brighter as the power built. They reminded Lethe of something, a rainbow shimmer that meant a gateway was opening between planes.

I've seen that dance of colors before.

Lethe tried to reach out with his mind and use the Locus to help him withstand the force of the attack. But the warding force formed by the ritual circle blocked him. He couldn't feel even the faintest evidence of the powerful stone. As if its very existence had been erased.

Lethe became desperate in the last few moments before the attack slammed into him, searching for anything to draw upon, any bit of extra leverage. Perhaps he could use their own power against them.

No chance. Meyer was an excellent mage, and he'd woven the spell cleverly.

There was nothing for Lethe to draw upon. He was alone with Billy, defenseless against the impending onslaught.

"Well," he said, "this is the end, my friend. I just wanted to let you know how much you've meant to me."

"The end?" Billy said, his voice still hazy. "Then I suppose it's time to say goodbye, my friend. Would you do me a last favor?"

"I will try."

"Show me Thayla again."

Lethe thought of the goddess of light, alone against the powerful ritual blood magic. The exquisite beauty of her song battling the chill silence of those who controlled the Locus. He tried to remember Thayla as she was before, pure white light. Unadulterated and wondrous.

He failed.

The spell filled Lethe's mind with nightmare images of consuming fire as he braced for impact. Memories of terrifying rage.

Lethe couldn't show Thayla to Billy. It was all he could do to say, "Goodbye."

31

"Jane, shut off those fragging alarms."

Ryan tried to ignore the incessant klaxons, tried to use his magic to filter out the loud wail so he could hear any voices or the bootsteps of approaching guards. He failed, the loud sirens rang in his head; he could hear nothing else.

Jane's voice came back tinny and weak against the volume of the alarms. "They're on a local system, isolated from the Matrix. I'm working on cutting the power."

"Hurry," Ryan said. He crouched at the bottom of the stairwell, using his stealth magic to its fullest, and glanced out into the adjacent hallway. He made a quick visual scan for threats, and he sniffed the air. His other senses would have to compensate for his hearing until Jane could cut the alarms.

The corridor smelled richly of incense, but the smoky aroma could not completely mask the odor of oil and sweat, of metahumans and—faintly—of blood. "Which way, Jane?"

"Left, then around the corner. You'll see the door five meters away, two guards standing ready."

The hall was clear of guards, so Ryan dashed out, sliding at his top speed. As he neared a turn in the corridor, he caught sight of several security cameras, and pointed them out to Axler and the others.

When Ryan reached the corner, he used his pocket mirror to take inventory of the opposition. Two guards, wearing tan uniforms with Leopard flash patches, stood at full alert, flanking a closed wooden door five meters away.

Both were human with dark skin and black hair; they carried swords and machine guns.

Looks too easy, Ryan thought.

Talon's voice grated. "They have a blood spirit waiting in astral space. A strong one. I don't think it noticed me, but if it did, they'll be ready for us."

"Acknowledged," Ryan said. "You and I will take it out. Axler, you and Grind eliminate the guards."

"Copy that."

"Douse them," Ryan said. "We're right behind you."

No hesitation. Axler immediately dove into the corridor, firing her Supersquirt in a wide spray.

Grind followed, his Ares Alpha Combatgun targeted to unleash death. Ryan had a dart ready in one hand and his silenced Ingram in the other. Talon came around the corner last, his hands open as power gathered around him.

The liquid from Axler's weapon caught the nearest guard full-on. Somehow, the other managed to dive clear.

The blood spirit manifested as Grind sprayed the corridor with bullets. The spirit appeared in the shape of a troll with patches of skin removed. Huge open sores all over its body oozed clear pus, tinged with rivulets of blood. Bone showed through in places where the muscle had been pinned back with dissection tools.

The spirit grinned as it absorbed the bulk of Grind's onslaught. It came on fast, blocking the dwarf's line of sight. Grind was an experienced merc. He dodged sideways instantly, moving to get a better angle.

The other guard's head disintegrated in a spray of blood and bone. Bits of red-laced pink brain matter splattering the mural-covered wall.

"Both guards down!" Axler reported.

The blood spirit was insanely fast, flying toward them, its massive arms swinging with scalpel-bladed fingers.

Ryan drew himself up and prepared himself for the attack. He focused his power, drawing strength from the Dragon Heart. He knew he could banish spirits now, and he was sure as frag going to try with this one. He felt

Talon's energy growing next to him as the mage worked on his own banishment.

Ryan unleashed his power at the same time as Talon. "Be gone!" he said.

"I banish you," Talon said. "So mote it be!"

As the spirit rushed them, Axler dodged one of the scalpel fists. The blow slammed into the wall just over her head, dislodging chunks of the masonry.

The spirit quavered before them, weakening under the banishment, but it did not dissipate. It merely reared back and lunged for Axler again. She was the closest target.

We failed.

Ryan focused his power again. He knew the *teocalli* was giving strength to the blood spirit. Helping to keep it alive. "I said, *be gone!*" Ryan thrust all his power as though he was making a telekinetic strike, but channeled into a disruptive force against the spirit.

The force hit like a shredding blade, chopping the spirit into morsels of dried flesh, bone, and blood. It crumbled to the ground and turned to dust.

I did it, Ryan thought, then he felt the energy drain out of him, and he lost his balance.

Talon stepped up and gave Ryan a hand to steady him. "You're experiencing drain," he said. "The effects should pass in a moment."

"Thanks."

"The door's unlocked," Axler said.

Ryan heard soft, wailing cries coming from inside the room as Axler threw open the door. She leveled her machine gun into the room, scanning for guards.

Ryan pulled his Ingram automatic, and stepped into the room, Talon and Grind close behind him.

"It's a ritual banishment," Talon cried.

Ryan looked into astral space and saw it—the swirling galaxy of mana inverting inside the hermetic circle that contained the spirits of the three mages. "They're trying to destroy Lethe."

The vortex of stars pivoted back toward the prone form

of Burnout, his cyberzombie body completely repaired. Brand-new, his innocent expression making him look more human, more like a little boy than the deranged killer he had been, the ripped-up monster Ryan had fought in Dunkelzahn's arboretum a few days earlier.

Talon cried out, "It's about to discharge."

Without hesitation, Ryan hurled himself into the circle. He flew through the air like a winged beast. And as his body crashed through the mana barrier, an electric charge sliced through him like a thousand razors into his guts.

The magic reached a crescendo as Ryan landed over the body of Burnout, focusing on the Dragon Heart, willing it to channel the ritual banishment energy into himself instead of Lethe. Ryan had no idea if it would work, but he had to try.

The magic force of the banishment slammed into Ryan like a battering ram, trying to force his spirit clear of his body. Trying to shred his soul.

He grasped for the Dragon Heart, drawing on its perfection, the unity of its pattern. And he felt Lethe touch the Heart as well, focusing to keep the essence of his spirit tied into Burnout's body.

Agony burned through Ryan, reaming through his body with immense force. The scene around him was lost in an instant of brilliant red, of screams of pain and long suffering.

Then it was gone. Leaving only the tingling of electricity prickling over Ryan's skin.

He looked up to see Axler and Grind plowing the guards and mages with a barrage of bullets. A dwarf in a white technician's coat tried to run for it, but a burst from Axler's Ingram took out his knees. He crumbled to the floor, dropping a small electronic device. The two mages came apart in a spray from Grind's Ares Alpha, their bodies riddled with holes, flopping to the stone floor, leaking blood over the fine lines of the hermetic circle.

The third was an elf who Ryan had seen before—Meyer. The same one who had worked for Roxborough. The man who had nearly erased Ryan Mercury from existence and replaced his empty brain with the personality and spirit of Thomas Roxborough.

Ryan jumped to his feet; he wanted this one dead.

Meyer had a look of dismay on his face as bullets ricocheted off an invisible magic barrier in front of him. He said some words in the elven language of Sperethiel, and thick smoke filled the room.

"He's gone," Talon said. "Fled out the door and down the hall."

"Frag!" Ryan said, almost running after him. He stopped himself. *Can't let a personal vendetta interfere with my mission.* "Let him go," he said. "We have to get Burnout loose and haul hoop out of here."

Ryan concentrated and used his magic to center himself. He noticed the alarms had silenced and the emergency lights had kicked in because of the power loss. "Axler," he said. "Can you cut through these bands?"

Axler waved smoke out of her way as she stepped up next to him, reaching into her backpack. "This'll take a few minutes."

"Better hurry," came Jane's voice. "I've just got vid of a whole cadre of Jaguar Guards closing in on your location."

"We'll be ready for them," Grind said, replacing a spent clip.

Ryan heard Lethe's voice in his head. *Ryan Mercury, what are you doing here?*

"I'm saving you."

You still have the Heart, Lethe said. *You should have taken it to Thayla.*

Ryan remembered the woman's beautiful song, remembered watching her hold off the zombies until the last possible moment, then plummet into the Chasm. "Just shut the frag up," he told Lethe, his anger showing. "Thayla's gone."

The stillness of the room was broken only by the sound of Axler working to cut away Burnout's restraints with her monowire shears.

Gone? Lethe said.

"The darkness forced her into the Chasm," Ryan said. "I got there too late."

Jane's voice cut in. "Guards have reached the bottom of the stairs."

"She said to get you, Lethe," Ryan said. "She said you would know how to wield the Dragon Heart."

Me?

"You."

I hope she's right, Lethe said.

"So do I."

Axler cut through the last of the restraints, but Burnout did not move. The cyberzombie simply lay there in a prone position.

"Lethe," Ryan said. "Get up."

Billy's cybernetics have been deactivated.

Grind stepped up holding the electronic device the dwarf technician had dropped. "I think this is some sort of remote deck for Burnout."

The technician used it to turn off access to our cybernetics.

"Grind," Ryan said. "Turn everything on."

"Copy."

Grind tapped some buttons, and abruptly Burnout stood.

The huge man shot up with amazing speed and grace, hulking over them all. He snatched the remote from Grind with a blinding move. "Thank you," he said. Then he gave Ryan a feral grin. "Let's get out of here."

Ryan nodded, but when he looked out through the door and peered down the hall through the smoke, he saw what Jane meant—fifteen or twenty guards were coming around the corner. Weapons brought violently to bear.

Frag, thought Ryan, *we're trapped.*

32

In her bedroom at Château d'If, Nadja Daviar sat at a huge wooden desk and looked at Gordon Wu's image on the small telecom screen. While Ryan was trying to stop Aztechnology from destroying the world, she was doing what she could to keep her affairs going.

The business of running the Draco Foundation and the politics of the upcoming vice presidential election seemed trivial now, though she knew they weren't. In the long run, her role was crucial. Perhaps it was more mundane than Ryan's, but just as vital.

On the screen, Gordon's lips formed a flat line, which was as much of a smile as he could give. Trying unsuccessfully to hide his fatigue. It was very early in the morning in Washington FDC.

"Also, Gordon, I want you to set up a meeting with each of the prospective members of the Draco Foundation board."

Gordon nodded, and Nadja stifled the overwhelming urge to yawn. She leaned back in the leather chair and took a deep breath.

The room around her was large and elegantly appointed. Beautiful, ancient tapestries hung over walls of hewn gray stone. A massive four-poster bed made of polished maple dominated the chamber, complete with a soft feather mattress. She and Ryan had tested it out earlier.

She remembered Ryan's face, the depth of his silvery blue eyes as they adored her. The hard muscles of his chest and abdomen as she ran her fingers across them.

"Miss Daviar?"

Nadja focused on the telecom. *I'm drifting,* she thought. She forced a smile, "Sorry, Gordon. I'm a little tired."

"What about your appointment with Lucien Cross?"

"I'll need to reschedule."

"I'll handle it," Gordon said. "When will you return to Washington?"

"When things are finished here," Nadja said. "One or two days, I think. I can't be more specific than that."

A knock sounded on the door.

"I must go now," Nadja said. "I'll contact you for an update." She disconnected.

She blinked against the sunlight streaming through the open window. Dawn had arrived here, even though she knew it would be several hours before it reached North America. Before Ryan's run would be finished, before she would know whether he had been successful. Many hours at the very least before she could see him again.

She stood and walked to the carved teak door. "Come in," she said.

A secret service guard opened the door, then stepped out of the way to reveal Jane Foster. Exhaustion made the young elven woman's eyes droop. Her blonde hair hung in a tangled mat, and her blue eyes had lost their gleam. "Aina has brought Harlequin back," she said.

Nadja almost hugged her. "That's great. Where are they?"

"Follow me." She turned and led Nadja down the hall, then into the main room. The early morning sunlight streamed through the macroglass ceiling, and gave a pink-yellow hue to the big, open room.

Harlequin lay on the blue velvet sofa, and Aina sat on the matching ottoman. Lines of stress showed on the dark skin of her elven face as she cast magic of some sort. Nadja could almost feel the power flowing through Aina, could almost see a tracery of scars across her brown skin as she placed her hands on Harlequin's chest.

Nadja stood at a distance and waited. Jane Foster slouched into an adjacent chair, struggling to keep her eyes open. Harlequin's breath came shallow and slow; his painted face was wrinkled and cracked, making him look very, very old. His eyes fluttered open as Aina's healing magic did its work.

Then Aina leaned back, almost falling.

Nadja moved to catch her if she lost her balance. But Aina recovered, swaying gently back and forth as she closed her eyes and seemed to concentrate on breathing.

Harlequin propped himself into a sitting position against some pillows. His eyes focused on the scene around him. When his gaze landed on Nadja, he spoke. "You seem to be out of place, Miss Daviar."

"I came with Aina," she said. "Ryan asked me."

"Is Ryan all right? I sent him back, before . . ."

Nadja gave him her warmest smile. "He woke up in great health. He is now in Aztlan, trying to get the spirit, Lethe."

Harlequin seemed to gather his strength, and he sat up fully, glancing at Aina, who slipped onto the sofa next to him. She was still recovering from her spell.

"He plans to get Lethe and bring him back here for another ritual."

Harlequin was quiet, though he seemed on the verge of speaking. He took a deep breath, one hand idly combing through the long strands of his hair. Contemplating.

It was Aina who spoke, "There's not enough time to wait for him."

Harlequin looked at her, nodding silently in agreement.

Jane Foster sat forward in her chair, giving Aina a look that would freeze steam. "What do you mean?"

Harlequin answered, "Aina is right. Darke has used the Locus far more effectively than any could have thought possible. He is close to completing the bridge. If that happens . . ."

Jane Foster's look did not soften. "I know what it means, but what do you intend to do?"

"I must go to Ryan Mercury and Lethe immediately," Harlequin said.

"But you've been through so much already," Foster said, her voice pleading. "You're not healed up."

"Actually, Aina's magic has made me almost as good as new. I feel great."

Aina gave Jane a sympathetic look. "I know you care for him," she said. "Just as I did long ago." She gave Harlequin a smile. "But this is for the whole of metahumanity. You cannot know what it is like to live with the Corruption, and I hope you never have to. It is worse than death. Believe me, I know."

"The bridge is nearly complete," Harlequin said. "We must go."

"They're in San Marcos, in Aztlan," Nadja said. "It's halfway around the world. How can you get there in time?"

"We'll go astrally," Harlequin said. Then he turned to Aina, "Will you join me? Your knowledge of such matters far exceeds even mine."

"I'm with you, Caimbeul," Aina said, though her voice gave away her fatigue. "Once more we fight together."

Foster stood, "I'm coming with you."

"I won't stop you," Harlequin said. "But I'd rather you remain with Miss Daviar. Watch over us. If we fail, she may need help."

Foster didn't hide her disappointment, but she said nothing.

Harlequin laughed. "Besides, I'd hate to face your father if anything happened to you."

Foster sank into her chair, a resigned look on her features.

When Nadja glanced back at Harlequin and Aina, they were already gone. Their bodies sitting side by side looked relaxed and content. More like two people watching the trid than warriors of ancient magic on a quest to save the Sixth World from an onslaught of evil.

33

Thick strands of gray smoke drifted into the hall as Ryan scanned the situation. He kept himself hidden from view, using his stealth magic, and assessed the opposition in a heartbeat. His magically enhanced senses told him all the details.

He saw the heat outlines of guards coming around the corner cautiously, expecting a confrontation. He heard their subvocalizations as the advance team sprinted into the hall, setting up overlapping fields of fire. They wore military-grade full combat armor with integrated helmets, which Ryan knew gave them infrared and low-light vision.

Ryan could even feel the pounding of their heartbeats. A slight pressure rhythm inside their suits. All these details came to him in a split instant.

Can't let them trap us inside the room, he thought. *We'll never get out.* The walls of the corridor were smooth painted stone. No cover. *A lot of people are going to die before this is over.*

Ryan quickly glanced the other way, the opposite direction from which they had come. No guards, no subtle indications that anything was coming to block their way. "Jane," he subvocalized, "is there another way out of here?"

"Yes, Quicksilver, but it leads to the main entrance."

"We'll take it," he said. "Axler, Grind let's go!" Ryan drew his MGL-6 pistol and fired a flash grenade into the hall.

The small orb flew into the midst of the guards coming

around the corner as Burnout edged up next to Ryan. The
third arm disengaged from its compartment in Burnout's
back and swung up next to his head like a chrome stinger,
a rotor-barreled M107 heavy machine gun attached to
the end.

"Ready to rock and roll, Ryan," he said.

A brilliant flash lit the dark hallway, a blinding light that
would overload their low-light vision and cause them to
blink simultaneously.

At that exact instant, Ryan called upon his telekinetic
strike, focusing his power through the Dragon Heart. He
opened his arms, releasing the force like tidal wave—a
tsunami of magic energy that slammed into the oncoming
guards.

The wave picked them up and hurled them against the
far wall like rag dolls.

"Let's move!" Ryan yelled. "Go, go, go."

Axler was first around the corner and gliding down the
hall away from the stunned guards. Talon and Grind followed closely behind, very difficult to see with the invisibility magic. Of course that wouldn't hide them from
thermal scans.

Burnout darted into the hall, his movement smooth and
nearly as fast as Ryan's. The cyberzombie didn't follow
Axler and the others, however; he headed for the downed
guards. The barrel of his M107 whined as it chewed up the
belt of armor-piercing rounds and spat them into the
stunned bodies of the six guards.

"Go," he told Ryan. "I'll be right behind you."

Axler and the others had disappeared around the corner
in the other direction. Ryan followed quickly, and Burnout
came right after as more guards burst into the hall from behind. Two held Panther Assault cannons, and the group
was accompanied by a combat drone that zipped along the
floor. It was big enough to have a mounted Vindicator
minigun.

Lethe spoke to Ryan through the Dragon Heart, "There
are mages in that group, and they've brought some nasty

blood spirits to help. I can banish them, but I need to draw from the Dragon Heart."

"Do it," Ryan said. "I brought the Heart for you anyway."

Ryan felt Lethe stretch his magic to touch the Heart where it rested in the sash around Ryan's abdomen. The spirit channeled his power through the artifact, then into the two blood spirits which had begun to manifest in the hall.

The blood spirits looked like orks or trolls with the skin removed. Naked eyeballs staring from bloody muscle sockets, nostrils flayed open and dripping. They moved incredibly fast, rushing toward them.

Lethe's force hit them and they flew apart, disintegrated into their constituent organs. They sank to the floor like a stew of body parts—bones, muscle and gut—then disintegrated.

The drone's minigun roared, filling the hallway with an onslaught of lead slugs. Ryan dove around the corner just in time, and Burnout came behind him. Ryan heard the distinct metallic ping of rounds ricocheting off Burnout's frame.

"Okay?" Ryan sprinted to catch up with Axler and the others.

The cyberzombie was on Ryan's heels, matching him step for smooth step as they raced up the corridor at breakneck speed. Burnout's voice came back with a note of laughter. "Fine," he said. "So good of you to ask."

Ryan watched Axler, Grind and Talon, their outlines difficult to see because of the invisibility magic, cut a sharp left down another passage. In the tacticom, he heard Jane giving Axler directions to the central staircase.

When he reached the left passage, Ryan ducked around the corner and stopped, simultaneously pulling a clip of fragmentation grenades from his belt and slamming it into his grenade pistol. These would frag them over, and they might even take out that drone. "Catch up with the others," he told Burnout. "I'll be right behind."

Burnout didn't even stop.

Ryan leveled the snub barrel of his MGL-6 and fired four grenades into the corner, watching them bounce down the hall and come to a rest a few meters from the advancing drone. He ducked into the passage before they went off, and he had nearly reached the others by the time the explosions shook the air.

Axler's voice came harsh in Ryan's ear. "Decision time, stairs or elevator?"

Ryan reached the group; they had paused around the corner from a small room. The hall continued on about twenty meters before making another sharp right. "Which is closer?"

"Elevators are here." Axler indicated the room. "The main stairs just a bit further."

Ryan used his mirror to peek into the space, noticing the three guards—two humans and a ork woman—standing in front of two elevator doors, alert and nervous. The ork paced back and forth, the emergency lighting flashing red and white over her tan uniform. The others stood still, trying to look confident.

Jane was insistent over the tacticom. "I can get you up the elevator shaft," she said. "It's faster and safer than the stairs."

"What about the power?" Ryan said.

"I'll restore it temporarily," came Jane's response. "Null sheen."

"I hate elevators," Axler said. "Too confining. One burst from an SMG could take us all out."

"You won't be inside the elevator," said Jane.

"We climb up the ladder then?" Axler's voice was thick with incredulity. "Or what about on top of the elevator car? They'd never think of that. Come on, Jane, they'll nail us either way."

"Not on top, Axler. Underneath."

Axler said nothing. It was a good idea.

"Let's do it," Ryan said, running up to the others.

"You have no choice," Jane said. "There's a hoopload of Jag Guards coming down the central stairs, maybe fifty or sixty. No way you can make it out that way. But if you get past them, you'll be almost to the main entrance."

Dhin's gruff voice broke in. "I can help you when you get there," he said. "My Wandjina is itching to see some action."

"I hope you'll get your chance, chummer."

Jane's voice came over urgent and all biz. "The power outage means that the sec cameras are dead. They won't see you enter the elevator shaft."

In Ryan's mirror, the ork guard paced up close and glanced out into the hall. Close enough that Ryan could smell her foul breath. But she didn't see him; his magic served as a cloak. Whether she noticed Axler and the others, Ryan couldn't be sure.

Her eyes went wide as she focused on Burnout, standing level with her, his perfectly proportioned head giving her a wry smile.

With a quick, precise jab Ryan sunk a narcotic dart into her neck. In seconds the drug made her slump to the floor. Ryan grabbed her weapon as she fell. "Axler?" he said.

On cue, Axler doused the room with her Ares Supersquirt.

The other two guards sank to the floor in seconds.

"Burnout," Ryan said. "Can't you go invisible?"

"That's Lethe's territory."

Sorry, I'm still a little rattled from the banishment.

"Well, spirit, pull your drek together before you get us all geeked."

On it, came Lethe's response.

Ryan watched in mild surprise as Burnout vanished into nothing more than a heat shimmer. "That's better," he said. "Now can you open the elevator doors?"

The vitreous cyberzombie stepped up to the metal doors and pushed them to either side as though he were opening curtains.

"Let's get these guards into the shaft," Ryan said. The elevator tube was dark and square with a hydraulic system instead of a cable and weight. In the center of the shaft, a silver pole gleamed in the dim light, telescoping up from the pump mechanism below to hold the elevator car.

They dumped the bodies into the opening, watching them fall the three meters to the bottom of the shaft. This was the lowest level, and Ryan could see that a maintenance ladder of round rebar rungs ran next to the door and up into the darkness.

"I've taken control of the elevator and put it on emergency power," Jane said. "It'll stop on the level above yours. But you need to haul hoop. I don't know how long I can keep control."

Ryan looked up and saw the elevator car come into view like a huge ghost of machinery. It stopped about four meters up, and Ryan searched the undercarriage with his low-light vision, trying to find enough hand-holds for everyone.

The bottom was made of smooth stainless steel that gleamed dimly in the low light. Along the edges of the car, a metal grating extended about ten centimeters below the floor of the carriage. Whether it would hold them all or not, Ryan didn't know.

The sound of movement came from the hallway behind. "All right, everyone in," Ryan said. "We'll have company any second."

"Let's go." Axler climbed nimbly up the ladder and swung out onto the grating. Grind followed, with Talon just behind him.

Ryan pulled a couple of smoke grenades and set them off in the passage. He could hear the team that was following them; they were close, but moving cautiously. Grenades had that effect. From the other direction, however, Ryan could hear a rush of guards. Coming fast.

Perhaps the smoke will make them mistake each other for us.

Ryan turned quickly and climbed into the elevator shaft and up the ladder. He latched onto the grating, joining the others, whose feet dangled over the darkness, looking like meat hanging in a smoke house.

Automatic gunfire sounded in the hall, followed by yells and screams. *They're shooting at each other.*

Burnout came last, swinging onto the ladder, the illusion magic unable to mask his massive silhouette, like a prismatic robot. Something had happened to the cyberzombie, Ryan knew. His entire demeanor had changed, and it wasn't simply due to Lethe's influence. It had happened too fast for that—ever since he and Ryan had fought in the arboretum. Burnout had nearly died that day, had nearly taken Lethe with him.

Now, Burnout sank his fingernails into the doors and slid them shut, first one then the other, plunging the shaft into utter darkness. A few seconds later, Ryan felt his weight on the grating.

"We're on, Jane," Ryan subvocalized.

With a lurch, the elevator began to ascend. Rising in the darkness. "You're going up five levels," she said. "To the fourth floor. The main entrance is on the third. You'll have to climb down and force the doors."

Grind's voice came on. "Nice thinking, Jane. Even if they think we've taken the elevator, they'll send troops up to the fourth."

"Maybe," said Axler, her voice sounding dubious. "But I still feel like a clay pigeon."

"Cut the cross chatter," Ryan said. "We go out by the numbers. Talon do you know how to levitate?"

"Yes."

"How many of us can you hold?"

"Two, maybe three."

"Do it," Ryan said. "Levitate yourself, Axler, and Grind. Float down to the doors while Burnout and I get them open. We can't afford to come out one by one, just in case they're ready for us."

"Got it."

The elevator slowed and came to a stop. At the limits of his low-light vision, Ryan could see the number three over the doors below.

"Burnout, do you want the pole or the ladder?" he asked.

"Call me Billy," he said. "I'll take the pole."

"Billy?"

"The man once known as Burnout no longer exists."

"Very well," Ryan said. "I'll take the ladder."

"Ready, Talon?"

"When you are."

"Let's go." Ryan swung over to the ladder and climbed down to the doors. There was a tiny, five-centimeter ledge between the doors and the shaft, and Ryan balanced on it, standing on his toes. Behind him, Billy slid down the center pole, stopping level with Ryan. Talon levitated himself, Axler, and Grind into position, holding them stationary, level with the door.

Everyone was ready.

Ryan put his hands into the crack between the big metal doors, and pulled. The doors slid back, letting in a shower of light.

A startled guard turned toward them in the alcove. A woman, her red-blonde hair pulled back against her scalp and tucked into the rear collar of her Leopard Guard uniform. She held an AK-98 up and ready to rumble, and as she pivoted toward them, her chrome cybereyes gleamed as they widened in recognition.

Behind the guard was an archway that led into a huge central chamber. The room's details registered in Ryan's mind in the fraction of a second before he made his move on the guard. The chamber had a high ceiling and was dominated by a massive sculpture of a dragon with feathers instead of scales. A feathered serpent, with plumage of purple and deep green.

Quetzalcóatl.

The walls and ceilings were a mosaic of tiles, depicting the sacred rituals of the ancient Aztecs in glorious reds and blues and golds. The main entrance was a huge archway, situated at the far end of the large chamber, beyond the sculpture. Next to the archway was a security station complete with weapons and cyberware scanners, and a lot more Leopard Guards.

The whole chamber was packed with people—acolytes and priests, guards and Aztlan military. There were perhaps a hundred metahumans between them and the main entrance at the far end of the chamber.

Frag me, Ryan thought.

A hundred people who wanted them dead.

Ryan gathered his focus and stepped toward the first guard. *Let's see if these Azzie slots are as tough as their rep.*

34

Blood gurgled inside Lucero. It boiled in her ears, reddened her vision as the pain of her death lived on and on in her mind. The vicious cut of the *macauitl* slicing its way from her sternum to her crotch. The sickening lurch of her intestines as they burst forth from her wound.

This pain defined her very nature, and it repulsed her.

Yet she must obey her master; she was bound to him now as she planted soul after soul, spirit after spirit into the tip of the outcropping. Somehow, the sound of drums reached her from across the metaplanes. The primal beat of an alien heart that drove her to snatch up the bloodless specters of the sacrifices as they piled up behind her. Drove her to heft the souls and slam them into the earth.

The rock beneath her was new ground, freshly created from earlier sacrifices that hardened beneath her feet as she advanced. She walked on spirits, on the ghosts of those who would remain trapped in the bridge forever.

Oscuro's commands made her move faster and faster. She created the bridge, extending it like a thin feeler across the bottomless Chasm between planes. How much time had passed? She had no way to judge.

How many sacrifices? How many spirits had come, channeled up from the Locus, through the column of fire and blood maintained by the Gestalt? She had no way of counting, but judging from the incredible distance she had come, it must be in the hundreds now, perhaps thousands.

She felt the presence of the *tzitzimine,* the creatures from the other side. They were much closer now, nearing with every passing beat of the drums. They spoke to her in delicate whispers, pleading for her to listen.

Winnowing their way into her mind. Lying to her with such sweetness. Telling her that she could be free of Oscuro. They could make her free.

When she glanced up, she was surprised at how narrow the gap had become. In the absence of Thayla's light, the creatures had redoubled their efforts. They had made much progress.

But it was Lucero's side of the arc that had grown at a phenomenal rate. She moved faster than she ever could have while alive, tireless in the completion of her duties.

She paused for a beat as she saw them clearly. Hideous monsters of sharp bones protruding through skin, alien shapes, flesh-ripping teeth and claws. But as she looked, they transformed into creatures of wonder, of misunderstood beauty. They were going to make the universe a marvelous place.

The eels in her mind slithered toward control.

The *tzitzimine* would free her. They would give her power. Whatever she wanted.

She believed them. For a fraction of an instant, Lucero succumbed.

The eels coiled around her sanity.

They yanked at her will then. Terrible, bone-crushing pain shocked through her.

She worked harder and the pain lessened. She plucked up the sacrificed souls and plunged them into the earth, moving faster and faster.

Blood dripped from her, bits of gelatinized flesh and chunks of internal organs flying as she tore into a frenzy. She began interring sacrifices, two and three at a time, then rolling over them to plant the next group.

Lucero's agony dissipated.

Her pain was gone. Her will was gone, giving way to a mounting ecstasy. A sublime shock of pleasure that increased as the bridge grew under her onslaught. The gap was only meters wide now. Soon the distance would be closed.

Soon the bridge would be complete, and the world would be forever altered.

35

Ryan sprang forward, leaping off the narrow ledge in the elevator shaft, and into the small alcove. Before he and the others could make a run past the dragon sculpture and across the entrance chamber, he needed to incapacitate the guard.

Red-blonde hair, chrome eyes narrowing on him. This close, his magic couldn't hide him. She could see him—a hazy shadow against the dark background of the elevator shaft.

Ryan struck at her just as she brought her AK-98 to bear. He stiffened his fingers and hit her in the neck with a precise attack to a vital nerve cluster, hoping that in her particular case, the nerves were biological, not cyber.

She never got her gun up. Her jaw clenched in pain, her red lips pulling into a grimace of agony as paralysis overtook her body from the spot where Ryan had hit her. She collapsed to the ground.

The whole combat lasted ten seconds. Silent and nearly unnoticed.

Abruptly, the chamber shook from the force of an explosion. Gunfire followed, the rapid staccato that could only come from a minigun.

"Rock'n'roll, Bossman," came Dhin's voice over the tacticom.

The Wandjina drone dove through the main archway like a swooping falcon, bullets from its mounted Vindicator ripping up the floor, scattering guards and priests. Creating pandemonium and chaos.

"Perfect timing, chummer."

Axler and Grind touched the floor and moved into the alcove, still somewhat hard to see because of the sustained invisibility.

Two guards who had been standing just outside the alcove glanced inside and saw their fallen companion. They stared for a second, bringing their weapons to a defensive posture as they took in the details—the open doors, the lack of an elevator.

Ryan knew they couldn't see him clearly, and were confused by the activity out in the main hall. People running everywhere, trying to get out of the line of fire.

Ryan fired one of his darts into the first one, a troll, watching as the flechettes appeared in his warty neck, just above the collarbone.

The guard lost his balance and stumbled to the ground.

Grind nailed the other guard with a burst from his combatgun. The man's chest blew out and he was tossed to the floor.

The troll guard didn't get up.

Talon came just behind Axler and Grind, and as soon as there was enough room, Billy leapt from the pole and landed next to the mage, the cyberzombie's form a waver of light.

"Let's go," Ryan said. "Dhin, try not to shoot us, okay?"

"I'll do my best," came the ork's reply. "Even though you and Billy are masked to my drones, I've got the thermal images of Axler, Grind, and Talon in sight. Just don't stray too far from them."

"Copy." Ryan crouched just inside the alcove and slapped in a clip of concussion grenades. "Let's help with the distractions," he said. "Then we run straight for the exit. Stay together."

"I'll toss a couple of fireballs," Talon said.

"Aim for the edges of the room," Ryan said. "Now!" he fired his entire clip of six grenades in a wide spread toward the corners and walls of the large chamber.

Grind aimed his combatgun and used its undermounted

grenade launcher to chunk several fire bombs. Axler and Billy brought machine guns to bear on the escape route.

Talon's fireballs went off first, one blowing out from an unsuspecting acolyte trying to run out of the hall to the right. The second targeted one of the guards by the entrance, sending sheets of flame out to cover several other guards nearby.

The grenades went off then, shaking the structure with the force of their explosions. "Patience!" Ryan yelled. "We bolt on my mark. Axler and Billy in front, carving out a path. I'll bring up the rear."

The last grenade went off a few seconds later, throwing bodies into the air. "Now!"

Billy's M107 whined into action, and Axler's machine gun spat lead as they ran for the entrance, a forty-meter sprint. Overhead, the Wandjina swooped and dove. Nearly everyone had taken cover now.

Bullets flew from all directions, but in the ensuing pandemonium, no one got between them and the exit. The Wandjina led them out, ducking under the main archway and into the night.

The entrance was three stories up from the ground, reached only by wide stone stairs that followed the steep angle of the pyramid. The drone showered the stairs with a hail of bullets, scattering guards and priests.

Billy and Axler followed in its wake. Outside through the archway and down the stairs. Behind them went Grind, then Talon, moving as fast as he could.

The drone exploded in a ball of flame just as Ryan reached the stairs. A missile coming from a guard near the base of the stairs.

Billy had blown the guard's chest out seconds later. A hint of the old Burnout showing through. Quick, decisive, extremely deadly.

"Dhin," Ryan said. "You all right?"

The ork's response was slow in coming. "Just a little dump shock, Bossman."

Then Ryan and the others reached the bottom of the

stairs and melted into the crowd. The people this close to the Locus hadn't even noticed all the destruction around them. They merely stared at the lake bed, mesmerized. None of them paid any attention to Ryan and the others.

Ryan felt the pull of the Locus as he moved through the crowd. Its power was phenomenal, alluring in a dark and sinister way. Like a drug rush.

Axler led them quickly, silently, through the crowd and around the lake. Toward the hillside where the drummers continued to pound their hypnotic syncopation. Their tapestry of sound.

Toward the old tower that stuck into the clear sky like a rusty needle.

"Jane," Ryan subvocalized. "Any word on the other runners?"

"Sorry, Quicksilver, but no. I haven't had time to deck into the army's communications to see if the runners have been captured or killed."

"Perhaps they accomplished their mission, but their com was knocked out."

"We both know how likely that is," Jane said.

"Yeah. I just hope they got those Nightgliders in place."

"Me too."

The crowd thinned as they came around the edge of the lake bed, moving toward an old hotel and restaurant that was part of the ancient amusement park, which had long ago fallen into ruin. Ryan shuddered as he saw it. After his capture by Aztechnology, he had been tortured inside.

Axler picked a way up the hillside, moving invisibly, quietly away from the smattering of guards placed near the old hotel. Billy moved behind her, then came Grind and Talon in single file, Ryan bringing up the rear. No one noticed them as they climbed into the live oak trees and the mesquite.

As they climbed, Ryan looked back over the lake bed. From this vantage, he could see that most of the army was clustered tightly around the Locus, protecting whatever ritual was being performed. The crowds blocked his view so he couldn't tell what was going on, but a feeling of nausea gripped him as he watched.

"Look at all those guards in the lake bed," said Grind. "They only sent a tiny fraction of their total force into the *teocalli* after us."

"They were far more interested in protecting the Locus than the temple," Ryan said.

"That explains the ease of our escape," said Axler.

They passed close to the drummers, hidden in the undergrowth on the hill above the hotel. Ryan caught glimpses of the musicians—men and women with naked chests, painted in swirls of color. Hair in long, thin braids, faces covered with carved wooden masks depicting demons and devils. They drummed with the abandon of the possessed. Never missing a beat. Coordinated chaos.

Their music pulled at Ryan, threatening to drag him under its hypnotic spell. *Perhaps it is the drumbeat that sustains the spell over the crowd.*

"Think about the mission," he told the others. "Let's just get the Nightgliders and get out of here." He feared one of them would fall under the spell.

They climbed and climbed, nearing the base of the tower where he had first encountered Burnout. Where he had first discovered the Locus. Ryan held onto the hope that even if Cluster hadn't made it out alive, he might have managed to leave the ultralights in position before being killed or captured.

"They're not here," Axler said.

Ryan caught up and searched the space around the concrete slab that served as the base for the tower. He and the others continued to search for several minutes before conceding that Axler was right.

No Nightgliders.

36

Under the knot of the tree canopy, Lethe watched as Ryan and the others searched for their missing Nightgliders. Next to him, the concrete slab rose five meters up out of the dirt, extending above the trees. Ivy and kudzu grew over the concrete, and out of the top the metal tower shot up like a huge needle into the dark sky.

The drumbeats formed a thickness in astral space around Lethe, tendrils of mana swirling into a vortex centered on the Locus. The tornado of blood that spiraled into the astral sky above the black stone sent electric shocks through Lethe. Dread and horror at what had happened to Thayla.

Billy spoke to Ryan. "You must have a backup plan."

Ryan sighed, disappointment at not finding the Nightgliders evident on his features. "Yes, of course." Then he subvocalized to his team. "Jane, Dhin, proceed to Plan B."

Billy wasn't wired into the tacticom, but he could hear the subvocalizations. His cyberears were amazingly acute. "What's Plan B?"

"Dhin will remote-pilot a helo to pick us up, and we run for it. It's less subtle, and we have to take our chances against the Azzie choppers, but it's better than staying here."

Something distracted Lethe then, two comets streaking across the astral sky, coming directly toward them. The spirits of two mages, extremely powerful. "Ryan," he said through his connection with the Dragon Heart, "we have company in the astral."

"What?"

The mages stopped next to Ryan and made themselves visible. They both appeared as elves, one male with a painted face and archaic clothing. The other was a dark-skinned female with close-cropped white hair and a patched appearance to her aura that frightened Lethe.

"Harlequin," Ryan said. "I'm glad to see you among the living. If indeed that is where you are."

Harlequin gave a little laugh. "Yes, well, once again Aina has rescued me," he said, indicating the other elf.

"Enough pleasantries," Aina said. "We have no time for it."

"That is true enough," said Harlequin. "We must get you and this spirit"—he turned to look straight at Lethe despite the fact that he was masking himself to the best of his ability—"across to the metaplanes at once."

"You want to perform the ritual now?" Ryan asked. "Here?"

"We have no choice. Thayla has fallen and the sacrifices that Darke is making on the Locus are extending the bridge. Even if we start now, we may be too late to stop the Enemy from coming."

"Can you perform the ritual from astral space?" Talon asked.

"No," said Harlequin. "You'll have to do it."

"What? I don't have anywhere near the kind of power it takes."

"Aina and I will assist you with that," Harlequin said. "We can't perform the ritual from astral space, but we can lend you some of our power and knowledge. I will teach you the symbols and their meaning. Do you have chalk or a candle?"

"I have a small candle," Talon said. "I use it for emergency summonings, but—"

"Excellent. It will do."

Ryan interrupted. "Okay, Talon will perform the ritual, but where? We can't just camp out here for several hours. Someone is certain to find us."

Billy spoke up. "The tower."

Ryan shivered but said nothing.

"There is some sort of observation platform near the top," Billy said. "No one's likely to notice us there."

"How wide is it?" Harlequin asked.

Ryan looked up, squinting into the sky.

Lethe followed his gaze. The tower was a metal cylinder that used to be white before the paint had flaked off. Now it was mostly rust. At the top, the observation platform bulged from the cylinder like a dark donut.

"I've been almost to the top," Ryan said. "Before, when I found the Locus for Dunkelzahn. The platform is circular, it used to rotate so that people could see the whole area. It's at least fifteen meters in diameter, at least as wide as the ritual circle you made at Château d'If."

"Let's go then," Aina said. "Now, before it's too late." Her aura shot up into the sky, fading from physical view as she rose.

"See you at the top," Harlequin said. He followed Aina up. Lethe watched him go, longing for the time he could move around at the speed of thought. But now, he had to use more mundane methods of getting to the top of the tower. Like the others, he and Billy had to climb the ladder.

Ryan led the way, climbing first to the top of the cement slab, then up the metal ladder. Billy followed in silence, the ground growing smaller and smaller beneath him.

And as they rose, Lethe tried to prepare himself. Thayla had told Ryan that Lethe would know how to use the Dragon Heart. That Lethe would be able to destroy the bridge with it.

The only hitch, Lethe thought as Billy continued to climb, *is that Thayla was wrong.*

Dead wrong.

37

The night air clung to Ryan like a wet blanket, causing sweat to prickle on his brow and run down his face as he climbed the metal ladder of the ancient amusement park tower. He tried not to remember the last time he had been on this tower.

The fall down the ladder was still a vivid memory, the sense of flying through the air just before crashing through the hard branches into the trees below. He had nearly made it out alive, and ironically it had been Burnout who had stopped Ryan then.

Now, Ryan grabbed the cool metal rungs of the ladder and continued his climb. Just below him Talon hung on, a grim look on his face. He had done exceptionally well thus far, but whether he could successfully cast and survive the powerful ritual that Harlequin called upon him to perform was a question no one wanted to ask. The chances were slim. Everyone knew that.

Ryan reached the bottom of the platform—a huge donut shape that hung onto the tower by rusted clamps on a welded track. There was no obvious way in from below, but the ladder continued up inside the center of the donut.

Harlequin appeared next to him, floating in midair. "The ladder goes up through the center. We'll have to put the ritual circle on the roof."

Ryan nodded, but kept his focus on climbing. He had no fear of heights, but he knew that any distractions, any slips, could mean death.

A few more meters in near blackness and Ryan came to

a metal hatch overhead. It didn't seem to be locked, but it was rusted shut. Ryan slammed a fist into it, jarring bits of flaking metal loose. He tried it again, pushing hard.

The hatch creaked open on hinges that hadn't moved in a hundred years, screeching with resistance. Ryan squeezed up through and onto the roof of the observation platform. The roof was rusted metal and curved down slightly at the edge. There were no safety wires along the rim, which meant they'd have to be careful. The drop to the ground was nearly two hundred meters, and Ryan could feel the tower sway in the light breeze.

Harlequin waited in the center, next to the lightning rods. "We don't have much time," he said. "If Darke manages to complete the bridge, we'll all die. Or worse. Even others like us won't be able to stop them."

Talon pushed his head through the hatch, and crawled up onto the roof. He lay there for a few seconds, breathing hard from the climb.

Axler, Grind, and Billy joined them. Axler immediately began measuring wire for safety harnesses. As she cut it, Talon stood and dug through his bag for the candle.

Harlequin moved next to Talon, talking to him in low tones.

Ryan watched as Talon went into a trance of sorts, taking in everything the elf mage was saying while pacing a preliminary perimeter for the ritual circle. Harlequin and Aina would lend their strength to the spell, but Talon would be required to perform all the physical components of the dance.

Axler and Grind attached one end of the safety wires to an eyelet in the center of the platform, then passed the other end to each of the runners. Ryan looped himself in, then made sure that Talon was secure.

The mage's frame was slight, thin compared to Ryan's bulk, and he was obviously exhausted from the run. Still, he seemed to be holding up and was in better shape than a lot of mages Ryan knew.

"Jane," Ryan said, "Axler and Grind will remain physical and watch over our bodies, but we don't know what kind of opposition to expect."

"Understood," Jane said. "Dhin and I are monitoring you. There's no sign of pursuit; their attention seems to be focused on the Locus."

"Bossman, I'm bringing a helo in from Carswell, and a T-bird as well. A little extra firepower in case you need it later."

"Thanks."

Talon pulled stray strands of his dark hair back away from his face and tied them into his ponytail. Then he began to chant in Sperethiel, the words whispered to him from Harlequin. Talon had lit his narrow blue candle, and was dripping it along the edge of the platform, creating an elaborate pattern.

"Billy," Talon said, fully entranced now. "Please lie in the center of the circle. Ryan, put the Dragon Heart next to him."

Billy complied with Talon's request, and Ryan unwrapped the Heart from its sash. He placed the sash on the rusted metal and set the Heart carefully on the sash.

When Talon had closed the circle, concentrating on the intricate patterns that Harlequin had instructed him to make, the mage walked slowly to where Billy was lying. Talon dripped hot wax around and over the cyberzombie's body. The candle wasn't big enough to cover all of Billy's body, so Talon dripped the wax in a crisscrossing lattice pattern. He continued his low chanting while he worked, the song helping to block out the beating of the drums that came from the hillside far below.

The smell of tallow and smoke met Ryan's nose as Talon finished with Billy and moved on to cover the Dragon Heart with the last of the candle wax. Ryan felt the power of the ritual, amazed at Talon's skill with the arcane. The young human had the gift in a way few others did.

Abruptly, Talon rose, trance-like. "It is time," he said to Ryan, then he began to pace a circle just inside the perimeter, and indicated for Ryan to follow suit.

Ryan complied, dancing exactly in the footsteps left behind by Talon. The sensation began immediately— the strange out-of-body duality creeping over him as he walked. They made one complete circle just inside the perimeter, then began to spiral toward the center.

The tapestry of power twisted around them, solidifying into a barrier of mana as the ritual neared its climax. Finally, they reached the center and Ryan's body slumped next to Talon's.

They rose into astral space.

A split second of recognition. Talon appeared, his stature much larger here in the magical realm. The astral forms of Harlequin and Aina hovered next to him, looking just as they had manifested.

There was a moment of gut-sinking dread as Ryan floated next to Talon, waiting alongside Aina and Harlequin. All waiting to see if Talon was strong enough to bring Billy and the Dragon Heart across.

Mana from the ritual glowed blue and green around them, a dense mesh that was nonetheless nearly overwhelmed by the huge forces of blood magic that swirled up outside the ritual circle from the Locus and the *teocalli*.

Then, as if in slow motion, Billy's body faded into astral space as it disappeared from the physical world. Possessed by Lethe, the cyberzombie shone like a beacon, a silver shimmer against the blue-green backdrop.

The Dragon Heart loomed into existence as well—a golden sun of pure power, casting its light over them all.

Ryan looked at himself. His aura showed turmoil. *Can Harlequin be right about me? Can I be more than I know? Who am I?*

For a fraction of an instant, the team hung in astral space inside the ritual circle. Then they were gone, shifted into the metaplanes. Projected into the worlds beyond.

38

Lucero scooped up unfortunate souls by the tens and slammed them into the extending rock outcropping. Screams ripped the air as she worked, ecstasy building inside her.

I must please them. The tzitzimine. *They will reward me.*

Lucero no longer cared that she was a creature of essence and blood, a stew of guts and magic. A blood spirit conjured up from the remains of her own dead and bleeding corpse. She barely felt the constant, searing pain of her nature. She hardly remembered being alive. None of that mattered now.

Everything of importance was here. Everything that had ever mattered to her coalesced on this one task. The completion of the bridge.

The gap closed, narrowed until she could see details of the creatures working on the other side. They were huge and hideous. Drones of black and red—faceless, veined slugs—worked in the front. Behind them were larger monsters of spectral green and burgundy with many barbed, spiny tentacles and an amorphous globular central body. White steam drifted in and around them, and Lucero smelled the wracking stench of it like the essence of a thousand rotting and maggot-riddled corpses.

Further back were more creatures, each unique, more powerful, and ultimately cunning than those in front. Pulling the strings. These were the true *tzitzimine*. The ones who would free her.

Such loveliness, she thought. *Such abject generosity and benevolence.*

Joy filled Lucero as she smashed the souls of more sacrifices into the stone beneath her feet. Sheer pleasure
coursed through her as she narrowed the gap. As she extended the span of rock to the brink of touching.

Oscuro moved up next to her, coming to help with the
last meter. "This is a glorious moment," he said to Lucero.

The two of them stopped when the two sides of the
bridge hung only a fraction of a centimeter apart, a narrow
membrane between worlds. Oscuro looked up to face the
horde of creatures. He bowed his dark head and spread his
arms wide. Lucero could see the bloodless crisscross
wounds on his forearms, where he had cut himself with
the obsidian knife.

The spirits of the sacrifices pressed in behind him like a
mounting wave of souls. Oscuro lifted his voice. "Welcome, my masters! I give you the world!"

He threw his head back, grinning wildly as his wounds
opened up. The gaping cuts passed through his body, forming crescent-shaped holes all the way through his flesh.
The sacrificed spirits behind him seemed to be sucked
toward Oscuro, passing into his back, then shooting from
his wounds in jets of blood.

Maniacal glee gripped Oscuro, holding his face in a ric-
tus grin. The gouts of blood shot from his arms and landed
on the last vestige of a gap between the two expanses of
the bridge. Sacrifices funneled into him, giving his skin a
glowing red hue. A ruddy, flushed appearance.

Lucero watched as the blood sealed the bridge, as Oscuro stood rigid against the onslaught of spirits. She
watched with growing anticipation as the last of the sacrifices plunged into Oscuro's body, as the last bits of the
crimson fluid spat from the gashes in his arms, spraying
the joint where the two spans met.

The red glow faded from Oscuro's skin, and he sank to
the ground. Overcome from the exertion.

A moment passed as the blood seeped into the cracks. A
single beat of a distant drum, a faint heartbeat followed by
utter silence.

An instant of hesitation.

Then, like a tsunami, the creatures surged toward them. They came in a mad rush, crawling over each other without regard.

Suddenly, Lucero knew they would destroy her. They cared nothing for her freedom. They had merely been controlling her so that she would help them.

She fled from the horde. She flew back the way she had come, the expanse much farther than she had thought possible. The cliff of her home plane seemed so distant, so small and remote.

The horde gained on her, trampling over the exhausted Oscuro as they neared. On her heels now.

I'm not going to make it, she knew suddenly.

Seconds later, she fell under their onslaught. The dense black of innumerable bodies surrounded her, and she was lost under their insane rush.

Trampled. Snuffed out just like the rest of the world would be once they reached the other side.

What have I done? Lucero wondered. *I have failed you, Thayla. I fear I have doomed the entire universe.*

39

Ryan floated in the dark void of metaplanar limbo. Gone were the auras of the *teocalli* and the Locus, the sacrifices and the drums. Gone was the aura of the tower jutting into the hot night sky, the observation platform rusting at its apex.

Axler and Grind had vanished, remaining in the physical world to protect the bodies of both Ryan and Talon. Even the auras of Harlequin, Aina, Talon, and Lethe had disappeared, giving way to a realm of his very own. The place in himself that he had to face solo.

Ryan drifted alone and in absolute silence as he waited for the coalescence that would come soon. The test.

The dweller on the threshold.

It came an instant later, taking the same shape it had the first time. A small dracoform of fiery red, standing on its hind legs. Its eyes were the color of Ryan's own—blue with flecks of quicksilver.

It had called itself a drake the last time, saying that it had once served Dunkelzahn, just as Ryan served him now. It had tested Ryan, showing him that he had the power to banish an elemental.

Dunkelzahn had never indicated that Ryan had this ability. *Why?*

"You have come again, Ryanthusar," the drake said. "Like the phoenix."

Ryan inhaled sharply. Then, "I bring Lethe and the Dragon Heart to stop the Enemy from coming."

"I know this, of course," said the drake. "I am like a mirror. I know what you know."

"What is the test this time?" Ryan asked. "Let's get on with it. I don't have time to waste."

The drake smiled. "Perhaps there is none," it said. "Your soul is pure, your heart clean. You are willing to die a hero's death in order to save the universe."

Ryan said nothing.

"Dunkelzahn chose you well," the drake continued. "Yet you are still more than you think you are. You must keep your mind open to possibility. It may save you in the end."

Then the dweller was gone and Ryan stood on a blasted, cracked plane of rock. A landscape darkened with black blood, and a sky of gray static.

The bridge.

Dread slicked through Ryan as he looked around at the corpses scattered across the tongue of rock. Harlequin and Aina stood next to him in the icy wind. Talon's hair whipped behind him as he gaped at the scene, shock and terror gripping the weary mage.

Lethe appeared, bringing Billy's body across with him. The cold and the dead seemed to have no effect on them. There was a sad expression on the cyberzombie's face. "It's so silent," he said, and now his voice was different. It was as if both Billy and Lethe spoke in unison. "So dark without Thayla."

Ryan saw that the Dragon Heart had made it across as well; he reached down to where it lay on the rock and lifted it. "Here," he said, and handed the artifact to Lethe.

"We're too late," Harlequin said.

Ryan looked out across the bridge—a hair-thin arc of rock that spanned the gap between cliffs. Dread threatened to overwhelm him as he realized that the structure had been completed, the connection made between the two worlds. Over the bridge poured armies of terrible creatures. Multitudes of hideous monsters the like of which Ryan had never dreamed existed.

They're coming straight for us.

He steeled himself. He would not succumb to fear. Despite their numbers and the obvious ferocity, Ryan knew he would stand and fight. He would fight for the things he loved—Nadja and the promise of a future of hope. Ryan vowed to resist until the very end. Until death or victory.

Ryan advanced onto the bridge, moving toward the oncoming horde. Harlequin and Aina joined him on his right. Lethe and Talon came up on his left.

It was the most powerful group of individuals Ryan had ever been a part of, and yet they seemed insignificant—a tiny resistance in a standoff against overwhelming force.

No one flinched; no one yielded to fear.

Lethe lifted the Dragon Heart in one huge cybernetic hand, holding it up over his head as they walked out onto the bridge.

Mana swirled around Aina, deep blue and forest green, mingling with the energies that flowed bright white and sun yellow into Harlequin.

Ryan gathered his own magic in preparation for the attack, and Talon beside him made a valiant effort to fight off the terror as he began casting.

They were as ready as they would ever be.

The wave of horror rushed up to meet them, faster and more ultimately terrifying than anything in Ryan's imagination. One thought raced around and around in his head as he braced himself.

This is the end.

40

Lethe straightened Billy's body and stood tall on the cracked earth as he watched the oncoming rush of vile creatures. They came like a stampede, trampling each other in their insane rush to cross the bridge. Soon they would reach this side.

Oh, Thayla, he thought. *My beloved goddess. Look what they have done to your beauty.*

Lethe held the Dragon Heart over his head. He and Billy worked in unison now, almost as though the journey to the metaplanes had fused their spirits.

Lethe felt the power mount inside him. There were no barriers to him here in the metaplanes. The suffocating restrictions that flesh and physical machinery had imposed upon him for the past days since he had tried to possess Burnout in Hells Canyon were gone now.

Lethe still couldn't leave the body of the cyberzombie, but he could control it completely, and he could move with it as he had moved before he'd tried to possess Burnout. Now, he could fly as before, traveling anywhere with a thought.

Lethe felt the familiar power that had been part of him what now seemed so long ago. And that power grew immeasurably as he touched the Dragon Heart with his mind, as he probed it for answers.

It's now or too late. Exactly how can I use the artifact to destroy the bridge?

Beside him, Ryan and the others fought the first wave of the Enemy. Harlequin and Aina unleashed a wash of such sheer intensity that it carved up the creatures like a monomolecular line. Each of them propelled a cool beam of mana like a scalpel, and the Enemy fell before it.

Aina seemed particularly vicious; she knew something of these creatures and wanted vengeance. As Lethe watched, she worked herself into a frenzy, the power coming from her on a level far above any that Lethe had seen from a mage. The front line of slugs and bulbous creatures burst into oozing black bags under her attack.

Harlequin was more precise, but no less effective. His strikes landed on the second line, tentacled creatures with luminescent green and burgundy bodies, the white fire of his magic charring them. Igniting their foul-smelling flesh.

Peripherally, Lethe was aware of Ryan and Talon, fighting those of the Enemy who escaped the elves' magic. Ryan moved with blinding speed, his blows striking with precision and perfect accuracy. And the human mage, Talon, despite his fatigue at bringing them across, held his own.

Still, the horde came on unrelenting. In a matter of moments, they would all be overrun. Lost under a bludgeoning of stench and razor-sharp bone spurs.

"Come on, Lethe!" Ryan yelled. "We could use some help here!"

Focus came to Lethe as he used all of his senses to examine the Dragon Heart. He saw millions of mana tendrils flowing toward and into it. As his mind touched the Heart, clarity came to Lethe. He felt the currents of mana around him like extensions of himself. He sensed the where and the why and the how of astral power.

It was a level of awareness that had been out of his reach without the Dragon Heart. A gift of sight that came as his spirit and the Heart connected.

Lethe understood that such a magnificent gift came with a price. He had been given the ability to comprehend. The ability to control. With such knowledge came a choice between self and selflessness.

Even as he knew the possibility existed for taking the

Heart and its power for himself, it flashed through his mind and was instantly discarded. The Heart must be used to destroy the forces of darkness. Lethe knew it as surely as he knew that Thayla had named him.

The answer came to him: the Dragon Heart was a lens of sorts for channeling mana. A tool for moving around magical energy. If it could handle a huge amount, perhaps . . .

Perhaps the bridge can be destroyed with it.

This place was a mana spike—a pinnacle of magic that had resulted initially from the Great Ghost Dance. And recently that pinnacle had been extended by the Locus sacrifices, the life energy of metahuman blood used to increase the mana at this point.

If I can move the mana out of the bridge, it should buckle.

Lethe exerted his will, channeling the mana flow. He focused the Dragon Heart at the apex of the bridge, and tried to draw the power out of the structure.

A few seconds went by. Nothing happened.

Perhaps I'm not using it—

Abruptly the bridge split, sending a loud crack through the air. The center crumbled and fell into the Chasm.

"Yes!" yelled Ryan, and he seemed to draw strength from the victory.

Lethe drew more and more mana from the bridge as he extended his will through the Dragon Heart. It was like a new limb, an additional part of himself, an extension of his mind that he wielded like a weapon. Mana tendrils of smoky black and rust red unraveled from between the stones of the bridge and flowed across the distance to disappear into the Dragon Heart.

The structure collapsed, this side of the span falling away from the center. The destruction moved back toward the cliff face. And as it fell, the Enemy followed the crumbling stone, swallowed up in the abyss.

As Lethe decimated the bridge, the mana built inside the Dragon Heart. Inside him. Giving him power and understanding. Images came to him as he enacted his destructive force. He saw the portal of swirling rainbows that had recurred in his mind. He knew now that it was the window through which he came to be.

He relived the burning fire that had plagued his waking mind, experiencing the agony of the fountain of lava. He screamed as he had once before, in a lifetime past. He saw things in the sharp relief created by the explosion. Rows of trees and cars scattered and burned, a facade of windows shattered from the blast.

A split second of agony pulsed through him. Then it was gone, and with it went the memories.

As the bridge crashed down in a thunderous avalanche of rock, taking the startled corpses of the Enemy with it, mana built and built inside the Dragon Heart. Lethe realized that he had to focus it somewhere, had to move it into the physical world. He knew only one way.

Lethe channeled the mana into Ryan and Talon, into Harlequin and Aina. The life energy of thousands and thousands of people passed out of the bridge, through the Dragon Heart, and into the four metahumans. Mana flooded them.

Lethe didn't know what it would do to them, but he had no choice. They were the only links to the physical world, the only way the mana could be diverted away from this place.

He just hoped the surge in power didn't kill them.

41

Ryan shifted his feet on the dusty rock of the bridge and buried his fist into the soft flesh of a blood-veined blob, killing it with one blow. He felt power building inside. His magic came stronger and faster than it ever had before. He fought at the limit of his magical ability, yet it all came easily to him.

He dodged an arcing tentacle and used his distance strike to pummel the chitinous skull of the attacking creature. The strike was like an extension of his aura, a magical pseudopod that landed with more force than Ryan had ever delivered. He felt the creature's head crush like an egg under the impact.

Ryan could feel more and more mana flowing into him. *What is Lethe doing to me?*

Beside Ryan, Lethe wielded the Dragon Heart, using it to rip up the foundations of the bridge and destroy the connection to the plane of the Enemy. It was a glorious thing to see, and it made Ryan wonder why he had ever considered keeping the Heart for himself.

The cracked earth quaked under his feet as the bridge crumbled in toward them. Huge chunks of rock fell away, massive boulders and crude pavement ripped off the main structure and vanished into the maw of the Chasm.

Hope and joy built inside Ryan as he watched the Enemy die as the bridge gave way under them. They slid down broken and cracking spans of the shattered bridge and fell into the abyss. Millions of the hideous monsters plummeted, screaming their vehemence as they dropped away, lost forever between worlds.

Still, there were thousands still alive. Trapped on this side of the expanse, they came rushing toward Ryan and the others, trying to outrun the collapsing bridge behind them.

With razor-sharp filaments of magical energy, Harlequin and Aina cut the creatures down in broad swaths as they came. Like two masters of monowire, the two elves created a barrier with their magic. They amazed Ryan with their ferocity, wielding magic on a scale far above anything he'd ever imagined. Intent that not one of the Enemy make it through alive.

Thousands of the Enemy died, hurling themselves with horrifying abandon into the vice of Harlequin and Aina. Burned to a bubbling goo or sliced into leaking black flesh or maimed and screaming. The shrieks of agony and terror grated against Ryan's ears, and it took all his will to block it out. This was a battlefield, a war arena. Atrocity had to be accepted. Ignored.

Talon was having a harder time. He fought well and his magic was stronger than Ryan expected it to be, most likely because Lethe was funneling mana into him as well. But Ryan could tell that the human was on the verge of succumbing to his fear, to his horror at the smell of death, the screams of the wounded and the visions of leaking guts.

"Hold yourself together, Talon," Ryan yelled. "Lethe's taking down the bridge. Soon this'll all be over." He tried to project sincerity in his voice, but the words came out hollow. Empty.

Talon could assess the situation just as well as Ryan. Even if Lethe destroyed the entire bridge, thousands of the Enemy would make it to this side of the expanse. Harlequin and Aina would kill as many as they could, but some would get through.

Abruptly, one of the creatures burst through the lines of

fire. It was a powerful one, a unique creature with a head like a hundred barbs of bone jutting from translucent blue flesh. Yellow, slitted eyes bobbing on tendinous stalks. It went directly for Lethe, and it was incredibly fast despite the wounds it had taken from Aina and Harlequin.

Ryan moved to intercept. He couldn't allow anything to distract Lethe until the bridge had been completely destroyed.

The creature turned its head on a neck of sharp bony ridges, quickly glancing toward Ryan. "Do not interfere," it said, the words materializing in Ryan's mind through telepathy.

Ryan responded with a vicious telekinetic attack, throwing all his power against the creature.

The blow hit hard and should have crushed it.

The creature barely flinched.

The brief hesitation was enough. Ryan used the split second to move between it and Lethe.

Ryan felt laughter bubble up from deep inside the creature's translucent blue gut. "Very well, then you shall die first."

Ryan struck with a barrage of punches, aiming for what seemed to be vital areas. His right hand chopped across the neck, his left connecting with the creature's midsection. Hands hardened into weapons by his magic.

Pain sliced through his fists as his blows landed. Both hands came back gashed and bleeding.

Those barbs are razor sharp.

He tried to ignore the wounds. They would heal.

The creature relented slightly under Ryan's flurry of strikes, stepping back.

Ryan moved forward, keeping up the attack. Looking for a vulnerable spot as he lashed out with his foot. Aiming for the eyes.

Abruptly, the creature's head struck with blinding speed. The blow was too fast. No time to dodge or block it. Ryan barely caught the blur of motion before the bony skull

slammed into his chest. Before the creature's massive bulk
threw him to the hard, cracked rock and pinned him there.

The scalpel-sharp orifice of its mouth sliced open
Ryan's chest as it went for his heart. The creature's razor-
barbed head cut through Ryan's body armor, his skin and
muscle and bone like piano wire through cheese.

Pain exploded in his chest—the agony of his soul
disintegrating.

With his last vestige of strength, Ryan clamped his
hands around the creature's head. He held it inside his
bleeding chest, and pushed against its body as he twisted.
He knew he was going to die here, but he wouldn't go
alone.

Blood flowed down Ryan's arms as he held on with his
wounded hands, cut to ribbons by the creature's jutting
bone. Ryan threw his entire weight into his last wrenching
twist.

A loud crunching greeted his ears, and the creature's
head snapped sideways and pulled away from his body,
completely severed. The body convulsed, spilling puke-
green and yellow ichor onto Ryan and the cracked rock. It
collapsed on top of Ryan's prone body.

Am I still alive?

He gasped desperately for air, smelling the foul stench
of its body fluid. His ears filled with the sucking pop of its
head coming free of his chest.

He tried to push the thing off of him, but his strength
was gone.

Blackness crept in. His breath gurgled through the massive hole in his chest.

I am dying.

He had always been prepared to die to prevent the Enemy from coming across. But now, when victory seemed
close, the irony of his own death was like bitter bile in his
throat.

He thought of Nadja in the last moments. How he
wished to see her face one final time, to put his arms
around her. To smell her hair.

Love was the one thing the Enemy couldn't feed on. The one thing they couldn't take from him.

Ryan's body had gone completely numb, and as breath rattled through his chest, it was the vision of Nadja that he held onto. A vision of hope that washed away the irony.

42

Pain wracked Lucero from all sides. Hooves and globular weight pummeled her as she was swept along in the tide of bodies racing for the cliff edge. Dark shapes of black surrounded her, veined with red fire. And there were the others, the tentacled ones, rushing in a mad dash to escape the crumbling bridge.

She had caught glimpses of the bridge falling into the Chasm far behind her, the edge of the abyss approaching rapidly. Now she pushed to move faster; it was her only chance to gain freedom without being completely destroyed.

If I can get off the bridge, she thought, *I can travel the metaplanes and escape.*

Suddenly she was tugged, jerked suddenly to her left and forward like a dog on a leash. She flew headlong through the grotesque bodies. It was Señor Oscuro who called her; she felt it in the nature of the pull, the subtle sensations that came from her connection to him.

So he is still alive, she thought. She'd hoped that the creatures had trampled him to death.

The rock quaked beneath her, splitting her ears as the foundations of the structure cracked and weakened. The bridge fell away, the magic that had held it together flowing out in a wash of color. As Lucero moved toward Oscuro, she plunged through the front line of the creatures around her and saw what was happening.

A creature of metal and flesh, glowing brightly like a silver star, held a blinding object over its head. It was wondrous and the light coming from it reminded Lucero of Thayla. It was this object that was destroying the bridge.

Next to this creature were others, metahumans. Some of them Lucero had seen before. The elf and the human who had tried to save Thayla. So long ago that seemed. Literally a lifetime ago.

Her lifetime.

The elf worked in conjunction with another, forging mana into a lethal weapon, and killing the creatures by the thousands, trying desperately to keep them from getting off the bridge. Lucero was flying directly for their line of defense.

The human lay prone under a huge creature of bone spurs. Miraculously, the creature was dead, but blood gushed from a massive hole in the human's chest, and he was not moving. Not even breathing.

Lucero knew he must be dead. Nobody could have survived that.

Another human—a mage it seemed—moved to try to help him. He looked to be weaker than the others, closer to exhaustion, but he was determined to help his friend.

Lucero felt the fragmentation of metaplanar travel hit her as she reached the end of the bridge. She was being called into the physical world. Señor Oscuro's doing?

In the last second of her existence on this plane, Lucero saw the glowing chrome cyborg with the artifact complete the destruction of this half of the bridge. He used the artifact to channel all the mana into the fallen human. Brilliant bolts of white mana slammed the man's lifeless body, making it twitch and convulse.

Perhaps it was a last, desperate attempt to save the human. A final attempt to maintain his spirit energy. Perhaps together the mage and the cyborg could bring him back.

Lucero wanted it to be so, but she held no hope. Thayla was gone, and those of her kind—these heroes—could never win. They could never succeed in bringing beauty back into the world.

Dust rose all around as the rock shattered and fell.

Screams of the fallen echoed throughout the Chasm, chilling enough to freeze Lucero's blood.

Then she was flying across the metaplanes, through the swirling silk currents. She manifested in the physical world next to Señor Oscuro. They stood side by side on the blood-drenched Locus.

Oscuro's body shivered uncontrollably in the hot night air. Pain drew sharp lines into his face, the muscles in his neck and back cinching up involuntarily. His dark hair dripped with blood, bits of flesh, and body refuse. For a moment Lucero thought he was going to curl into a fetal position on the hard stone.

Around them, the Gestalt continued to chant, sitting cross-legged in a circle around Lucero and Oscuro. Oblivious.

Technicians continued to monitor the ten human mages, making certain that the catheters that formed the blood circle were secure and flowing well. The Gestalt maintained the swirling column of astral energy, the sanguine tornado that connected the Locus and the sacrifices to the metaplanar bridge.

Oscuro gathered his strength and stood. He screamed at the Gestalt, "STOP!"

The blood mages did not respond. They seemed not to hear him.

He looked at Lucero. "Make them stop. The conduit must be severed before—"

A subliminal rumble sent a wave of shivers through Lucero's spirit. *What the frag is happening?*

Oscuro cast a spell on himself.

The rumbling grew into a shaking, and in the astral Lucero saw it coming, a pulse traveling down the conduit. Like a circular tsunami, bulging the column in a toroid of white as it descended.

It came too fast. Too powerful.

Shaking became an earthquake, an ear-splitting shock wave. Oscuro saw it too and ran for the edge, plowing over one of the mages, and leapt from the stone at the last second. Lucero followed, clearing the circle as the pulse hit.

The Gestalt exploded as the tsunami wave reached the Locus. They blew up in a blast of fire and burning flesh, sending a wave of searing energy out from the stone.

The blast hit Lucero and her master, carrying them up and up. The force of the explosion plowed into Lucero, slamming into her on the astral as well as the physical. Like a huge battering ram of rock-hard energy that crashed into her spirit and hurled her across the dry lake bed.

She wavered on the verge of disintegration as the explosion enveloped her, wrapping around her in a rush of liquid fire. She focused herself, trying to concentrate. To hold herself together against the shower of mana shards.

She found herself on the astral plane behind the *teocalli*. Shivering and feeling hollow. Like a ghost of icy wind.

Purged.

Purified.

Her spirit still intact.

Lucero felt her freedom come then. A sensation of liberation that overwhelmed her, and she knew that she was no longer bound to Oscuro.

Perhaps he is dead.

She didn't wait there to find out. She raised herself into the astral sky and flew away.

All around her, the destruction of the Gestalt wasted the landscape. A chromium sun shone from atop the obsidian black Locus, sending out rays of power that scorched everything around it. People burst into flames and exploded, their spirits thrown clear of their disintegrating flesh. The bodies and blood at the bottom of the lake bed vaporized.

This is the result of the bridge's demolition.

The army could do nothing to stop the ferocity of the magic sun. Soldiers merely atomized against the onslaught. Tanks and Thunderbirds flew back from it like dry leaves in a hot breeze. The *teocalli* melted from the heat, and she realized that the structure had protected her, had shaded her from the cyborg's magic.

For the first time in her existence, Lucero had been lucky.

Exhilaration filled her as she flew. She was free at last. Free to decide what to do with herself. The constant pain of being a blood spirit had dwindled. Faded until it was no more than a dull memory.

As she flew, feeling the crystal-clean air of the astral surround her, cool and fresh, she realized that she could do anything she wanted. Go anywhere she desired.

She briefly considered going after Señor Oscuro, to make sure he was dead. The fact that she was free indicated that he had either died or come close to dying. She hated him, abhorred his wanton desecration of all that was good and beautiful.

She didn't stop. Oscuro was part of her past now. Her history. She wanted to move beyond the dark part of her existence. Start anew.

What now?

The answer came to her instantly, and she knew it was the right path for her.

She had been used in both life and afterlife, manipulated and commanded in a malicious effort to destroy beauty and light. To rid the world of all that was good and wondrous.

She thought of Thayla, the goddess whose song was the essence of beauty, whose light defined goodness. And Lucero knew that she would search the metaplanes for that beauty. Lucero would seek out the one thing that had touched the speck of compassion and love inside of her.

Perhaps she would find Thayla.

Lucero vowed to keep looking for bits of Thayla's beauty and song. She would spend the rest of her existence repairing the damage to her own soul.

Lucero wanted to undo her wrongs, and she knew just where to start.

43

Time slowed as Ryan died.

In his mind, he hears Nadja's gentle laughter, feels the tickle of her fingertips on his neck.

Pain coursed through Ryan, spreading out from his opened chest to fill his entire being.

He remembers that it was Nadja's love for him that saved him in his battle with Roxborough. His gun to her head, she talked soothingly to him, telling him how important he was to her.

Cold wind blew through his spirit like a blizzard of icicles.

I guess my luck has run out, my love.

He was drowning, suffocating, as the hole in his ribs filled with his own blood and the foul ichor of the creature above him.

I will miss you, sweet Nadja.

Ryan felt the bolts from Lethe almost peripherally, on the edge of his awareness. Out of the corner of his experience.

Goodbye.

Tremendous strokes of mana lashed out from the Dragon Heart and slammed into him as he faded from the pain and weakness.

The creature had drained him, had sucked his life force out somehow even though Ryan had managed to kill the thing at the last.

Lethe is trying to force the life back into me with all that mana, Ryan thought.

In the distance, like a faint tickle through thick fabric, Ryan sensed healing magic touch him, coming from Talon. It seemed so far away, so removed. But as the mana from the Dragon Heart continued to arc through Ryan's spirit and into his physical body, the magic combined with Talon's healing spell to coalesce into a synergy.

Ryan felt the world shift and change around him. His perception grew and grew until he was in many places at once.

He lay dying on the cracked plane of rock.

He flew across the metaplanes in the body of the dweller on the threshold.

He perceived in the physical world, inside the ritual circle atop the amusement park tower, his awareness hovering over the unconscious bodies of Talon and himself.

Is this what it feels like to die?

Talon's healing spell. The synergy with the increased mana gave the spell far more power than Talon could safely use. The spell slammed into Ryan, purging the poison, knitting the wounds. The magical construction stabilized his astral body, reassembled the shattered fragments of his soul.

Flying across the metaplanes, Ryan transformed. As the mana built inside him, his spirit metamorphosed. Awakened.

Power surged through him, magic of such a level that he thought he would explode from it. His spirit swelled, and he emerged in the physical world. Whole and complete.

His nightsuit and body armor shredded on his physical body as he manifested in a new form. The fabric stretched, then ripped, then fell away. Ryan's weaponry and arsenal hit the metallic roof of the observation platform as his new body emerged in place of his old.

Ryan manifested in the body of a drake—a small dragon like the dweller on the threshold. His human shape was gone, his head elongated into a reptilian beak, spines jutting from his mouth. Sharp horns protruded from his brow, curling back.

What the frag?

Ryan's gut burned with fire and wings unfolded from his back, his skin replaced with blue and silver scales that glowed from the mounting mana inside him. A tail coiled behind him and his arms and legs appeared with talons, claws like scythes.

His consciousness expanded and he found he could perceive astrally without effort. He saw the ebb and flow of mana instinctively. Those around him were no longer just physical forms, they were now essences and auras—Axler and Grind turning toward him with their weapons brought to bear.

White and silver flames flickered off his scales. He could still feel the mana that Lethe was channeling into him. He felt whole and completely healed. Powerful as he stretched out his wings and stood upright, more completely himself than he had ever felt.

It made sense in an odd way. The dweller had told Ryan that it was a mirror. That Ryan was more than he thought.

Ryan spoke to Axler and Grind telepathically. *Don't shoot,* he said. *I am Ryan. I don't know how, but I've manifested in this shape.*

Axler's look never melted. "Don't move!" she commanded.

An explosion on the Locus shook the tower beneath their feet, causing it to sway and rock. Unconsciously, Ryan used his wings to hold himself aloft while the others tried to keep their footing on the moving rooftop.

Axler, you'll just have to trust me. If you listen to that cold heart of yours, you'll know I'm the real thing.

Axler kept her distance, but did not fire. She wasn't ready to trust him, but didn't want to take the chance of shooting him if he was telling the truth.

Ryan looked down on the scene far below. He did not need binoculars now. His eyesight was extremely keen. The area around the Locus was surrounded by dead and burned bodies. No one moved within a half-kilometer perimeter. Everyone dead.

Ryan winced at the stench of charred flesh rising from below. Trees burned all around, sending black smoke into the cloudless night sky. The *teocalli* sat like a crooked mound of melted slag. On the side nearest the Locus, the stone had been blown away and charred, melted from the heat.

The Locus sat intact and unmarred in the center of the destruction. Its surface was a dull black now, not shiny, except for the faint scintilla coming off the hairline threads of orichalcum that passed through the stone. Ryan could feel the magic dwindling inside the Locus, and knew that Lethe and the Dragon Heart were responsible.

Next to Ryan, Axler and Grind still maintained defensive posture. Axler subvocalized to Jane, "Can you see this?"

Suddenly, the tower swayed again in a gust of wind, listing violently this time. It had sustained damage from the explosions. The ancient amusement park ride was on the verge of toppling over with all of them still on top.

Ryan might survive; he could fly now. But his friends would certainly die when the tower fell. There was no way he could save them all.

44

Nadja paced around the room as sunlight filtered hazily in through the skylight above. She walked from the Louis XIV chairs, past the huge stone hearth, around behind the blue velvet sofa where Harlequin and Aina sat unconscious, then back again. Completing the circle.

As she paced, she shivered and rubbed her arms. Harlequin's Château d'If was cold in the morning.

The two slumped elves had not moved in hours. Sitting side by side on the sofa, their expressions slack, revealing nothing of their success or failure. Nothing of Ryan.

Nadja had been in touch with Jane-in-the-box, but the decker could not follow the mission into astral space, and did not know what had happened. Whether they were succeeding or being destroyed.

Jane Foster sat cross-legged on the ottoman, facing the sofa. She wore a Missouri sweatshirt over her mauve dress, and absently turned her coiled-dragon ring around and around on her finger. She was another elf mage, an apprentice and powerful in her own way, but much younger and far less experienced than either Aina or Harlequin.

Foster was meditating, not asleep. Meditation was just her way of passing the time and trying not to worry. There wasn't room enough for *both* of them to pace.

Nadja's portable telecom rang, and she straightened abruptly and walked to the end table where it sat. She turned the screen toward her and tapped the Connect key.

Jane-in-the-box's icon filled the screen, ridiculous

cartoon breasts bulging under a tight yellow leather halter. Huge pouting lips of the brightest red. Gigantic blue eyes.

"Yes, Jane?" Nadja said.

"Something's happened," Jane said. "Look."

The screen image shifted to show a halting, grainy view of the top of an amusement park tower. The human bodies of Talon and Ryan lay unconscious in the center of the ritual circle. The cyberzombie and the Dragon Heart had vanished, moving completely across into astral space or to whatever metaplane they all went.

"This happened just moments ago," Jane said. "I pieced together feeds from the headcameras of both Axler and Grind."

Suddenly, Ryan's body jerked. He began to glow silver and cobalt blue as though a cold fire shimmered over his skin. Then his clothes tore and fell away as the transformation of his flesh changed him. In instants, his skin grew metallic, and his head elongated into a dragon's snout, horns curling back from his brow and protruding from the edges of his mouth.

Wings appeared, beautiful silver and blue scales shimmering as his body armor and equipment fell to the metal roof. A small dragon had taken shape from Ryan's body.

Nadja watched this with fear and fascination.

There was movement next to her, and she noticed that Aina and Harlequin had awakened. Harlequin leaned his head back and let out a long slow breath. His face paint couldn't hide the dark purple-black circles that hung under his bloodshot green eyes, the droop of his shoulders, or the obvious pain evident in even the simple task of drawing breath.

Aina was in similar condition. Her head hung forward as though it were too heavy to lift. Her yellow-white hair was tousled, and her Rolling Stones T-shirt was wet from exertion. After a minute, she managed to sit up and see what Nadja was looking at.

"He's a drake," Aina said. "It's still Ryan, but he's manifested his drake form." She gave a tired laugh.

Nadja looked at the drake on the screen. Ryan? Then as the creature turned toward her, she caught a close-up of the eyes. Blue eyes, flecked with silver. How many times had she stared into those eyes?

She loved the man with those eyes.

Ryan.

"Jane," Nadja said. "Did you hear what Aina said?"

"That drek about Ryan manifesting his drake form?" Jane's tone was incredulous.

"It is Ryan," Nadja said. "I don't know how, but that's him."

"That's what Axler thinks too," Jane said. "Dhin is on his way to pick them up."

"Good."

Jane disconnected and the screen went blank.

"The increased mana caused him to manifest early," Aina said, laughing again. "We never suspected drakes had survived the wane in magic."

Harlequin stood up from the sofa with Foster's help. He arched his back and stretched. "The dragons must have hidden them in their lairs."

Nadja looked at the two of them, scanning from one to the other. They were exhausted, but whole. "Did you win?" she asked. "Did you make it to the bridge in time?"

Harlequin nodded. "Yes, I think so."

Aina gave a harsh laugh. "Barely," she said. "But for once I agree with you, Caimbeul."

Harlequin smiled and turned back to Nadja. "Ryan and his team got to Lethe in time. Talon took them to the meta-planes, and Lethe used the Dragon Heart to destroy the bridge. He was still working on the far expanse when he sent us back. He was worried that our strength would give out.

"Besides, we had killed all the Enemy who had made it across—all we could find anyhow. There may be one or two still here, but they'll pop up sooner or later and we'll destroy them."

Aina put her hand on Nadja's shoulder. "Ryan succeeded,"

she said. "Dunkelzahn chose him well, trained him well, and he still surpassed all possible expectation."

Nadja turned to look at the dark-skinned elf. Lines of fatigue held her face in sharp relief, but she was smiling. Nadja guessed that Aina rarely found occasion to smile.

"It's strange," Aina said. "But this experience has given me renewed faith in Dunkelzahn's plan."

Harlequin's jaw dropped open in astonishment.

Aina narrowed her eyes on him, but she was smiling. "I think I've got the first glimmer of the hope I was promised in the will. Perhaps that was his plan all along."

"I can't believe my ears," Harlequin said.

"I want to join your Draco Foundation, Nadja," Aina said. "I'd like to accept your offer."

Nadja felt a surge of excitement. "Thank you."

"I believe a celebration is in order," Harlequin said. "Shall I call for champagne?"

"Not for me," Aina said. "I need a rest."

"And I'd like to go back to Washington right away," Nadja said. "I want to see Ryan."

"I'll go with you," said Harlequin. "I'd like to see the drake myself. Will you come, Aina?"

"As long as I can sleep on the plane," she said, stifling a yawn.

"Just don't snore," Harlequin said. "I'd like to get some rest too."

Aina started to say something in retort, but she laughed instead. "Let's just go," she said.

Nadja nodded, then she started to make plans. They could leave in less than an hour. The helicopter would take them to Marseilles where they would transfer to the Draco Foundation Platinum III jet. They could be in Washington in four or five hours.

Nadja couldn't wait. She needed to see Ryan. Needed to make sure he was still the same inside that reptilian body.

One question haunted her as she packed up to leave: did the Ryan that she loved still exist?

45

Ryan balanced on the swaying observation platform, easily keeping his feet. The choking stench of burning bodies thickened the air all around them, smoke filling the dark sky. The Azzie army seemed to have retreated to a wide perimeter and the helicopters had vacated the area.

Axler, Ryan said, projecting his thoughts, *get Dhin down here to pick us up, pronto! The tower's about to fall.*

Axler cocked her head slightly to the side. She was listening to Jane, through the tacticom. She did not lower her Ares Combatgun.

Grind followed her lead, keeping Ryan targeted.

They don't think I'm me.

Ryan didn't blame them. He didn't feel like himself in this drake body. Even though it clarified a lot of things— the dweller's talk that he was more than he knew. Dunkelzahn's choice of him so long ago. His special abilities—fast healing, his ability to banish spirits, his ease with the magic of the Silent Way.

How could I not know what I was?

Ryan didn't know the answer to that, except he knew that many orks and trolls had been born human and had transformed into their true nature through an agonizing process called goblinization. Many of them hadn't known they were metas.

Dragons didn't goblinize, however. Ryan knew that much. Even elves and dwarfs were born in their true form. And dragons weren't even metahuman.

Shapeshifters were sometimes animal, sometimes human. Maybe I can. . . .

Ryan gathered mana to him, and it seemed to come so easily now despite the foul and polluted stench of astral space around him. He focused on his own physicality, the very nature of himself. He saw how his aura and his physical nature were connected.

The magic he had been capable of before seemed child's play now. Tweaking his aura to look like the surrounding astral landscape, hiding himself physically. It was all fundamental—the first tentative steps of a toddler.

Ryan used the gathered mana to change his aura in a fundamental way and thus to alter his physical shape. He forced his bones to shrink and his muscles to stretch. His head grew rounder as he morphed from drake shape, his wings disappearing as he regained his previous physical body.

In moments, Ryan stood in his human form in front of Axler and Grind, naked and sweating. The tower creaked again, throwing him off balance as it swayed violently in the breeze. "What the frag are you waiting for?" he said. "Let's get out of here."

Axler cocked her head to the side again, listening to Jane inside her head. She still eyed him suspiciously, but she and Grind lowered their weapons. And in the distance, Ryan heard the faint rhythm of an approaching helicopter.

"That should be Dhin," Axler said. "Sorry, Ryan, we had to check with Jane to be sure you were you."

Ryan nodded, then kneeled to get his gear. There wasn't time to get dressed, and his clothes were in tatters, but he wanted his weapons and his wristphone. "How could Jane tell?" he asked.

"She showed Nadja the recording from my headcamera. Harlequin and Aina have returned, claiming success at the bridge. They know what happened to you and told Nadja. She told us."

Ryan nodded as he gathered up his gear. Even in human form, his senses were higher than they'd ever been and he saw the astral continuously.

Talon still lay unconscious on the metal platform, his face pale and slack. The mage's spirit hadn't returned from the site of the spike. He had been the one who'd healed Ryan at the last.

I hope you make it back, friend, he thought.

"Well, Ryan . . ." Axler said. "What happened? Were you successful?"

Ryan nodded. "Yes, I think we were." But there was melancholy in his voice. Ryan touched Talon's face. The human's aura was far, far away.

"Is he dead?" Axler asked, a rare tone of sadness in her voice.

Ryan shook his head. "His vitals are stable, but I fear his spirit may have been trapped or lost on the metaplanes."

"Why do we always lose the mage?" Grind asked. "We're going to get a bad rep."

Ryan allowed himself a smile. "We haven't lost him yet," he said. "Talon is very resourceful; he has surprised me again and again. I'm just hoping he has one last trick in his bag."

The sound of an approaching Hughes Airstar grew louder and louder as Dhin arrived with transport. Wind gusted around them as the ork rigger brought the helo close. He couldn't land on the metal roof so he hovered over them.

"Grind," Ryan said. "Can you carry Talon?"

The dwarf inclined his black head. "I got him."

He bent and lifted the mage with his third arm as Dhin lowered a rope from the chopper. Grind used his two free hands to grab the rope.

Another explosion shook the tower as a blinding white toroid of energy rolled out from the Locus. The wave was massive. Ryan watched it expand out from the stone like a tsunami. In seconds, it plowed up the hillside, flattening trees and blowing out buildings as it rose. It slammed into the base of the tower like a volcanic explosion.

The world tilted under Ryan as Grind hauled himself and Talon up the line and into the helicopter. The tower lurched and toppled then, its base sheared by the force of the explosion.

Axler yelled as she jumped for one of the ropes from the helo. But she hadn't released her safety line, and her waist was still connected to the eyelet on the observation platform. The line jerked taut and pulled her down. She never reached the helicopter rope.

"Drek!" she yelled as she fell with the observation platform.

Ryan fell after her, riding the falling tower like he was surfing a crashing wave. "Axler," he yelled, "cut your safety line!"

If she was still attached when the top impacted with the hillside, she would die instantly, her body whiplashed into the unyielding rock. All her bones pulverized.

Ryan might die too, but he didn't think about that. He focused his magic and concentrated on changing his shape again. The mana came as easily as before, and in seconds, Ryan was in drake form for the second time.

He flapped his scaled wings and hovered in the smoky air for an instant. The sense of weightlessness, of flight, sent a thrill through him. Then he dove.

Axler, push away from the tower. I will try to catch you.

Ryan watched in absolute clarity as Axler, flying through the air, cut her tether to the observation platform, and sailed through the sky like a tiny doll. Out and away from the tower.

Ryan twisted in the air, nearly overcompensating and losing control as he swerved toward her.

Axler maintained an amazing calm and poise as she plummeted. Facing down death without flinching.

Ryan swooped in, his control over his new body growing by the second. He extended his hind legs and snatched at her. The claws that had been his feet protruded now with sharp talons, and he used them, sinking them into the flesh of her gut and leg as he latched onto her.

"Ahh!" Axler yelled, gritting her teeth against the pain of her flesh being pierced.

The ground rushed up at them as Ryan tried to bring himself level. Her extra weight pulling him down. Even in this form, he massed only slightly more than Axler. He tried to tap into his magic to help him. He didn't know if his ability to fly was physical or magical, but he would try anything.

Meters behind them, the tower hit the ground with a deafening crash, sending a shower of tiny rock fragments over Ryan and Axler. Metal screeched and buckled behind them as the observation platform blew apart from the impact. Twisted bits of shrapnel and fragments of glass plowed into them.

Ryan ignored the pain of the bombardment, the agony of the hundreds of tiny cuts that sprouted across his flesh and made him bleed. He ignored the imminent collision with the ground. He maintained focus on his own aura, and the connected aura of his friend, Kaylinn Axler. His friend who had saved his life more than once. He spread his wings and he willed himself to fly.

Tree tops brushed against Axler's body as Ryan finally leveled out and brought them back up. He held onto Axler and flew higher.

"Thanks, Ryan," Axler said. "I don't know what happened to you—this new body—but I'm glad it did."

Ryan grinned. *Me too, my friend. Me too.*

As he rose into the sky, Ryan projected his thoughts to Dhin in the helicopter. *Dhin, lead on. I can carry Axler a ways. At least across the border.*

With his acute hearing, Ryan caught Dhin's response in the physical world, coming softly across the distance. "You got it, Bossman." The helo's nose dipped and it angled north.

A thrill of exhilaration rocketed through Ryan as he shot into the sky, following Dhin. *We won,* he thought. *We fragging one.*

We beat Darke and the Enemy, and we're still alive.

All of us except Talon.

46

Lucero materialized on the plane of cracked rock and looked around. She seemed continually drawn to this place, and it seemed like a good location to start her search for the remnants of Thayla's light and song. The site of the metaplanar bridge. A place once of immeasurable beauty and heart-wringing song. Transformed into the most hideous and foul-smelling hell.

Now, a verdant forest, rich with trees and ferns, grew at her back as she stared out across a white-washed desert at the spirit-cyborg standing on the edge of the cliff. Brilliant silver light radiated from him and the artifact that he held high over his head as he decimated the final span of the bridge on the far side.

When the cliff faces on both sides of the Chasm had been made completely flat and smooth, the cyborg-spirit lowered the artifact and the light abated somewhat. Lucero noticed that the forest around her was growing quickly, and she had to continually advance toward the cliff edge to avoid being overtaken.

Lucero had learned that with freedom she had gained control over her spirit form, and she had changed it to look like her old physical body when she had been alive and young. Now she took the form of a petite human woman with delicate features. Beautiful fine lines and bone structure. Her skin showed no sign of the runic scarring that had come from the use of blood magic.

The cyborg before her did not move even though he had

completed the demolition of the bridge. It seemed to Lucero that he was resting.

I am called Lethe, came a voice into her mind. *You are the seed of darkness, or what remains of her. You are the one who breached Thayla's light.*

"I am Lucero. I have come to repair the damage I have done."

Thayla has fallen.

"I know. Perhaps her beauty can still be found."

I understand, Lucero. You seek hope.

"Yes."

May I ask a favor of you?

"I am free, Lethe. I do not have to obey."

The cyborg had not turned; he seemed to be studying his hand. The extendible fingers that wrapped around the heart-shaped artifact had become fused, and he could not retract them. The artifact was welded to him.

I do not order you to obey, Lucero. I am merely asking your help, one free spirit to another.

"What do you want?"

I managed to save all my friends, but one. A human mage named Talon. His spirit was taken away or thrown into an adjacent metaplane. I'm not sure what happened, but he is gone.

Lucero understood. "I will look for him," she said. "I have much to atone for."

Thank you.

Lucero left Lethe, still standing in an apparent stupor, the excess mana from the bridge's demolition resonating through him. Making his metal and flesh body vibrate and give off light. She left him and searched the forest.

She searched across the planes, shifting from forest to grassy plain to scorched desert. She traveled as fast as she could, her urgency for atonement—even a tiny amount of it—driving her. Across wastelands and frozen tundra, glaciers and urban hellholes where millions of strange creatures lived in the midst of their own defecation and urine.

She knew what the human looked like; she knew the smell of his aura. And she knew she could find him.

How much time had passed before she came upon him, she did not know. He was staggering and nearly dead of thirst. Lost in the salt flats of a remote metaplane. The carcass of a tentacled creature—one of the agents of the *tzitzimine*—lay a few hundred meters from where she found him.

Their struggle must have brought them here, she thought. *And he had barely managed to kill it.*

"Are you Talon?" she asked.

His nod was a slight drop of his chin.

He had no strength to resist her. She scooped him up and carried him, flying desperately with his spirit in tow. She would carry Talon back to Lethe, who would send him into his physical body.

Talon looked at her with grateful, intelligent eyes. A look of such gratitude that she would never forget it. She was trying to save his life, and he placed his trust in her.

No one had ever counted so much on her before. She had never saved anyone before.

In life, she hadn't even been able to save herself.

As she raced across the metaplanes, Lucero felt a glimmer of the light touch her. A peek at goodness and self-sacrifice. It was the best feeling she'd ever felt and it kept her warm for a long, long time.

47

Back at Dunkelzahn's Georgetown Mansion, Ryan reclined in the overstuffed leather chair and sipped his cognac. Nearly asleep, his muscles relaxed and his cares gone for the moment, Ryan was in a state of extreme contentment.

Late afternoon sunlight streamed into the sitting room, filtering through the cherry trees in the garden outside. The smell of the cherry blossoms mingled with the aroma of the warm liquor, filling Ryan's head with a blissful fog.

Ryan blinked to try to stay awake, focusing on the painted elf who sat in a matching leather chair across from him. Harlequin. Despite the early hour, Aina had retired to her room. Jane Foster sat on the floor with her back propped against Harlequin's legs. Her blonde head lay to the side, resting on the soft leather upholstery. Asleep.

Harlequin gave Ryan a tired smile, and raised his own glass of cognac.

Ryan nodded, and lifted his glass. Hours had passed since he and his team had made it in safely across the Aztlan border and landed at a private airstrip in Austin.

Talon had awakened shortly after, and his aura seemed remarkably undamaged. He'd sat up, looking like he'd been tossed into an Urban Brawl match without body armor—bruises on his face and body. But nothing that wouldn't heal. He was mostly in need of rest.

Ryan had changed back into his human form, and he immediately authorized a month of corporate-funded R and R for the whole team. Then Ryan had said goodbye to the others and had hopped a private plane for Washington FDC.

Axler, Grind, and Talon went with Dhin to the Assets, Inc. compound. And from there they'd probably take separate vacations to Fiji, the Caymans, or wherever they wanted.

Nadja had been waiting at National Airport when he stepped off the plane. She had looked into his eyes, long and hard, searching for the truth of who he was.

"It's still me," he said, though he wondered if he knew what that meant anymore.

She put her arms around him and held him tight. "I know," she said. "I know."

"Believe me," Ryan said. "I'm more surprised at what happened than anyone."

Nadja laughed. "Guess we know who Dunkelzahn's successor is."

"I hope that doesn't mean my daily job will consist of fighting the supreme forces of darkness."

"Quit whining," Nadja said. "It pays well and you get a full benefits package." She stepped away from him and modeled her body so that he knew exactly what she meant.

"Well, if you put it that way . . ." Ryan swept her into his arms. He had held onto her, letting her guide him to the limousine. He had found himself whispering, "I love you." Over and over. His face had been wet with tears.

He had cried all the way home.

Now, in the living room of the mansion, Nadja silently entered the room. She wore her green silk robe and matching slippers, and Ryan saw fatigue in her eyes. She said nothing as she slid into the big chair next to him and draped her arm across his chest.

The smell of her filled the air around him as she nuzzled her head into the hollow of his neck. The fragrance of her essence. The warmth of her body, lazily cuddled next to him, was the most perfect and comfortable sensation in his entire existence.

There can be nothing better.

Harlequin looked up at Ryan. "Before we all fall asleep," he said. "I'd like to propose a toast to Dunkelzahn." He raised his glass.

Ryan opened his eyes and lifted his drink. "To Dunkelzahn," he said. "May he rest in peace."

"A truly heroic creature," Harlequin said. "Whose sacrifice saved the world from impending destruction."

Ryan gave him a puzzled look.

Harlequin was nodding, knowingly. "The Dragon Heart," he said. "I figured out how it was created, how such a powerful item could exist so early in the cycle. Its power came from Dunkelzahn. He killed himself in order to give his essence to the Dragon Heart."

"Is that possible?"

Harlequin just continued to nod. "It all makes sense. The inexplicable explosion in front of the Watergate Hotel. The manastorm left behind."

Harlequin gazed into Ryan's eyes. "Dunkelzahn knew that Darke and the Azzies were trying to extend the spike at the Great Ghost Dance site. I had told him myself, and boy was he pissed off at my solution. In retrospect, he was right. Thayla was a good temporary solution, but she was vulnerable. In my hubris I couldn't see that."

"So when I told him about the Locus—" Ryan started.

"He realized that time was getting short. He had been stockpiling orichalcum, and had secretly fashioned the Dragon Heart—an item designed to manipulate mana on a scale such that it would be able to destroy unnatural spikes. Dunkelzahn had his solution then, but he needed to power it. I believe he'd been set up to sacrifice himself all along. It was just a matter of when."

"So he gave up his life to power the Heart?"

"Like I said, he was a true hero." Harlequin drank once more from his cognac, and when he spoke again his voice was thick with emotion. "He gave himself completely to the salvation of the world, and he took no credit for it. This was no lightweight personal vendetta, no false pride."

Harlequin bowed his head, and his voice went soft.

"Ryan, I have done my share to keep the Enemy at bay, but I could never have imagined making the sacrifice that Dunkelzahn made. Even had I conceived of the dire urgency, which I didn't because in my pride, I expected Thayla to be practically invulnerable."

Harlequin looked up, staring into Ryan's eyes. "You realize that Dunkelzahn was powerful enough that he could probably have survived the Enemy, but that wasn't good enough, he wanted *everyone* to survive. He saw hope in the future of metahumanity, and he wanted to ensure that future even if it meant giving up his belongings, his place among the immortals. His very life."

Ryan sat and watched as the tears flowed down Harlequin's cheeks.

"He is the hero, and I sit humbled."

Ryan took a sip from his glass. The sweet burn of the cognac soothed the back of his throat and nudged him toward sleep. Exhaustion and alcohol threatened to carry him under the soft blanket of slumber.

"You are like him, Ryan Mercury," Harlequin said, his makeup smeared from crying. "You share his heroic qualities, I have seen that. And your nature is most uncommon."

"How is that?"

"A drake, my friend. A dragon servant."

"What do you know of drakes?" Ryan asked.

Harlequin considered for a time. Then he spoke, "Other than you, there are no known drakes in the Sixth World. Long ago, before the magic fell, many drakes existed. They were perhaps created by the great dragons, or enslaved in order to serve them. In that way we are not dissimilar."

"How do you mean?"

"Some elves were once bound to serve the great dragons."

"How do you know . . . Never mind."

Harlequin smiled. "You are right to be wary of certain questions," he said. "But I will tell you this; there are those who will seek to destroy you because of what you are."

"Why?"

"Again questions." But Harlequin was still smiling. "For your longevity and magic. Drakes are magical creatures, perhaps even more so than dragons. It is too early in the mana rise for you to have manifested. It's only because of the extreme surge in mana that Lethe sent through you that you changed so soon.

"Over your lifetime, which could easily span the entire Sixth World, you will gain power. You may be hunted now while your power is modest because of your potential to upset an ancient balance of power when you are older, stronger. Or you may be in danger from other great dragons whose agendas' conflict with Dunkelzahn's. It is best to keep your nature completely secret."

"What about those who already know?"

"Do you trust your runners?"

Ryan considered for a minute. "Yes," he said.

Harlequin nodded. "Good. And you can be certain that I'm not going to tell anyone and neither will Foster. Aina and I are both at odds with the others who share our . . . gifts. We don't agree with those who manipulate and plot for power, presuming to know what's best for all the world. Anyhow, I think Aina is on your side for a while; she was impressed with your performance at the bridge."

Harlequin paused to finish off his cognac. "Your conduct has been truly heroic, my friend. I congratulate you."

"We've all made sacrifices," Ryan said. "Aina, Lethe, Nadja, Foster. Everyone. Including you."

Harlequin merely nodded.

Ryan took a last sip from his glass. "Can I ask you a favor, Harlequin?"

The elf looked up.

"You say that I am magical in nature," Ryan said. "You are the best mage I know. Will you teach me how to use my magic?"

A smile broke through. "I would consider it an honor, my friend."

"Thank you," Ryan said as he sank deeper into the cushions, running his hands through Nadja's dark hair. The flush of sleep overtook him as he sat in the waning rays of sunlight coming through the window. The love of his life cuddled next to him.

What could be better?

Sleep overcame him and pulled him into a world of pleasant oblivion.

Epilogue

Lethe straightened up to his full height, Billy's physical body under his complete control. Billy had become part of him, their spirits fused somehow by the rushing flood of mana that had pulsed through them and the Dragon Heart.

He stood on the edge of the cliff and stared out across the Chasm. No evidence of a spike or bridge remained on either side now. Lethe had used the Dragon Heart to level out the mana. He knew what its purpose was now.

He knew that it had been created not only to decimate the bridge, but to even out all of the mana spikes. To prevent premature contact.

Trees grew up around him now, the cracked rock desert replaced with a forest full of life and energy. His work here was nearly complete, and soon he would move on to the next spot. The next unnatural spike of mana.

Lethe would use the Dragon Heart to smooth it out, then move on. And on until every point of abnormally high mana had been leveled flat, its energy dispersed throughout the world.

The Dragon Heart was fused to his body now, and it had become a part of his spirit as well. Lethe had remembered things as it merged with him. He recalled the burning fire and the rainbow portal. He recalled anger and frustration at the elf with the painted face.

Suddenly, as the mana inside him, inside his Dragon Heart, merged with his expanding consciousness, everything clicked into place. The fire was an explosion, a bomb that immolated him. The portal was created by a magic ritual, it was a conduit for life energy.

Lethe remembered much more. Flashes of a life before being named by Thayla. Smells and images came back to him. Memories that spanned millennia came rushing back with wonderful, exquisite clarity.

He had not known what would happen when he died. But the sacrifice had been absolutely necessary.

Now, as he began moving along the edge of the cliff, he remembered the one thing that had evaded him. The one thing that defined his existence.

He remembered his previous incarnation.

He recalled his name.

Dunkelzahn.

ABOUT THE AUTHOR

Beyond the Pale, Book Three of Jak Koke's Dragon Heart Saga, completes the story of Ryan Mercury and the Dragon Heart which began in *Stranger Souls* and continued in *Clockwork Asylum.*

Koke has also written two other novels set in FASA-created universes. His first, *Dead Air,* was a stand-alone book in the Shadowrun® world and was published by Roc books in 1996. His second, *Liferock,* is his only fantasy novel so far and will soon be published by FASA Corporation as part of its Earthdawn® series.

Both solo and in collaboration with Jonathan Bond, Koke has also sold short stories to AMAZING STORIES and PULPHOUSE: A FICTION MAGAZINE, and has contributed to several anthologies such as *Rat Tales* by Pulphouse, *Young Blood* by Zebra, and *Talisman,* an Earthdawn® anthology.

Koke invites you to visit his web site at http://ursula. uoregon.edu/~jkoke. You can also send him comments about this and any of his Shadowrun® books care of FASA Corporation.

He and his wife Seana Davidson, a marine microbiologist, live in California with their five-year-old daughter, Michaela.

MEMO

FROM: JANE-IN-THE-BOX
TO: NADJA DAVIAR
DATE: 20 AUGUST 2057
RE: THE LEGEND OF THAYLA

Dunkelzahn's Institute of Magical Research just un-earthed this document. Thought you'd be interested. Text follows:

Ages ago, before written memory began, lived a queen of great beauty and even greater heart. Thayla reigned over a rich green valley nestled between two mountain ranges that rose like spikes into the heavens. Under her rule, the land she loved prospered, and her people lived their days in joy.

Each morning Thayla greeted the rising sun with a Song. She sang in a voice as clear as the air and as bright as the great burning orb itself. Nothing foul or dark could prosper in her land, for her voice was too pure for such abominations to bear.

One night an army of dark creatures made to enter the valley, seeking to overrun the prosperous land and corrupt it with their vile presence. Thayla rose that morning as she always did, and upon seeing the black army, sang. Her voice filled the valley with power and hope.

The evil horde, shown the depravity of their existence by her voice, had no choice but to flee. And as they did—running and flying with wild abandon for refuge beyond the valley—one black soldier slowed and, for the briefest of moments, listened to Thayla's Song.

Days passed, and the terrible army remained beyond the valley, fearful of the Song. Finally, driven by their dark masters, they surged forward again. And again Thayla sang.

As before the foul creatures fell back blindly, unable to stand even a few pure notes of her voice. But again the lone, tall warrior with hair and eyes of dark fire lingered and listened, if only for a few moments, before fleeing the valley.

The next time the creatures approached Thayla's domain, less of the army came. The rest were unable to marshal the will needed to enter the valley. But again, the lone dark soldier fell back last, so that he could hear her Song.

Finally, not one of the black army would come. Not even the terrible threats of their vile masters could push them forward. But still a single warrior in ebony and red armor would slip into the valley before each dawn and listen, and after a time, watch as well.

The black figure advanced to where he could see Thayla standing high upon the terraces of the great sprawling city that surrounded her palace. And he would watch her every morning as she rose and greeted the new day with the Song. And as he listened, blood flowed from his ears and his skin blistered from the powerful purity of her voice, but he would not turn aside. He would not flee from her Song. And so he stood, listened, and watched.

Then one night, the dark warrior slipped into the city as Thayla slept. He crept into her citadel, sat at the foot of her bed and watched her.

When she woke and found him there, she called for her guards, but none were strong enough to move the dark warrior. She called her sorcerers, but none were wise enough to banish him. She sang to drive him away, but though his body and spirit were wracked with pain, he stood strong and firm, enraptured by her beauty.

Unable to drive him away, the great Queen Thayla decided to ignore him. Though he stood at her side, she ate without speaking to him. Though he ran alongside as she took her horses out for exercise, she did not look at him. And though he stood silently nearby as she slept, she did not acknowledge his presence.

Each morning she would rise and greet the sun, singing loud and strong so that the dark army waiting beyond the valley could not enter. And each morning he stood beside her and cried tears of blood and fire at the pain and joy her voice gave him.

And so this went on for some time. Thayla slept, sang, and performed her royal duties. But the black warrior stayed at her side, and slowly the land began to darken from his presence. The animals of the field sickened, as did the people. The crops would not grow, and dark and terrible clouds filled the sky over the valley.

Thayla knew the black soldier was the cause of all these things, and so she asked him to leave. He did not even answer her. She tried to trick him into leaving, but he would not be fooled. Then she tried to force him away, but he could not be broken. Finally, she begged him to leave.

"But I do not wish to leave," he replied. These were the first words he had ever spoken to her, and his voice was like dried leaves blown on the autumn wind. "Your beauty is like none I have ever seen."

"But you cannot stay," she told him. "Your presence is destroying my land and my people."

"I care not for your land or its people," the warrior told her. "I care only for you."

Faced with his determination, Thayla wept. Slowly her people died. Finally, she called her greatest advisors together and told them what they must do.

"As you know, the presence of the dark warrior is destroying our land and our people," she said. "However, he will not leave my side. We cannot make him leave, and so *I* must leave the land and take him with me."

Her advisors wailed at her words. "But you cannot! It

is only your voice that holds the black army at bay! If you leave, we will certainly die!"

Thayla nodded, for she knew this to be true, but said, "I will leave, but my voice will remain." And with that she charged her most powerful sorcerers with the task of placing her voice in a songbird that would greet the rising sun each morning as she had.

They searched the land and found the finest songbird of all. And as the sun rose, they performed the ritual. When the first light appeared the next morn, the bird sang with Thayla's Voice, and the Song held the dark army at bay.

The sorcerers rejoiced at this, but when they turned to congratulate Thayla, she and her dark shadow had gone. They searched the land but could find neither of them.

But the Songbird rose each morning. And with a voice as pure as the clear air itself, it sang the Song, and the black army trembled in its tracks, unable to enter the valley.

An exciting excerpt from
the next in the Shadowrun series
TECHNOBABEL
by Stephen Kenson

I never believed in the Ghost in the Machine until I saw one. I always thought that computers were something predictable and known. There wasn't anything really mysterious about them—challenging, yes, even exciting, but nothing Unknown, nothing that we did not create and intentionally put into the complex ecosystem of the world-spanning computer Matrix. I learned to explore the glittering virtual world of the Matrix from the time I could sit up to use a keyboard, and I have seen amazing things that cannot even exist in the real world, but nothing changed me as much as when I discovered that the Ghost in the Machine was real.

—Fastjack, decker

My name is Babel and my life begins in an alley—a dark, hidden place in the shadows of the city. I awaken there like being born: weak, blind, and helpless, new to the world and all of its strange sounds, smells, and experiences. And alone, but not for very long. The first thing I become aware of is the darkness and the noise. I cannot see, but I can feel and smell and hear.

I can feel the ground beneath me. It is hard and cool. The roughness of it is not unpleasant—like someone scratching your back—and I lay there for I don't know how long just enjoying the sensation of being supported by the ground, feeling its cool and strong embrace. I can feel the air stir around me, a gentle breeze brushing across the bare skin of my face and hands and ruffling my hair. The breeze brings smells and sounds to me as I lay there.

I smell the harsh smells of the city: a smell of burning. Burning fuel, burning trash, burning wood, and people burning with hope, despair, misery, and joy make up the smell, mixed in with the decaying smell of the city as metal, mortar, and stone slowly crumbled to rust and dust, ground down beneath the force of the elements. I smell my own sweat, cooling on my skin.

I hear the distant sounds of the city, the constant rumble of noise that most city-dwellers ignore almost completely in their daily lives. I hear the voices of cars, from the bass rumble of diesel engines to the high whine of electric motors driving small commuter cars. From time to time a horn blares out its distant cry of anger or warning. The voices of the city whisper and speak to me, and I know there is danger.

Then I hear another voice, much closer, that is speaking to someone else.

"There he is," the voice says and I know he is talking about me. The other's voice replies, deep and gravely.

"Just like Crawley said he would be. I'll give him this, Weizack, that freak may be weird, but his intel is right on the money." Weizack laughs, more like a humorless bark.

"You should talk, chummer. You ain't winning no beauty prizes yourself." Weizack's partner growls, a low, throaty sound.

"Watch it, chummer. I ain't like that fragging thing. I may look like something outta somebody's fragging nightmare, but at least I don't act like it. Let's just do this job and get the frag out of here. This place gives me the creeps."

A rough hand grabs my jaw and I feel a jolt of fear and surprise shoot through my nerves. I want to push away the hand that touches me and fills my nostrils with the stench of overripe sweat and the smell of decay, but my body refuses to obey me. My muscles remain limp and I lay like a dead fish on the cool, hard ground as the hands turn my head to the side and blunt fingers brush against the side of my neck.

"Hey," I hear Weizack's comrade say, his hot, rank breath blowing past my face. "He's still fragging jacked in."

"So unplug him. What's the big deal?" The fingertips brush my neck again. I hear a faint metallic click and feel an immediate and yawning sense of loss open up within me. He has taken something from me. Something very important, my connection to something larger and greater than I am. I am truly alone now, and helpless against these strangers. I try to move, or even open my eyes, but I can't. It feels like my brain is detached from the rest of my body. Like I've forgotten how to use it somehow. The part of me that is awake and aware floats somewhere, detached, unable to make the connection to make a move or a sound.

"Fragging chipheads," the deep voice grumbles. "Why they wanna burn out their fraggin' brains beats the drek outta me. Feedin' stuff right into your head is totally fragged up. All of that techno-trash, just for the sake of gettin' high."

"You ever try slottin' sims, Riley?" Weizack asks his partner.

"No way, chummer. Those things'll frag you up for good. Not even beetles, just the soft-core drek. My cousin was into sims and he spent the whole fraggin' day sitting around slotting chips and living in a fraggin' fantasy world. Couldn't hold down a job or nothin'. Finally cooked his brain slotting something he shouldn't of. Cheap Hong Kong trash. You wanna get trashed, I say do it the old fashioned way: with a bottle or something. These brain-burners frag you up good."

"What about all this drek?" Weizack says, his voice coming from close by and above where I lay. He must be standing near my head, looking down at me.

"Leave it," his partner replies. "Said you don't wanna mess with this drek. It's bad biz."

"Why not? As long as we're here . . ."

"No," his partner says, his tone flat and cold. "Bad enough we're comin' here for him, but I ain't messin' with some of the weird-ass mojo that goes down around here. Chipheads are bad enough, but this place gets used by some real hoodoo. Once we're done, we're out of here. But if we mess with this place we could end up cursed or worse."

"You really believe that hoodoo curse drek?" Weizack asked.

"Take another look at my face, drekhead, and tell me there's no truth to curses. Ever since the magic came back it's been nothing but trouble for the whole world, chummer." The other man's voice was heavy with bitterness. "It mighta made some of the elves and their wannabes happy to be able to do magic, but it's just another way to screw over the rest of us. Proof that mother nature is a slitch with a sense of humor. Now shut the frag up and give me a hand. We need to move this fragger before somebody finds us here."

A strong pair of hands grips my ankles and, a moment later, another pair slides under my shoulders and grips me under my armpits. I am lifted off the ground like a limp rag, all of my muscles still stubbornly refusing to respond to the demands of my mind to move. Just a little movement, a twitch or a blink, to indicate to these two that I am awake and aware. That's all it would take. But I can't seem to figure out how to do it.

I feel vaguely sick and dizzy as I am carried a short ways, swaying gently between my two carriers. They set me down again on a surface that is slick, dry, and soft over the hardness of the ground.

"All set?" Weizack asks, and for a moment I think he's talking to me. Riley grunts in response and Weizack says, "O.K., let's get going. Crawley doesn't like to wait much."

"Frag him," Riley says. "I don't take drek from some fraggin' ghoul."

I hear the sound of a zipper and feel the slick vinyl-

coated cloth slowly close around me like an embrace. The
zipper passes up above my head and I'm completely sealed
in . . . oh no. They don't think I'm unconscious. They think
that I'm dead! But I'm not! I feel panic grip my heart like
a cold hand as my mind frantically screams at my body to
obey. I just need to move, to make a sound, something to
tell these men that I'm really alive, that they've got the
wrong guy. Dammit, move! I feel my breathing begin to
quicken and I hope the sound will penetrate the heavy
vinyl, but there's no response from outside it.

Two pairs of hands lift me off the ground and swing me
a few times like a sack before releasing me. There is a moment of cold, stark terror as I fly through the air with no
sense of balance and no idea where I'll fall. Then I drop
onto something firm but yielding and roll just a bit before
coming to rest on my side.

There's a clunk of metal on metal and the retreating
footsteps of the two men. Then the sound of doors opening
and muffled talk from somewhere ahead of me. That's
when I realize I'm lying on top of a stack of bodies,
wrapped up for delivery just like me. But delivery to
where? And are they dead, or like me, trying desperately to
gather the strength to cry out, to shout, "I'm alive!" in
hopes that someone would hear them?

The thought hits me: is this what death is like? Maybe I
really am dead and just don't know it. Perhaps when you
die all you really do is become a helpless prisoner in your
slowly decaying body, aware of the world around you but
unable to move or communicate in any way. Maybe your
mind hangs around until your body rots away in the
ground or you get the quick and merciful release of crema-
tion. The idea that this paralysis is what the afterlife is
nearly makes me scream and collapse in terror, but another
thought bubbles up into my mind from somewhere. I know
I'm not dead. I just know it somewhere deep down inside.
I know that I've been dead before and this isn't what it
was like. I'm alive, reborn, and I have to figure out how

I'm going to stay that way. Be a shame to start my new life only to end up dead again.

An engine rumbles to life and we start to drive. The meat-wagon slowly pulls away from the place of my awakening and heads out into the city.

MORE EXCITING ADVENTURES FROM
SHADOWRUN®

◼◼ BRINGS THE FUTURE TO YOU